RETURN TO STONEMOOR

COM	DIA	GRE	HAG	H/L	MAR
					6/99
BRE	BRI	DG	BET	RD	WOO
ADS	BRA	CH			NEG
CL	CB	CR			SS

Recent Titles by Kay Stephens from Severn House

STONEMOOR HOUSE
HEIR TO STONEMOOR

THE BRASS RING
DARK BEFORE DAWN
FELSTEAD
SIGN OF THE MOON

RETURN TO STONEMOOR

Kay Stephens

This first world edition published in Great Britain 1998 by
SEVERN HOUSE PUBLISHERS LTD of
9–15 High Street, Sutton, Surrey SM1 1DF.
This first world edition published in the U.S.A. 1999 by
SEVERN HOUSE PUBLISHERS INC of
595 Madison Avenue, New York, N.Y. 10022.

British Library Cataloguing in Publication Data

Stephens, Kay
        Return to Stonemoor
        1. Yorkshire (England) - Social conditions - Fiction
        I. Title
        823.9'14 [F]

        ISBN 0-7278-2228-4

Typeset by Palimpsest Book Production Ltd
Polmont, Stirlingshire, Scotland.
Printed and bound in Great Britain by
MPG Books Ltd, Bodmin, Cornwall.

One

"Something terrible's happened! I've got to talk to Dad."

It was Tania, and she was calling from Dallas, only she sounded upset. Mihail didn't understand. She should be excited after singing at that reception for the American President.

"Whatever's wrong?" he demanded.

His half-sister wouldn't tell him. "Isn't Dad there?"

Their father was beside him now, taking the receiver. "Tania, what is it? What has happened?" Andre's Russian accent intensified as he realised his daughter was crying. "Are you hurt? Has there been some accident? What about Ian . . . is he all right?"

Andre turned, gestured to Mihail to lower the volume of the Beatles belting out the 'Yeah, yeah' of their recent hit *She Loves You*.

Pamela stopped tidying the room and hurried towards their son. It no longer mattered if the youngsters spoiled the effect of carefully chosen Regency furniture with the customary scattering of possessions.

"What did she say, Mihail?" she asked when the record dulled to a murmur. "Whatever's wrong?"

Watching her husband's anxious face made her afraid there was a crisis serious enough to ruin today's family celebration.

"That's what I asked her, Mum. She wouldn't say – just wanted Dad. But she sounded sort of . . . strange."

He'd expected Tania to ask how he was, they'd always been so close. And she had been sorry to leave for the States while he was still injured in hospital.

"Oh, my God – no!" Andre exclaimed. "And you saw what happened . . ."

"We were looking down on the motorcade when we heard the shots," Tania sobbed down the line. "Couldn't believe it. Still can't. He somehow collapsed in his seat, then Mrs Kennedy leaned over him. We could see the blood; she was covered . . ."

"Where were you, did you say?" Andre, his face ashen, was appalled that his daughter had witnessed such a terrible attack.

"At one of the windows. They'd told us to take a break and watch the President go by. Oh, Dad, there was blood everywhere."

"But Ian was with you? He will see that you are all right."

"Not then, no. But he's here now, at the hotel. It was just the other performers – we were having a last rehearsal for . . ."

Andre swallowed, sighed. "Let us hope it is not so serious as it looked. That they will be able to save President Kenn—"

"No, it's too late. That's what I'm saying. It's been announced – he died at the hospital."

All his old need to protect Tania surged up again. "You must come home, at once. Tell Ian to get you away from there."

"Don't worry, we will. But it's complete chaos here. It's taken ages to be able to get through."

"Let me speak to Ian."

"He's on the other phone, trying to get us a flight."

"Take care then, both of you. If you let me know when you will arrive, I shall meet you at the airport."

Andre replaced the receiver, turned slowly to face them all. "Very bad news, I am afraid. President Kennedy is dead. Shot."

2

"But how? Why?" Pamela was bewildered. "Why on earth would anyone want to – I mean . . ."

Andre shook his head. "Who can say? Some fanatic, I suppose, or someone with a grudge."

"But Mum is all right? She is, isn't she?"

Everyone looked at Pamela Anichka, Tania's daughter. Moments ago she'd been dancing with Sonia, laughing, fitting to the Beatles' tune last year's craze, *The Locomotion*. Both girls were gazing towards the rest of them, alarm erasing their exuberance.

Andre smiled reassuringly. "Your mother is fine, Pamela Anichka, only shaken by witnessing that dreadful shooting."

Pamela crossed swiftly to the girl who'd been special to her since the day that Tania named the baby for her as well as in memory of her own mother. That gesture had been a lovely surprise; becoming a stepmother to Tania hadn't always been easy. Putting an arm around Pamela Anichka now, she gave her a little squeeze.

"You heard what your grandfather said – your mum's fine. We'll soon have them home again."

"Won't she be singing at those other concerts in Texas now?" the girl enquired.

"Doesn't sound like it. I expect all entertainment will have been cancelled." Even here in Stonemoor House, everything felt different already, this elegant room with its striped green wallpaper darkened by the bad news. Andre looked terrible. Pamela knew how he would be feeling. He hadn't wanted Tania to go to America. But she knew this need to shield his daughter was generated years ago, before he got her away from his own country to England.

"They'd have to drop the shows out of respect, wouldn't they?" Mihail hurried towards them across the pale green Wilton carpet.

"That's right," his young sister Sonia agreed. She liked to appear as well-informed as Mihail. And now that they knew Tania herself hadn't been in any danger at all, she suspected Pamela Anichka was creating rather a fuss.

3

"I'm going to make a pot of tea. Why don't you girls give me a hand?" Pamela suggested.

The three of them had reached the oak-panelled hall when they heard the doorbell.

"That'll be Gran," Sonia exclaimed, rushing to welcome her.

Mildred Baker came in and straight into Sonia's hug. She only moved aside to make room for Tom and Gwen as they ran up the front steps from their car.

Giving Sonia a kiss and disentangling herself, Mildred glanced towards the rest of them, her greeting as cheery as ever. She gazed all around, noticed their sombre expressions. "Where's Mihail? It's him we've come to see. He *is* all right, isn't he now?"

"Here, Gran. And I'm much better, thanks. Good as new." Mihail had emerged from the sitting room, and strode across to grasp his grandmother by the shoulders. He kissed her cheek. "Let me take your coat."

"What is up then?" Mildred persisted as soon as Tom and his wife had greeted the rest of the family.

Andre had paused to turn off the Beatles' record. It now seemed quite inappropriate.

"You have not heard the news, I think," he said, walking towards them.

"Not Tania? Don't for God's sake tell me something's happened to her?" Mildred exclaimed.

"Not to her, no," Andre assured her swiftly. He'd always appreciated the fondness between Pamela's mother and Tania. "But she has had an unpleasant shock."

"We all have, Mum," his wife added. "Not five minutes since. There's been a shooting, you see. In Dallas. The American President's dead."

"Kennedy?" Her brother Tom was as disbelieving as any of them.

"Are you sure?" Gwen asked, hesitating with one arm half out of her coat sleeve. The coat was new, black with a fashionable cross-over collar of Indian lamb. Tom provided well for his wife and family.

4

"Tania saw it happen," Mihail told them. "The blood and everything."

"Don't," Pamela Anichka protested.

To his mother's surprise, Mihail hurried to comfort the girl the moment he'd hung Mildred's coat on a hook.

"Sorry," he was saying, smiling into the blue-grey eyes of this girl who was only an inch shorter than himself. "You mustn't be upset. You heard Dad – your mum's on her way home now. And we're all looking after you, anyway."

"So, you're well enough to be caring for somebody else, eh, Mihail love?" Conscious of the original reason for this visit, Mildred was forced to place family concerns before international events, however tragic.

Grinning across at his grandmother, Mihail kept an arm about Pamela Anichka while leading the way into the sitting room. "It was only the concussion that kept me in hospital so long." Tapping his forehead with the free hand, his grin widened. "It'd take more than a bash during a rugby try to crack this thick skull!"

Checking dark hair and pert features in the mirror, Gwen followed her sister-in-law into the kitchen when the others trooped after Mihail.

"*Is* that lad of yours really okay now?" she asked, her brown eyes concerned. The whole family had become involved in the dread generated when he was rushed into the Royal Infirmary.

"So the doctors say," Pamela assured her. "He's supposed to take things a bit quiet for a while, but you know what they are at fourteen."

Gwen, with three boisterous sons aged between four and eight, could be in no doubt of the disturbance lads created. "Don't we just – or all the years leading up to that age! Tom was only saying in the car how odd it feels when they're not around. Sort of dead, like."

"Are they with your mother?"

"Not this time. Our Sally's come round to sit in. We

weren't sure how long we'd be over here, and my mother likes to be ready for bed by ten."

Distantly, Pamela heard some newscaster's grave tones from the room where one of the others had switched on the television.

"That's if anybody gets to bed so soon tonight, now this news is coming through," she observed.

"President Kennedy was *shot*, was that what somebody was saying?"

Filling the kettle, Pamela nodded. "Aye. According to Andre's account of what Tania said. I think it must have been outside, in the procession of cars or something. If you want to go through and see what they're reporting on TV, I'll manage in here. All the food's ready." Their housekeeper had left everything prepared.

Gwen shook her head. "Nay, I'll give you a hand, if only to take stuff through. No doubt we'll hear all the details soon enough."

"And over and over again. It's such a catastrophe. I wonder if the ordinary programmes will be taken off tonight?"

Accounts of the killing and its aftermath became more than any of them could endure. Once they had learned the circumstances of the President's assassination Andre strode across to turn off the set.

"We have seen enough for one night, I believe." He turned to look at his son, a smile on his lips although his grey eyes remained solemn. "We still have reason to celebrate. Because our Mihail is well again. Pamela and I are pleased that you all have come to Stonemoor House this evening, and we thank you also for your many kindnesses during those anxious days." Everyone had been so very thoughtful, calling here at Stonemoor with offers of help, as well as visiting Mihail in hospital.

Mihail surprised his father by rising to speak. "Yes, I want to thank you too. For coming here like this, even if the news from America has stopped it being a proper celebration. And it was lovely of you to visit me when I

6

was so terribly bored in hospital." His smile growing, he looked straight at Pamela Anichka. "You'll never know how glad I was to see you."

Noting the glance between her brother and Tania's daughter, Sonia turned her head away. She had visited that ward a lot more than Pamela Anichka. *And* she had saved some of her spending money to buy Mihail chocolate and sweets.

He had seen her reaction; Sonia observed his momentary hesitation.

"Sonia was quite good as well," he added, too late. "For a sister."

She ignored him. He needn't patronise *her*. She might be only twelve, but she wasn't stupid. And she knew why Pamela Anichka and Mihail had become so friendly. You could see it in their eyes, in those lingering glances when they thought nobody was looking. They were the ones who were stupid, though, couldn't they understand that attraction between them was all wrong, forbidden?

Relationships within this family were complicated enough, with Mum being Dad's second wife, and Tania the child by his first. This meant Tania's daughter was closer than a mere cousin. Didn't the fact that she was *Pamela* Anichka remind Mihail she was almost a sister!

"What time does your Sonia go to bed, these days?" asked Gwen. She had been watching her niece's growing resentment, and wondering if overtiredness was making the girl appear sulky.

Pamela smiled, anyway. "Earlier than this, midweek. But we arranged this get-together for a Friday so it wouldn't matter."

Sonia smiled back towards her mother. During the TV programmes about President Kennedy everyone had made comments concerning his life, and his actions in office. She loved current affairs at school, and didn't mean to be prevented from contributing to any family discussion which might develop.

Her father began, unsurprisingly, with sincere regret

that John F Kennedy had not lived to further his efforts to secure world peace. "I would never have believed when the war ended that there was much real hope of dialogue between America and the staunch Communists in my old country. However, I reckoned without that man who was killed today. He had opened the door with talks which could have led to eventual nuclear disarmament."

"You mean they might have created the assurance that we'd allus have peace?" asked Mildred. She never really followed politics, always switched off the wireless when folk were on about that sort of thing.

Andre nodded towards his mother-in-law. "Indeed, yes. Two years ago in 1961 – at his inauguration, I believe – the US President appealed to Soviet Russia. In words to the effect that both sides ought to start afresh their search for peace."

Sonia sat up very straight beside her grandmother on the sofa. "It was just a year ago last month that Mr Khrushchev gave his word about missiles based on Cuba. I think he said they would be – immobilised, or something."

"That's right," her Uncle Tom confirmed. "And didn't Kennedy then tell the Russians that the US wouldn't land on Cuba?"

Sonia smiled across at him. "Excellent, isn't it? That the West is developing a more friendly attitude towards Russia? Dad is hoping that one day this may encourage his sister to come to England."

"Are you really, Andre?" Gwen enquired. "Is it on the cards that she could live here?"

Pamela watched the shadow cross her husband's eyes. When he eventually replied his tone was cautious.

"I do not know. That time when I went back to see Irena, she would not commit herself to coming all this way. We rarely hear from her, you know. Communications are not very easy."

Surprised that Andre should sound daunted by such difficulties, Tom raised an eyebrow. He was working on one of the major newspapers, aware of the advances made since 1945. "Happen now there's that Telstar communications satellite, it's going to be simpler to keep in touch with folk worldwide."

"And with artists like my mother appearing all over the world, a greater understanding will develop between people of other nations." Pamela Anichka had been impressed when Tania was invited to sing in America.

While Andre still appeared sceptical, Mihail was pleased to agree with her.

"You're right, love, of course. The freedom to move between countries of different persuasions is bound to lead to that understanding you mention."

Mildred had been listening, her forehead furrowed. "But I thought that awful killing in America just now was by somebody foreign. Weren't they saying they suspected a chap that sympathised with Communists – the Cubans or summat?"

Oh, dear, thought Pamela, and just when everyone was beginning to consider something a little brighter, like the things John F Kennedy had achieved. Understandable though the reaction to the President's assassination was, this wasn't the mood she'd wanted tonight. She did wish that they might have been permitted to celebrate Mihail's recovery in more cheerful spirits.

Mihail himself was more philosophical about the way his party had been overshadowed. When his mother and father had first mentioned that they should celebrate his return from hospital, he had been less enthusiastic than they were. Fourteen wasn't a particularly comfortable age, he'd decided already. And a part of his perpetual unease was awareness of the rapid changes in his appearance. He had grown so much during the past year that he now was taller than both parents. Only at school, where everyone in his form was suffering alterations in voice and looks, did he feel quite normal. He'd been afraid that, surrounded by all his relations, he'd have too much attention riveted on him. If the news which had given such a different slant to the occasion had been happier, he might have been relieved to have had the focus shifted away from himself.

That accident had shaken Mihail up in more than one sense. Every member of the family had been so concerned that he'd been surprised. Although he wouldn't have told anyone, he'd also felt quite moved. When they'd visited the hospital – individually, or perhaps in twos – he had relished the way in which they had been so interested in him. Interested, but without ever making him feel that he was something of a curiosity.

Since he hadn't particularly looked forward to that party, he couldn't understand now why this feeling of anticlimax plagued each day. Except that he was forbidden to return to school before his own doctor declared him completely fit. That made him restless.

Mihail loved his life at a grammar school in Halifax. He was bright enough and enjoyed learning. Since the day that his mother's insistence had prevailed against his father's wish to send him away for a private education, Mihail had determined to do well there. Fortunately, his ability on the sports field and in the gym made him sufficiently popular to prevent anyone calling him a swot.

It was his friends he was missing now. A few of the lads had visited the hospital ward, some called at the house; but at this stage serious attention must go into preparing for exams. Time was often scarce.

Mihail was glad to have his father around. Andre was between rehearsals for playing the solo violin, and they were enjoying an even greater affinity than in the past. Man to man, they discussed matters which only a short while ago would have bored someone younger. Their hours together were becoming increasingly important to Mihail, compensating for the absence of the comradeship normally found at school. Somehow, he'd always known how greatly Andre Malinowski loved having a son; these days it was good to sense that he also appreciated him as an individual.

Both parents had fussed terribly after that head injury, making a thing of their reluctance to have him go wandering far on his own. The walks which he and his father began taking became vital, and not only for the exercise provided.

They were coming home together to Stonemoor House just as the November daylight was slipping away. They had tramped uphill towards Blackstone Edge, challenged by the rough terrain as the gentler green landscape of the slopes surrounding their Yorkshire home gave way to moorland turf. Mihail liked the prospect of boulders and heather drawing them towards the black crags beyond. With thick scarves and heavy coats, and warmed by the exercise, they had scarcely heeded the wind keening across from the Stoodley Pike monument.

Perhaps the wild nature of the countryside before them had inspired their discussion: the possibility that, one day, the international space race really would take man to the moon.

Andre had always allowed that he might feel proud of Yuri Gagarin and other Russian achievements, without subscribing to the political ideals of his homeland. He was pleased to be discovering steadily that this son of his also felt some degree of pride in his inheritance.

Closer than ever, they hurried up the steps and into the hall where warmth was flowing through from a huge sitting room fire.

"At last," a feminine voice exclaimed from within the room. "I was afraid no one would ever arrive to make me feel welcome!"

It was Tania, rising from the elegant sofa, beautiful in a knee-length woollen gown whose honey shade enhanced the gleam of her long golden hair.

Wow! thought Mihail. If she wasn't my half-sister, I would really fancy her. Old though she is!

But Tania was looking anything but old. Andre saw his

little girl who had fled from the tragic events in Dallas – fled to seek comfort from him. Rushing to draw her to him, he covered the distance in energetic strides which belied the fatigue induced while walking.

"Thank God, you are home. You should have called me, I would have met your plane. How are you, my sweet?"

Her voice muffled against the comfort of his chest, Tania sounded quite childlike to Mihail listening from the doorway.

"I'll be all right now, Daddy. Just so thankful to be here. And glad now that you are home. Mrs Singer let me in, but I gathered that you had gone walking or something."

"With Mihail. You knew he was out of hospital?"

"Of course." Over their father's shoulder, Tania looked towards her half-brother. "Okay now?"

"Yes. Sure," he responded, hurt already because the question had sounded dismissive, unfeeling.

Andre half-turned towards him. "Find Mrs Singer, eh? Get her to make tea."

Heading towards the kitchen and their housekeeper, Mihail tried not to heed his intuition. It wasn't really asserting that now Tania was home his father wanted him less. He glanced at the clock, wished it was time for his mother to close her antiques business for the day. And where was Ian – why had Tania arrived alone?

Mrs Singer smiled when Mihail strolled into the big white kitchen. As always, the pad and pencil which provided her contact with the family lay on the work surface near the door. The elderly housekeeper pointed to the message she'd written already. 'I have made tea now that Tania is home'.

"Thank you, that's good," said Mihail, although well aware that Mrs Singer's inability to hear was the reason she'd never learned to speak.

While the housekeeper carried the tray through to the sitting room, he remained in the kitchen. Ever since he was small he'd loved it in here, had enjoyed a special rapport with Mrs Singer, watching while she baked bread

12

or cakes, tasting casseroles and stews. They had needed no words when she understood the need for tempting treats. He supposed now that she could have relished having him around – someone who helped compensate for her own lack of children.

Today, however, the housekeeper returned to shoo him away, and frowned at his reluctance to rejoin his father and Tania.

The pair were still standing close. Andre was holding his daughter by the shoulders, speaking softly, in that earnest way he had of making you certain you were important to him. But no matter how he tried, Mihail could not rationalise. Reminding himself that Andre Malinowski treated his offspring equally did not convince. Tania was here: those two had eyes for no one else.

The front door crashed open and banged to again. Pamela Anichka was back from school. Still wearing outdoor shoes and a winter coat, she heard her mother's voice and dashed straight through into the sitting room.

"Mum, you're home!" Hurtling across to be embraced, the girl was drawn into Tania's arms and kissed as soon as Andre stepped back.

Suddenly, overeager to learn everything about her mother's visit to America, Pamela Anichka became tongue-tied.

Tania smiled towards Andre who'd remained close by. "She's looking well, Daddy. You've taken good care of her, I can see." Her attention swung back to her daughter. "Only I notice you've not been kept up to standard – since when have you been allowed to charge around the house in outdoor shoes?"

Mihail quelled the impulse to protest. Couldn't Tania recognise Pamela Anichka's desperation to be with her again?

"Where's Ian?" the girl enquired.

A frown narrowed Tania's grey eyes. "Your *dad*'s at home." She'd believed she had cured Pamela Anichka of using his christian name, which was neither courteous nor fair. Hadn't Ian always treated the child as though he was her natural father? He would have adopted her as his own if Gerald hadn't refused to permit that.

"I'll go see him now," Pamela Anichka decided. "Aren't you coming?"

"Not yet, darling. I've got lots to tell your grand-father."

"I'll walk you home," Mihail offered. He remembered she'd been sleeping at Stonemoor while he'd been in hospital and Tania and Ian had been away. "Want to pick anything up from your room?"

Pamela Anichka shook her head. "Later. Let's just go."

Closing the outer door after them, he made himself smile. "She was like that with me as well. You know what she is when my father's around. Nobody'd guess she was thirty-three."

"Didn't she even ask how you were?"

Mihail shrugged as they strode down the drive. "Sort of. You know how it is – makes you wonder if she's listening to your answer."

"Poor you. Bet you hate having your nose pushed out just because—"

He interrupted her. "We shouldn't be saying all this. She *is* your mother."

"And your sister. Well, half."

"Suppose I'm being silly. Mum would say I've grown too fond of everybody being especially nice since I had that crack on the head."

Pamela Anichka grinned, thrust her hand into his. "And why not? Anyone who knows you understands you don't normally want any fuss. There were those few days, after all, when we wondered if you'd ever be really okay again."

"That's beginning to seem a long time ago. Must admit I have enjoyed the last few days, being with Dad, talking *properly*. Rather wanted to hang on to that."

"Don't blame you, it's not that often he isn't travelling all over to play the violin."

"Could be why he wants to catch up on things with your mum – while he is still at Stonemoor."

She gave him a look. "You reckon? You don't have to make excuses for them. Not with me. Remember our pact, the reason we'll be there for each other. Always. No one else would dream of hinting at what the problems are. But that doesn't alter the truth."

Mihail grew pensive. "Not sure we were right. Or not concerning you. I'm certain Tania scarcely remembers her first marriage . . ."

". . . Or the fact that I was the cause of all the trouble? Grow up, Mihail – nobody forgets being forced to marry."

"She *doesn't* blame you, I'm sure. She's very good really."

"As mother's go?" She laughed. "Tell you what, though – yours is nicer."

"Mine?" Mihail smiled. "She is quite – special." Not that he had any substantial regrets about his father, except – well, life might have been different had Andre Malinowski not already had a daughter born in Russia. In his other life.

Surrendering all possible misgivings about their respective parents, they changed the subject, glad to discuss something more exciting.

"Have you asked about going to that concert?" Pamela Anichka demanded. Some of the others from school were planning a trip to see the Beatles playing. She was determined to go along, and suspected that permission might be granted more readily if Mihail were included.

"Haven't got around to tackling Dad yet. Sounded Mum out first – naturally, she insisted he must be consulted."

"They're an absolute pain, aren't they! Never mind, if they stop us doing that, you and me'll think of somewhere else."

For years now the two youngsters had enjoyed being

conspirators, and were both of an age when their gender differences were beginning to add spice to their schemes.

Ian had watched them walking towards the grey stone cottage less than a mile along the hillside from Stonemoor House. Flinging the door wide, he extended both arms towards his stepdaughter and drew her into a powerful hug.

"Come on in, PA love, come in, come in. It's great to be back home at last. To see you. And you, Mihail – hi! Glad to know you're so much fitter. Are you as well as you look?" he enquired as he released the girl whose name he abbreviated affectionately to 'PA'.

"Yes, thanks, Uncle Ian."

His uncle turned back to the girl. "Your Mum decided to hang on a bit at Stonemoor?"

Pamela Anichka grinned. "How did you guess?" She glanced sideways to wink at Mihail.

Ian seemed unsurprised. "I expect she wants to see our Pam. Had she come in when you left Stonemoor?"

Mihail shook his head. "Business seems quite good just now, and she is trying to make up for taking time off because of my accident."

His uncle smiled. "Aye, well – I dare say it'll be enough for her that you're no worse for it. Have you returned to school yet, lad?"

Mihail shook his head. "I'm seeing the doctor again next week, just hope he signs me off then."

"So we might all be back to our routine before too long. I've just been having a word with Ted Burrows, let him know I'm home."

Ian's sherry-brown eyes narrowed and his smile faded slightly. He wouldn't trouble anyone with his misgivings, but he might have been happier if Burrows had sounded thankful he was returning to work.

There'd always been this unease between himself and the man who now was manager of Canning's. Years ago when Pamela was still actively involved in the interior

16

design business she'd built up, Ian had been obliged to accept that he himself was too young for shouldering responsibility within the firm. At thirty-two, and still only the foreman, kowtowing to Burrows rankled.

As their Pam had long since ceased to be more than a member of the board, he could expect no favours from her. Not that he was given to demanding favours, Ian reflected: he'd always proved he knew his job. It just seemed unfair that, no matter how much he put into the work, his ambitions were thwarted.

That trip to the States had opened his eyes. The Yanks were so go-ahead, nothing held them back. One day – and he didn't mind admitting that he didn't yet know *how* – one day he would thrust himself out of this situation.

There were shortcomings enough in his life, and this was the only thing that seemed to have even any prospect of a solution. He'd always loved this work, whether it was simple redecoration of somebody's home or the restoration of a public building. Today, he was determined, he would fight to have his skills acknowledged.

Two

"I am not about to argue with you, Mihail. You shall not go there!" Andre's accent was more intense than Sonia had ever heard it.

She was listening unashamedly from the upstairs landing, her smile widening as her brother's dismay became increasingly evident. *She* wasn't surprised that Mihail and Pamela Anichka were being forbidden to attend that Beatles concert.

Mihail knew better than to attempt to change their father's mind. Most times, Sonia also knew how fruitless it was to try and talk him round. Andre Malinowski was so old-fashioned. Whenever they really wanted something she and her brother usually approached Mum who tended to be more easily persuaded.

This time, Sonia gathered, Mihail had already tried that, only to be referred to Dad. One day she might sympathise with her brother. Today she simply thought he'd been an idiot to believe he would be permitted to go off like that for the evening.

Saddened by his son's disappointment at being refused permission for the outing, Andre strode pensively through the panelled hall and out into the large rear garden.

The day was bitingly cold, yet he needed the air blowing down over the valley from the moors, needed perhaps to feel this autumn chill savaging him. Needed something to root out his dismay. Generous by nature towards his children, he hated to deny them anything, but that must not encourage him to indulge them too recklessly.

Mihail would not be fifteen until next July, Pamela

Anichka was younger still. And a simpler man than he would have concluded that, had he consented to Mihail watching the Beatles perform, the girl would have used that as leverage to ensure her own attendance! Andre knew Tania well enough to suspect that, whatever her misgivings, she would have difficulty in preventing her daughter from going off to join other fans drooling over those four young men.

Reluctant though he was to accept that role, Andre had learned over the years that containing the enthusiasms of all these young people often fell to him. Only too aware of Tania's history and the way her wilfulness had plunged her into that disastrous first marriage, he'd always wondered just how firm she would prove with her own daughter. And Ian, sensible as he undoubtedly had become, was only Pamela Anichka's stepfather and should not be expected to impose too much discipline. Or not to the degree that a natural father might.

Shivering as the wind strengthened to bend the surrounding trees while it surged about the house, Andre glanced past fields and woods towards the hills. Still concealed by the slopes behind him, the sun was rising now, shining across to Stoodley Pike, the obelisk erected to mark British success at Waterloo. For that moment when nothing else was in sunlight the landscape took on an eerie ambience. Woods and even the meadows appeared darkened; Stonemoor House – despite its gold-toned stone – looked quite forbidding. And then the sun came over that nearby hill, lighting his surroundings, enhancing every familiar detail, somehow reassuring.

Exhaling slowly, Andre turned to go back into the house. All would be well, given time. Neither Mihail nor he himself bore grudges.

Listening again, Sonia recognised that her brother sounded dreadfully put out. "Anybody'd think I'd no idea how to behave, that I wasn't to be trusted," he was saying into the phone. Sonia could almost hear PA (as Mihail called her now) agreeing. "I know," she would be saying. "Terrible, isn't it. We're not children, after all . . ."

The pair of them were always claiming to be grown-up, these days. It would be pathetic, if it didn't annoy *her* so much. Mihail was only a couple of years older than Sonia herself, and PA younger than he was. They chose to overlook how small that gap was, of course, when they were ganging up to lord it over her.

Last night, for instance, when they'd had their heads together in front of the television. Sonia herself was having a bit of a struggle with her French homework. Concentrating might have been easier in her bedroom, but she'd been determined to stay with the others: she wasn't going to miss anything. She hadn't been aware that she had sighed, but suddenly there PA was – dashing to the table, looking over her shoulder.

"God, but that is so easy!" she'd exclaimed. "Can't you manage it, Sonia? We did this in the first year. You are twelve now, aren't you?"

Humiliated, Sonia's only consolation had been when Tania appeared in the doorway to reproach Pamela Anichka for blaspheming. Uncle Ian had followed, and had come to place a hand on Sonia's shoulder while he looked down at her books.

"I think that's excellent, anyway. I never did French properly."

Sonia felt comfortable with Uncle Ian, but more for his being her mother's brother than for the marriage to Tania. She could still recall that day when Ian Baker came back to Stonemoor, it had changed so much for the family. Gran and everybody had been here, they were all going to watch Queen Elizabeth's coronation on the television. At first when Ian had walked up towards the house, somebody – it might have been Mihail – had thought it was Uncle Tom.

Discovering it was Ian home from working abroad had been exciting. People had been almost too thrilled

20

to concentrate on watching the coronation. Sonia could remember now that she'd felt quite relieved when everybody kept interrupting to talk. That service had gone on and on for such a long time.

Sonia had always been pleased about Ian marrying Tania. Her half-sister had been transformed. She understood now that Tania had been quite fragile after leaving her first husband and bringing Pamela Anichka to live at Stonemoor. Even while little more than a toddler herself, Sonia had recognised that Uncle Ian's reappearance had somehow brought Tania back to life again.

When the pair eventually were married everyone began to relax. They no longer needed to behave quite so carefully – because Tania no longer snapped at them or shouted. And, of course, they took Pamela Anichka and went to live in their own house.

No matter how frequently the three of them visited Stonemoor it was always all right. Tania would always monopolise their father (who would seem to notice no one else), but she would go away again. Pamela Anichka would hang around Mihail in a positively sick-making fashion, but in the end she would have to leave.

Sonia didn't resent PA's interest in Mihail all the time; some days she herself could hardly bear to speak to her brother. She did wish, though, that she had someone who was special just to *her* – one person out of all the world who always showed that she mattered.

She supposed really that what she longed for was that the years would pass until it became her turn to fall in love. Whenever she thought about the manner in which Uncle Ian and Tania had got together, she dreamed of having somebody arrive without any warning like that; someone who would love her.

"Anybody would think that PA and I weren't related, that she was some girl I'd met away from here."

Mihail had taken his disappointment to the antiques shop, hoping perhaps that his mother would discover some means of altering the decision which had been such a blow to him.

Pamela was performing her customary morning inspection, pausing now and then to wind one of her many clocks.

Could it be that it's *because* you are related that Andre is being particularly circumspect? she wondered. Dismissing that notion as unnecessary while the pair were so young, she smiled at her son.

"I'm sure it's only that he feels you're neither of you quite old enough yet for tripping off to events of that sort. There'll be masses of folk there, won't there, love? And most of them overexcited because of being let out for an occasion like that, to see their favourite stars." Pamela bit back her own concern – that Mihail wasn't sufficiently recovered from that injury for going far without them. Would she always be uneasy about him now? Being told that he'd been rushed to hospital had been a dreadful shock.

Aware already that pestering his mother with further pleas wouldn't achieve a thing, Mihail didn't speak. Instead, he hurried through into the back of the shop. Here, amid furniture awaiting restoration, silver in need of polishing and books requiring repair, were more clocks.

Since the day that he'd first noticed the longcase clock given to his parents by the Norton sisters, Mihail had adopted Pamela's love of old timepieces. His father had explained that those two elderly ladies had once lived at Stonemoor House, and that particular clock was special to them because it had been made in Halifax. It was about as old as the house itself.

During the years that Pamela had been in the antiques trade she had acquired a great many clocks. Some of these were in excellent condition, others needed mending, some were in bits.

Disappointed because his doctor had advised yet another week away from school, Mihail had been reading one of the books his mother had obtained when she first began

22

as a dealer. Always clever with his fingers and keen to discover how things worked, he had become fascinated not only by timepieces but by how they were put together. Pleased about her son's interest, Pamela had given him a pocket watch that was contained in one lot bought in a recent auction. Made in the 1930s and cased in chromium plate, it was neither an antique nor of particular value, and it kept poor time. She had told Mihail he could have a look at the thing.

Surprised by the care he had taken, she had glanced his way whenever she wasn't occupied with serving a customer. Sitting at a table in the back room here, her son had laboriously cleaned that watch and had fine-tuned the adjustments until its timekeeping became perfect.

Smiling down at his shining golden head, and congratulating him for his patience, Pamela had been surprised again by Mihail's response.

"I enjoyed it, Mum. I just wish there was something more difficult you'd let me tackle," he'd told her, blue eyes gleaming.

Remembering this today, she handed him a cardboard box.

"So far as I know, there's only one clock in here, but there could be pieces from another. You can see what a state it's in – you can't do any harm trying to put it together and get it to work. That's if you don't mind trying something that'll take you ages?"

"Not mind? I'd be thrilled to have a go. I'll be really careful."

Pamela smiled. "It's good to see you relishing a challenge, love. Just remember you can take as long as you like. This came from one of the houses where I offered for all the contents; I never anticipated that I was likely to pay someone to make it good enough to sell!" Thinking of something, her smile widened. "Of course, if you do turn out better at it than I expect, I'll consider paying you for the work you put in."

Mihail needed no such offer as inducement. He set to

immediately, removing each bit from the box and setting them out before him in a semicircle on the table. Even the casing of the clock had suffered. The door hinge was broken and several pieces of the pale inlay decorating its wood were missing. Worst of all, though, was its mechanism. From what Mihail could see, someone at some time had tried to repair it. He could imagine that they might have become irritated when nothing would come right, or maybe there had simply been an accident. Whatever the cause, the movement was in so many pieces that he could believe it had been dropped.

"Well, I did say I wanted to have a go at something harder," he remarked wryly.

His mother laughed from the sink where she was washing a tea service that had come from the same household. "Thought that might keep you quiet for a while. If you like, you can take it home and carry on with it there as well."

"I might be glad to. But it won't be tonight. I'm going to Tania's."

And I can guess it's not Tania you're eager to see, thought Pamela. If I know you two, you and Pamela Anichka will be commiserating with each other.

She could have told Mihail how sorry she was that neither she nor Andre were able to agree to all his wishes, but they didn't encourage their children to go on and on about a matter, and she had no intention of doing so now. It really wouldn't be all that long before Mihail would be old enough to go wherever he wanted. Within reason, she added silently.

"I managed to mend its broken hinge, and I'm going to find out what kind of wood was used for the inlay and fill in the bits that are missing," Mihail was telling PA that evening.

"That's nice," she replied without enthusiasm. She'd had her hair cut on the way home from school. As short as she dared and with a fringe down to her eyebrows in the style Vidal Sassoon had designed for Mary Quant. Mihail hadn't noticed.

That had been *so* disappointing. Especially after all the bother.

"What on earth have you done to your hair?" her mother had demanded the minute Pamela Anichka walked into the cottage. "When I said you should have it cut I didn't mean you to come home resembling a boy."

Ian had said it looked nice and neat. PA wished, for once, that he was her real father. He was quite often on her side. At least he wasn't always issuing regulations.

"All you can think about is that broken old clock, isn't it?" she said to Mihail now.

He grinned in that way he had of making her want to spend more time with him, to have the whole of his attention. "Sorry, but it is interesting. Don't mind telling you – I'd love to work with clocks."

"As a job, you mean? Properly?"

When he nodded Pamela Anichka groaned. "They'd never let you. What about going to university and all that, wouldn't it be wasted?"

He shrugged. "I'd have to find out if they do courses in clockmaking." That's if he went to university; he didn't want to go.

"That's more likely to be at a tech. Your dad wouldn't like that at all. Anyway, this isn't why we're here now. I thought you said we were going to think of something really special that we'd do, to make up for missing the Beatles."

"We are, we are." The trouble was he'd been too busy today, too fascinated by what he was doing to give a thought to finding ideas.

"There must be somewhere they'll allow us to go," PA persisted.

"The pictures?" Mihail couldn't face another battle at home over his wish to go anywhere contentious. "I've been dying to see *Lawrence of Arabia*."

Pamela Anichka wrinkled her nose. "Have you? I hope

we'll find something better than the pictures. We can go there any time. I'll have a think, give you a ring."

She glanced at her watch. "Hey – have you seen the time? *That Was The Week That Was* is on in five minutes."

The television show cheered PA considerably. Her mother and Ian professed not to like it, which made her relish the programme all the more. Tonight she even felt less perturbed that Mihail was still somewhat preoccupied with that wretched clock.

Since Mihail's head injury, his father was being terribly boring and insisting that he must not walk back to Stonemoor late at night. PA heard the car arrive, then the doorbell, and Andre talking to Ian in the hall.

"Better say goodnight," she told Mihail, and added, "In here . . ." before he could dash from the room.

They got up from the sofa in front of the TV set. When he made as though to give her the usual kiss on her cheek, Pamela Anichka slid her arms about him.

"Goodnight, love," she said, and kissed him full on the mouth.

Taken aback, Mihail grinned. He couldn't pretend he'd never noticed how attractive PA was, and he didn't mind her demonstrating that she was aware of him. He didn't mind that at all!

Mihail was wondering how fervently he should respond to that kiss, how she would react if he held her really close, when he heard his father's voice approaching.

"Are they in there? I know they like to watch that thing people call TW3." Andre himself did not appreciate English satire.

"See you," Mihail told Pamela Anichka.

In the car his father was trying to make amends for denying him permission to see the Beatles perform. "Do you wish us all to go somewhere during the weekend perhaps? Even this time of year, there are some places sufficiently interesting for a visit."

"We'll see," said Mihail, and smiled in the dark interior

of the car. He'd just realised he sounded like a parent himself, a parent cautious about making promises. Not believing in entirely wasting opportunites, he thought for a few moments, smiled again. "We could go and see *Lawrence of Arabia*."

"So long as it's somcthing your mother would enjoy."

It was Sonia who didn't wish to see that particular film, so Pamela suggested that she should take their daughter to watch *The Pink Panther* instead. "That way, you menfolk can revel in the exploits of T.E. Lawrence undisturbed."

Mihail was delighted by the prospect of an evening out with his father, a further occasion to indicate a beginning to a future where he'd be treated as an adult male.

Andre was thankful just to go somewhere and relax. He would not be sorry when 1963 was over. Mihail's injury had made them all so worried. Even now that he could see how well his son had recovered, he still felt anxious. Whatever would they do if the doctors had missed some additional symptom – something which might flare up in the future?

Further from home, the news had been too uneasy for comfort. The Profumo affair had brought spying to the forefront of public attention. Andre could have done without that reminder of the period, over a decade ago now, when people had been afraid that his own Russian roots mean that he could be a Communist spy.

Watching Andre and his son driving away on that Friday evening, Ian had felt that familiar profound envy surging right through him yet again. No matter how frequently he reminded himself how much Andre had endured, he never seemed able to accept that the man had three children, while he himself had none. No one ever understood. Sometimes it appeared that Tania understood least of all. Deeply though he loved that wife of his, he couldn't feel she shared this yearning.

"You love Pamela Anichka," she'd reminded him more than once. "You always used to say that we make a good family. You even wanted to adopt her, give her your name."

All of it was true. PA's likeness to her mother had, right from the start, ensured the girl his affection. Only Gerald Thomas's refusal of permission prevented Ian from assuming total responsibility for her. The trouble was that while Ian had been strengthening the bonds between himself and this daughter of Tania's first marriage, he'd considered that as merely the prelude to increasing their family. His desire to make Pamela Anichka entirely secure in his love had grown from the expectation that she would have brothers and sisters.

Even though Tania assured him she was as eager as he was to have his children, he saw no signs that she was perturbed by the absence of them. She had her classical singing which now took her all over this country and abroad. When she was at home she and PA were closer than many a mother and daughter. And she had her father.

Ian had always been conscious of the devotion existing between Andre Malinowski and Tania. Hadn't he himself, all those years ago, been the one who'd sympathised with her while Andre took that hazardous journey into Eastern Europe to visit his sister. He had seen then how anxious Tania was for her father, and afterwards recognised the depth of love which bound them together.

Being unable to talk to anyone about his own sense of deprivation made everything all the harder, Ian acknowledged that night as he went slowly up the thickly carpeted stairs.

Tania and PA were in the girl's room now, chattering and laughing while they evidently went through her wardrobe. From what he could hear, they were obliged to discard several items which PA had outgrown, in order to accommodate the clothes that Tania had bought for her daughter in the States.

If only we had a child which *I* had fathered, Ian thought; if only I needn't always feel just a little bit left out. It was years now since he had ceased to resent Gerald Thomas for being the first to marry Tania. But that fact did not mean he had ever for one moment forgotten who the girl's real father was, even though the reminders had ceased. They hadn't seen the man for years – so long in fact that Ian could scarcely recollect how uncomfortable he had felt during those brief meetings when Gerald had called to either take PA out or to drop her off.

The life when Ian and Gerald had played popular music in the same band felt now to have belonged to someone else. Looking back, he recognised how carefree he'd been in those days; on occasions even quite irresponsible.

From Pamela Anichka's room the two chattering voices started to make Ian feel irritated. He could appreciate the closeness between those two without denying that he wished Tania would come more readily to him. At times like this, with his longing for children so raw, he became afraid that his wife could be turning away from him because of the ferocity of this need. Tania said very little yet he sensed her reluctance to make love, which was creating the sort of barrier that he'd once have believed impossible. From the day that they had met, the attraction between them had been so very potent – had even in the early days become so insistent that he himself had been alarmed. And those years they had spent apart had in no way dulled their desire. When he had returned from Africa he'd scarcely been able to endure until Tania was free to marry him.

His chief fear then had been that he might fail to provide adequately for his wife and her daughter; but he had managed that, had succeeded in giving them this home. It hadn't mattered then that Tania earned substantial fees whenever she sang. Ian was satisfied they were relying on his earnings for day-to-day living, while his wife's money provided little luxuries and additional comforts.

Granted children of his own, he would be so happy. Was it too much to ask that he should be allowed such a normal satisfaction? Was it so wrong of him to feel

29

incomplete without the offspring which so many folk took to be their right?

It is time we talked, he decided. I'm not going to have this sour everything for me. Tonight, while I'm ready to reveal my own emotions. When Tania comes in to the room I must make her understand.

He was in bed and reading when he finally heard his wife call goodnight to Pamela Anichka and walk along the corridor.

"I didn't know you had come upstairs," Tania said as she opened the door. "We were enjoying ourselves making room for those new things I bought for her in Texas. Fashions change so swiftly, especially for young people – dresses she wore a year ago already look ludicrous."

Ian forced himself to smile. "I know she appreciates all the new clothes you buy for her; she's a good girl."

"Most of the time," Tania agreed, thinking of the recent tussle over going to see the Beatles. "I just wish she would realise that she is too young yet for doing exactly as she wishes."

"Do you remember how your father used to react to your determination to sing with the band?"

Tania gave him a look as she struggled to undo the fastening of her dress. "Of course. But that was very different. I was much older than Pamela Anichka is now. And we were not travelling more than a few miles from Stonemoor."

No, thought Ian, and despite all that you got yourself pregnant by Gerald Thomas.

"Never mind," he said. "Are you coming to bed?"

"When I've been to the bathroom."

Tania always took ages over cleansing her face and teeth, then brushing her beautiful pale hair. He ought by now to have accepted how long the procedure took. Tonight, he suspected she was delaying the moment when she would join him.

The room was still warm. They'd had central heating installed some months previously, and relished the ability to move around the house without shivering; a rare quality in the West Riding of Yorkshire during autumn and winter.

Her nightgown was alluring, silk-textured, the shade of cinnamon. Against his side in the bed, she was fragrant, her limbs smooth and inviting. Ian moved nearer, kissed her neck, the lobe of an ear. Tania was reaching sideways for her book.

"Just let me read, darling, eh?" she said gently. "It's what you're doing."

"I was, you mean. Only while I waited for you."

Tania opened her book, said nothing.

"I wanted to talk," Ian persisted. "About us."

"Tomorrow, eh? Or we might not sleep."

"D'you never think that *I* might have difficulty sleeping? Not just one night, but lots of times. And don't you even wonder what might be wrong?"

"Have you had another bad week at work, love? Ted Burrows throwing his weight around again?"

"Well, yes. But this isn't about work. When did I ever expect to involve you in that sort of problem? This is about us, Tania. Time passes that fast, and I can't help thinking we're never going to be any different."

"Different?"

She sounded quite vague, had only half-closed the book with one finger still keeping her place.

"Oh, love, don't pretend. You know what I mean."

Tania sighed. "That again! Oh, Ian, do you have to be like this – do you not realise what you are making me feel? I have never felt so, so unad – *in*adequate in all my life. It is not only my fault that we do not make a baby," she finished, her accent strong, as it always was when her feelings rose.

"All right, all right. I'm sorry, lass."

But as Ian reached for her he felt her tense again and realised his mistake in calling her 'lass'. Not long after their wedding Tania had made plain her reluctance to hear him speaking as he used to years ago. The Yorkshire dialect which once had been natural to him and to the rest of his family had, to a degree, disappeared while he had worked abroad. The rest he had tried to discard, especially for occasions when accompanying Tania. Succeeding had pleased Ian himself, a fact which had surprised him. He'd always been too down to earth for putting on airs. But he did relish discussing matters with well-educated people, in the kind of language which would make no one flinch.

"I need you, sweetheart," he reminded Tania now. "Need you just as much as ever I did when we were younger and hardly able to keep our hands off each other."

"I hope you are not suggesting that I do not need you. You ought to be fully aware by this time that—"

His mouth prevented further speech, kissing fervently, his tongue searching and probing. Tania responded, her arms going about him, welcoming his warmth and his strength to her. Ian began to believe that he need give no further explanation.

She did understand, did know how he felt, how earnestly he ached for his own family. She was showing him yet again that she would always, always be here for him like this. That she would receive his loving no less fervently because this great yearning of his was not simply for its anticipated release.

When they both lay, breathless and sated side by side, Ian felt for her hand, held it in his grasp, fingers caressing hers. "You're a wonderful lover," he murmured, thinking to reassure her that he needed her *just for herself* as fiercely as ever in the past.

In the darkness he felt Tania sigh before she spoke. "I only wish you did not make it seem each time that you only want me as a baby-making machine."

Three

The three years which had passed hadn't made life any easier. Deeply though Ian loved Tania, he seemed unable to dismiss those words of hers. Whenever he tried to introduce more spontaneity into their lovemaking, he would wonder yet again if his wife really could believe that all he wanted from her was a baby. Attempting to talk the matter through only led to greater unease between them. And the time they spent together was becoming rarer; Ian had no wish to ruin what they had.

Tania was busier than ever in this summer of 1966, taking more bookings to sing abroad as well as in the major cities all over Britain. As she had explained, Pamela Anichka was almost sixteen and quite capable of coping in her absence. True though this was, Ian missed his wife a great deal whenever she was away. PA never stayed in very often of an evening. Fond though she might be of her stepfather, he had no illusions that she could prefer his company to that of her friends.

Ian suspected that much of PA's spare time was spent with Mihail, certainly they visited each other's homes frequently. Occasions when some pop music programme like *Ready, Steady Go* would blare out from the television, and Ian would long for Glenn Miller's melodies which he himself had loved. Between broadcasts from Radio Caroline and the TV the house never seemed to be quiet.

I must be getting old, Ian reflected, wondering one time while Tania was away where on earth the years had gone. He didn't seem able to get any help from their Tom either.

But then, with three small children, his brother was in such a different situation that imagining Tom any older proved difficult. Perhaps that was why his advice was disappointing. Only a couple of years separated them in age, but on the day that Ian was invited to join them for tea it had felt closer to ten or more.

Since Tom's promotion in the art department of the newspaper in Manchester the family had moved into a larger house. Although still modest by the standards of anyone familiar with Stonemoor, it was far more spacious than the cottage Ian had bought. The difference was not so much in the size of the surroundings, though, as in the liveliness. With three growing boys making free in every room, no one could be oblivious to the toys, games and hobbies very much in evidence.

Gwen had long since adapted her house-proud nature to accept that for the foreseeable future happiness rather than tidiness must be the criterion. Tom was the one who played with their sons, behaving in an uninhibited way difficult to reconcile with the quiet brother who had grown up alongside Ian.

"I suppose that's what keeps you young while I feel like Methuselah!" Ian had exclaimed with a laugh, realising that getting Tom to listen to his anxieties would be anything but easy.

Tom *had* listened finally, when Gwen was marshalling the children for bed, but his advice hadn't been much comfort.

"You could both go for tests, couldn't you?" he suggested. "Aren't doctors looking into infertility now that the pill has been brought in to regulate the size of families?"

"It isn't as simple as that," Ian responded, wishing already that he hadn't begun this conversation. "Happen this sounds daft, but it's spoiling things between us, ever since Tania got it into her head that I only want, well, sex because it might give us a baby." And, he thought miserably, *she's* proved she's all right in that

34

department! He didn't relish the prospect of having his own fertility investigated.

In the absence of any constructive advice, Ian wasn't sorry when Tom turned to the subject of their mother. Mildred Baker wasn't at all happy living on her own, and evidently considered that Tom's move to Manchester had taken him almost beyond reach.

"I know," said Ian. "It's awkward, isn't it. We try to get her to come out to us pretty often, but she takes some encouraging. And she's no better at visiting Stonemoor House."

For some long while the brothers discussed their mother's situation, but without reaching any satisfactory conclusion. The real source of the problem wasn't that Mildred needed care; quite the opposite, she was no longer looking after anyone. From the day she was widowed, while Pamela was still a schoolgirl and Ian and Tom were small, she had lived for her family. Since Tom and Gwen had moved to their new home, she wasn't even required for occasional baby-sitting.

Driving home over the moors from the outskirts of Manchester, Ian began to feel quite desperate. There wasn't one thing in the whole of his life which seemed to be right. And arriving back at the house would only remind him that for several days yet Tania would still be away.

If only the atmosphere at work had improved, he might have learned to accept the absence of a child of his own. Unhappily, Ted Burrows was making life there more trying than ever. Canning's had taken on a big contract to redecorate the interior of a school which was being renovated. Ian had been the first to learn of the scheme and, even before tenders were invited, had suggested that Canning's should put in for all the renovation work, not simply the final decorating. Burrows hadn't agreed, but then he hadn't been involved during those early days when Pamela had built up the business, principally by renovating the interior of Stonemoor House.

35

Expecting her to support his ideas now in 1966, Ian had spoken to his sister about the extent of their involvement in the work ahead. Pamela had refused to back him against Canning's manager.

"No, love, I can't overrule his decisions. After all, Ted's in charge of the day-to-day operating of the company. He knows the men, and what our commitments are; he's got to have the last word on how much we tackle."

"We could employ more chaps, temporary-like, while we were doing what has to be done afore the actual decorating of the place."

Pamela had remained adamant. And from that day Ted Burrows appeared even more assertive than he'd become already.

Arriving back at the house that evening, Ian was glad to see lights shining from within, even if the Rolling Stones' latest hit was shaking the windows. Pamela Anichka was good company, these days – when she and Mihail didn't have their heads together over some scheme or other!

There was no sign of the lad tonight, and PA came into the hall to greet her stepfather. "How were they all?" she asked, making him glad that she had remembered whom he was visiting. Pamela Anichka had reached the age when she wasn't particularly interested in family outings.

"Fine, fine. They send their love." Tom especially had always had a soft spot for PA as, indeed, he had for her mother.

"Where did you go?" Ian enquired, and wondered guiltily if she had told him where she intended spending the afternoon and evening. He must try not to be so weighed down by his own difficulties that he paid his stepdaughter insufficient attention.

"Over to Stonemoor. Then to the shop. Mihail wanted to show me a watch that he's managed to repair."

"And did you go anywhere afterwards?"

PA shook her head. "We were helping his mum. Quite fun really, we unpacked a load of things she'd cleared out of a house in Hebden Bridge."

"Was there plenty of good stuff among it?"

Pamela Anichka grinned. "Not sure yet. Most of it was filthy. It was one of the old houses on the way up to Heptonstall. Mihail thinks it'd never been cleared out since the day it was built! He was very happy, though – they've got several watches and clocks."

"He's been keen on them for a long time now, hasn't he?"

"You're not kidding. Still, they know where to find him when he's not busy with homework."

And at least we know you'll be all right when you're with Mihail, thought Ian, wondering how they would feel when PA became more venturesome and went out with young fellows about whom they knew nothing.

"You don't mind if I go out tomorrow, Dad, do you?"

"No, love, why should I?" he responded, while supposing already that he was going to hate Sunday lunch alone. "Are you invited to Stonemoor again?"

"Actually – no." Suddenly her manner changed; she glanced down at her hands. "I'm having lunch with my father."

"He's back in Yorkshire then?" Ian had heard that Gerald Thomas had opened up a London head office of the family firm. They were doing well, exporting a great deal.

"Just for a visit, I think. There was a piece about him in the *Halifax Courier*, didn't you see it? You needn't put on your anxious face, Dad – Mihail's going with me."

Ian said nothing. Pamela Anichka hadn't seen her natural father for years; it was quite normal for her to wish to go over there. It wasn't her fault that this was making him feel so conscious of merely being a substitute – and a somewhat ineffective one, if he was any judge.

Mihail was thankful to be spending Sunday away from home. Breakfast had been an uncomfortable meal, and only because he had asked his mother if he would be allowed to have a go at one, at least, of those clocks.

"Why not, you know by now that I expect you to take care. And as always I'll have a look through them first to see which are so good that they justify qualified attention."

He had grinned across the table. "And then those are the ones you'll give me?" he'd asked, with mock innocence.

"That's wishful thinking, and well you know it! But I dare say there'll be more than one that comes your way." Pamela was proud of the concentration Mihail employed, and his considerable skill.

"Just so long as you do not let this interfere with your studies," Andre put in. He didn't like his son to be so absorbed in this antiques business, any more than he had really wanted Pamela to continue running it for so many years.

"I'm not stupid, I know better than to neglect my homework," said Mihail indignantly. He would never let them down by failing to work. When that rugby accident had kept him off school, he had put in hours with his books until he'd caught up with the rest of the form.

"It is not simply that," his father insisted. "These months leading up to your final exams are of the utmost importance. You will need excellent results to ensure you a place at university."

"*If* I go there," Mihail murmured under his breath.

Andre heard, and was infuriated. "The matter is not in question, Mihail. You will go to university; only in that way will you be fully prepared for the life ahead."

Mihail had looked towards his mother. She knew that all he wanted was to work as a clockmaker, nothing else in the whole world fascinated him so completely. And he was good at it. He'd taught himself so much since that time three years ago when he'd spent hours on that old clock almost broken beyond hope of repairing.

"Your father is right, I'm afraid, love," Pamela told him gently. "If you'll only agree and continue to study, you will have that better education behind you, whatever you decide on for a career . . ."

*   *   *

38

"I shan't go there, you know," Mihail assured PA as they sat in the bus on the way to the Thomas's house at Hebden Bridge. "It's my life – they've got to let me have some say in where and how I spend it."

"I suppose university could be fun," Pamela Anichka reflected. "At least, you'd get away from all these restrictions." She could fancy going there herself, if she and Mihail got to the same one . . .

"But what's the point, PA? I'd not be studying what I wanted. I can't waste time like that."

She slid her hand through his arm, beamed up at him. "Okay, then, that's fantastic! We'll be able to go out together like this, and in another year or so, they won't be placing embargoes on anywhere that we want to go. I shall have a job by then."

"Oh, yes? Doing what?" She wasn't at all musical like her mother or grandfather, and, despite his own mother's original career, the decorating business wasn't really girl's work.

"Something in fashion, of course. I'm going to be another Biba or Mary Quant."

"You've never said."

"No – well, I've only just decided." Until today, she had been so certain that Mihail would be made to continue studying that she had resigned herself to a few more years of learning. Suddenly, though, everything seemed to be coming together. Today would be ideal. She was going to talk to her father. Her real father.

The Thomases were in the textile business; her father would know all about the clothing industry, fashion. He would want her to get on, would introduce her around; through him, she would meet people who could help her learn all she needed to know. She fancied designing, although she wouldn't mind running her own exclusive shop. Perhaps her father might eventually set her up in premises somewhere glamorous.

It was years since Pamela Anichka had visited this

house. She'd forgotten it was so impressive and was thankful for Mihail at her side. When Gerald Thomas greeted them at the top step she was relieved that neither his parents nor a maid opened the door to them.

"Hello, Father!" she exclaimed. "You remember Mihail, don't you?"

Gerald nodded, shook hands with the lad, and drew his daughter to him as he welcomed them into the house. For once in his life, he felt awkward. Pamela Anichka had grown into a lovely young woman, very like Tania, but also with a haunting resemblance to his own mother. As she had been in his earliest memories.

"Do come right in," he insisted. "My parents are looking forward to seeing you."

Mihail couldn't avoid noticing that the man seemed hypnotised by PA, to the extent that he received little more attention from him than that first glance. Dismally, he followed them into the elegant sitting room. Thelma and Barry Thomas looked quite old, seated either side of the hearth while a Chopin concerto played on the radiogram in the corner.

As Mr Thomas rose he glanced sideways at his wife and then towards the young people. "Pleased to have you here again, Pamela Anichka, Mihail. You will understand my wife's arthritis prevents her rising."

"But my welcome is no less sincere," Thelma added.

Pamela Anichka and Mihail noticed simultaneously that the woman's chair had wheels. Embarrassed when she sensed that she was staring, PA blushed. Stumbling slightly against a low table, she went to grasp her grandmother's hand.

Thelma Thomas's flinch was controlled, but it was a flinch nevertheless. Young people never realised how sensitive one's hands could become.

Gerald took charge after the preliminary greetings, offering to take their coats which were handed to the maid who had appeared at the open door. She's not a bit like Mrs Singer, thought Mihail, noting the dress of good navy-blue cloth which looked stiffer than the woman's own back.

Gerald and his father were doing their best – a skilled best; this family was accustomed to entertaining people, ranging from local friends to business acquaintances. Mihail wished they did not remind him of the kind of formality one would expect in church. He was experiencing the urge to whisper.

Whispering, however, was not something that Mihail relished. Ever since those awful weeks when his voice had played alarming tricks in the process of breaking, he had felt comfortable only when speaking without first thinking!

PA was doing well, chattering to them all while drinks were proffered and accepted. But, of course, these people were her family, however rarely visited. He tried to accept that Gerald Thomas was her father, but could not.

"You know I've married again, of course," Gerald was telling them now. "At last. Someone I knew years ago, and met again in London. She's not here with me this trip. Couldn't make it, not with the twins born just ten days ago."

Mihail watched Pamela Anichka's face alter. Her cheeks paled, and then flushed. He knew how upset she was, and longed to grasp her arm. They had been seated apart, PA on the sofa beside her father, he himself on a curiously uncomfortable chair; low, with upholstery so soft that he felt to be sitting almost on the floor.

Valiantly, Pamela Anichka smiled around at everyone. "How exciting, congratulations. I wish I'd known, we could have brought something for the babies."

Smiling across at her, Mihail felt his heart lifting. She was doing them all proud, as his Grandmother Baker would say. He certainly had to acknowledge that PA had acquired massive self-possession. No one but he would have known how shaken she was.

Dinner was served in the dining room which Pamela Anichka recalled from previous visits, but it had been redecorated in a lavish paper that gleamed in the sunlight streaming through the large windows.

"Gerald darling, do close the blinds," urged Thelma Thomas. "Gladys has been so busy that she overlooked them."

Venetian blinds were lowered and adjusted, until the room took on the ambience of a dull November. Pamela Anichka only just checked herself in time before remarking what a shame it was to exclude such a glorious day. She didn't know all that much about her father, but enough to be aware that the family cherished all these signs of material wealth.

She hadn't foreseen that the presence of her grandparents would naturally continue throughout her visit; somehow her vision of discussing her future with her father had been as a tête-à-tête. Mihail being there wouldn't have counted, of course, they had shared everything forever. And besides, she wanted him to see how well she handled explaining all her ambitions.

Not getting her father alone was difficult, but must not prevent her from putting across her ideas. The opportunity came when they were returning to the sitting room. Barry Thomas with his wife in her wheelchair led the way, and Mihail hung back for the other two to precede him.

Hesitating until her father was at her side, Pamela Anichka smiled up at him. "I've been longing to talk to you," she declared. "About my career. Your factory produces cloth, doesn't it?"

"Our factor*ies* do, yes." Gerald paused, wondering what the girl could be contemplating. She surely would be the last person to wish to work there!

"Well, in a way, that's connected with what I've set my heart on. All I want is to work in the fashion business, perhaps on the design side. Or I wouldn't mind running my own shop . . ."

Gerald cringed, anticipating her idea of how he might become involved. Had this daughter of his really got so little notion of how much setting up a business would cost?

42

"And what does your mother think about all this?" he enquired carefully. From the publicity he'd come across, Tania was earning well as a professional singer.

"Oh, I needed to talk to you first, Father. Mum doesn't have all that much time when she's at home. I thought – well, if you could help or something, I'd be able to tell her it was all arranged."

"I see. Well, I'm afraid this isn't a very good time. With the twins having just arrived, and all that. I'm sure you understand. We've recently taken on the new house, you see, and London prices . . ."

"That's all right," said PA very swiftly. "I wasn't really thinking. Just forget I said anything."

She sounded extremely cool. Once again, Mihail admired her composure, but was he the only one to notice that she clamped her lips together to halt that slight quiver?

Her composure lasted only until they were waiting at the bus stop. "How terribly mean! He hasn't done a thing for me in all these years, and now when I ask for help he won't give it."

"Perhaps it really is that he can't afford," Mihail suggested, not wanting PA to be upset by believing her father could be so ungenerous.

"Of course he can! You saw that house."

"Which belongs to your grandparents, surely. And don't forget she's not very well; they probably have to spend a lot on—"

"No, it's on this new family of *his* that the money's going. All I wanted was an investment – in my future," Pamela Anichka added, and thought that sounded rather good.

Mihail put his arm around her shoulders. "Why don't you speak to your mother about it? Or my dad – he is your grandfather, after all."

PA shrugged dejectedly. "Oh, I don't know. Maybe I'll do something else. I suppose I could begin in a shop, so long as the things it sold were really cool." If Mihail was going to be working at his mother's business in Cragg

Vale, she would be glad to remain somewhere near. "I don't like him much, anyway," she declared as soon as they were seated on the bus. "My father, I mean. He's never showed any interest in me, has he?"

Had Ian known his stepdaughter's feelings about Gerald Thomas, he would have been happier. Since PA tended to conceal her vulnerability, he didn't learn of her disappointment. When she bounded into the house after Mihail had seen her to the door he assumed that she'd had a wonderful few hours.

"How did it go?" he asked, looking up from the *Radio Times* where he was trying to find a programme to take his mind away from the reality of his own dissatisfaction.

"Fine, fine, thanks. They've had someone in to redecorate again, the dining room looked really posh. Oh, and my father's got a big house in London now, very expensive."

They might have asked Canning's, thought Ian; they know we're in the decorating business. It wouldn't have hurt them to suggest we at least estimate for doing the place up. But then, he supposed the Thomases – and especially Gerald – still felt awkward about the past.

"What does he look like, these days?"

PA gave him a curious glance as she removed her coat and tossed it over the bannister at the foot of the stairs.

"Oh – you know, a bit older, but so smart and sophisticated you never notice the few grey hairs." Looking at Ian now, she couldn't help wishing that he'd brighten himself up. Not for working, she understood there'd be no point in that, but at weekends like this. He had some nice clothes, especially those that Mum had persuaded him to buy in the States. Admittedly, they weren't particularly trendy three years on, but they'd so rarely been worn that everything still appeared new.

Ian read in her eyes the gist of what she was thinking, and suspected yet again that everyone thought he was an old fogey. What was he doing, letting himself become reduced to this?

44

Tomorrow, I'm going to change, he decided. He'd begin as he had promised himself for years, by being assertive at work. He would leave Burrows in no doubt that Ian Baker was indispensable to Canning's, then he'd ensure that he was justly rewarded for all that he did. The years of experience and sheer hard slog had honed his skills; it was high time that fact was appreciated by everybody.

They were trying to complete a restoration job in order to be ready for the immense task of decorating the school. The current work was on a big old house in Halifax, close to Manor Heath. Ian had quite enjoyed the journeys each morning as Mihail's school was in the same area and he regularly gave the lad a lift, as he did the next day.

Although Ian was preoccupied with assessing how best to raise the subject of his future with Burrows, he mustn't have Mihail believe he was unhappy with his company.

"I gather you and our PA had a right good time yesterday," he began. "She seemed well suited with everything at the Thomas's."

Mihail didn't know what to say. He shouldn't be surprised perhaps that Pamela Anichka hadn't let on about her disappointment. She did always say that it was only to *him* that she revealed her true feelings.

"Yes, it – it's a splendid place, and her grandparents are very – sociable."

"As, no doubt, Gerald is."

"Well, I hardly know him," Mihail began, and clammed up.

"I knew him, once, you know. Used to play in the same band. Mostly Glenn Miller's music."

The conversation slid onto easier ground, even given their differing tastes. Ian heard enough pop music, didn't he, to be able to discuss groups like the Beatles, or the Kinks?

Ted Burrows was at work at the old house already, even though Ian had made sure of arriving five minutes early. A couple of the other men were getting their tools

45

together and picking up pots of paint ready for going off to the rooms nearing completion.

The sound of a motorcycle approaching assured them that their apprentice Eric was on his way, and reminded Ian of his intention. The lad had been working closely with Burrows. Ian was going to suggest that he should now take him under his wing. That way he would demonstrate that he ought to be given more responsibility. Had Burrows forgotten that Ian Baker had been teaching apprentices their trade over ten years ago?

"I've been thinking, Ted," Ian began, and wished that Burrows would turn from whatever he was fiddling with on the workbench and pay attention. "About yon apprentice – Eric. It's wasting a lot of your time having him round your neck. Now if you'd only let me . . ."

At last Burrows faced him, but slowly; Ian guessed he was reluctant. There was something sort of strange about his eyes, as though he couldn't quite see straight. If Ian hadn't known him for the assertive beggar he was, he'd have believed the man was confused, or agitated; he was breathing noisily, and his cheeks were turning red.

"What do you say then?" Ian prompted him. He had heard the engine of the bike cut out, and Eric's footsteps in the entrance hall.

Ted Burrows opened his mouth to speak, and no words came out. Ian was beginning to realise there was something wrong when Burrows clutched at the bench. It toppled with him as he collapsed onto the tiled floor.

"Well, I'll go to heck!" Ian exclaimed, bending over the man as Eric hurried to them. "Fetch t'others, lad, quick!"

Eric stared, horrified, at their boss whose breath was emerging with alarming rasping sounds.

"Look sharp then, this is bad," Ian insisted.

The other men were running towards them anyway, drawn by the clatter of paint cans and other equipment crashing to the floor with the workbench.

"He passed clean out," Ian told them. "What do you reckon?"

"Looks serious to me," the elder of the two workers said. "Could be a stroke."

"Aye," his colleague agreed. "Better get an ambulance here fast as we can." He darted out of the house, and off in the direction of the nearest telephone box.

"Should we give him summat to drink?" Eric suggested. "Can't just leave him stuck there like that." He was terrified that Mr Burrows was going to die while they all just stood there, staring.

Ian shook his head. "Best not do owt till the ambulance gets here. Don't want to make matters worse." He noticed now that Burrows's limbs were twitching.

He knelt down beside him, tried to feel his pulse but didn't seem able to locate it. This is stupid, he thought, all us lot here and nobody knows what to do. At least, we can tell he's still alive, there's no mistaking the fact that he's breathing.

The ambulance crew assured them that they had been right not to interfere with the man. "You need to know what you're doing afore you assist folk that's having a stroke."

Confirmation of their diagnosis shook every one of them. They stood around awkwardly, feeling useless as well as perturbed while they watched Ted Burrows being placed on a stretcher and carried out to the ambulance.

"One of us ought to go with him," the oldest of their team suggested.

"It'll have to be me," said Ian. "And I'll take the van, then I'll be able to get back here after I've seen him settled."

The ambulance sped ahead, its bell clanging, while Ian coped with the morning traffic, thankful that the General Hospital was only a short distance from where they were working.

By the time he had found a parking space and hurried into the hospital, Ted was out of sight.

"He's being resuscitated, love," one of the nurses told

47

him. "It'll be a bit yet before they'll let you see him. Is he a relative, like?"

"No, my boss. We were just going to start work when it happened."

"So, his family will know nowt about him collapsing then?"

"Nothing at all, no. Are you going to let them know?"

"Somebody will have to. He is married, is he?"

"Yes. But I can't for the life of me remember exactly where they live – somewhere Pye Nest way, I think."

The nurse gave him a harassed smile. "Well, if you're not that close, we'll see they're told. Happen he'll have a driving licence or summat, with his address."

Waiting and wondering while he sat on a bench, Ian felt terrible. Seeing Burrows collapse like that had been a shock, and never having liked the man made him feel even worse. He watched the wall clock, thinking how he was wasting time here; he could do nothing, yet he knew in his heart he would feel compelled to remain until they could reassure him about Ted Burrows's condition.

When a doctor came eventually to tell Ian that they had stabilised Ted, and taken him to a ward where he would receive special care, Mrs Burrows was with him. If Ian had ever met her in the past, it was years ago, so long that he had no recollection of the middle-aged woman with greying hair scraped back into a French pleat.

"Thank you for looking after him," she said, her voice revealing the strain she suffered.

"I didn't do so much," Ian began. "Didn't know what to . . ."

"You made sure they got him here, that's the main thing."

"Are you stopping here for a bit, or do you want a lift or anything?"

"I'm stopping. See how he goes on, you know. My daughter's on her way. In any case, I have the car when I'm ready for home. Thanks for offering, though. You've been ever so good, love."

Before leaving the hospital Ian telephoned Pamela to tell her about Ted Burrows. She needed to know – the only other directors of Canning's were on the financial side, not really concerned in how the work was organised.

"This is dreadful," she exclaimed. "Does Mrs Burrows know?"

"Aye, she's here at the hospital now."

"I'll have to have a think about what we're going to do. Can you come round to the house after work? I'll shut the shop early."

All Pamela had decided by that evening was that Ian should continue as Ted would have done: sorting out which of the men should do each task, and attending to such routine matters as ordering supplies.

"If you keep in touch, Ian, I'll know what's going on. And we'll get together again in another week or so, see what's to happen from there."

Ian went to see Pamela on the following Sunday morning. The news from the hospital wasn't good. Ted Burrows was partially paralysed by the stroke and he could barely speak.

"There could be a full recovery," Ian told his sister. "The hospital people are confident of that, but it's going to be a long business, even after they discharge him."

Pamela nodded; she had made her own enquiries, telephoning Ted's wife several times. Although it was so many years since she herself had done any of the actual work for Canning's, she was deeply conscious that it originally was the firm she had built up. Nothing could alter this feeling that she was responsible for their workers.

Ian had done a lot of thinking during that week. He'd never been the kind of person who'd be glad to seize an opportunity generated by another man's misfortune, but he was realistic. Learning what an age it would be before Burrows would be fit again, he had recognised that someone would have to step in to manage the company. He was damned sure who that person was going to be.

Putting this to Pamela would be tricky, but he'd had time to weigh that as well. Diplomacy might not be his second name, but he did know his sister.

"So, we'll have to get our contingency plans running," he began. "We've a lot on, with this big house to finish, and that school job coming up. The chaps'll need a manager on the spot, just to keep everything on schedule. I shall understand if the position has to be on a temporary basis, at least until we know a bit more about how he—"

"Now wait a minute, Ian," his sister sighed, thrusting a hand through her short blonde hair. "Ian love, you'd better hang on, see what I have to say."

"You're not going to give it to me, are you? Even now, when Canning's is desperate for somebody to take charge, you're refusing to make me manager."

"I can't, love, don't you see? I can't take Ted's job away from him now. He needs an incentive to make him get better; I'll never deprive him of that."

And what about me? thought Ian. You've deprived me of the right to feel I was getting somewhere ever since the day I began working with you.

"You'll be given an increase in pay, naturally," Pamela continued. "It shouldn't matter to you that you're still only called the foreman. I shan't try to interfere, you'll have total responsibility."

Ian was too upset to even listen.

Four

"Ian darling, do you not think that you are worrying unnecessarily?" Tania was smiling in that way she had of encouraging him to believe her. "We both know Pamela – she would no more wish to hurt you, than she would hurt anyone."

Ian smiled back despite his misgivings. He not only knew his sister, he knew himself – and was aware of his shortcomings. He'd always tended to feel slighted, when no slight was meant. And these past few months had proved that none of the men appeared to care whether he was called their foreman or the manager. They did work as well for him as ever they had for Burrows, and young Eric was really putting his back into learning the job.

"So – are you feeling a little happier about one thing now?" his wife enquired.

"I suppose so, love. You've been patient, yet again, putting up with me moaning on about Canning's."

Tania laughed. "It is not very difficult to live with your complaining, when I know how much you really love your work. I am just glad that I have not been away too often recently. And not only on your account."

"Oh, what do you mean? Is there something else that I should be getting anxious about?" Ian was beginning to realise that the firm had been taking his mind off other things.

"That daughter of ours, of course," Tania said, and Ian recognised that she never really made him feel that Pamela Anichka wasn't his.

"She's not been doing something she shouldn't, I hope?"

Tania shook her head, although her expression remained solemn. "Perhaps it is simply that she is young; yet not so young that she will accept much guidance from anyone. I had to be quite cross with her the other day. I do not think you were around when she went out that afternoon; you did not see that miniskirt she was wearing."

"I've seen what other young lasses wear. It's a wonder their backsides aren't numb with cold in winter time!"

"This is not funny, Ian. Pamela Anichka seems totally unaware of the dangers. These girls go around revealing so much leg that any male over the age of, of, oh, I do not know, *fourteen*, will be attracted. And all the time they are children still, would not know how to cope if someone tried to seduce them."

"What did PA say when you put this to her?"

"But I have not done so. How could I?" Tania's accent was steadily increasing. "Do you wish for me to place such thoughts within her head, to convey to her these ideas?"

Ian grinned. "Nay, Tania love, just think! Youngsters today know that much about sex, they can't be oblivious to where attraction starts."

"You think? I am sure I would not know. I was never brought up in such a way. Things were so different in Russia."

That's as may be, Ian thought. But you, my love, seem to have forgotten how young you were when you succumbed to Gerald Thomas! He would not mention that, of course. He'd hate his wife to even suspect he could be hinting that PA inherited some sensuality from her.

"I dare say things have altered a lot everywhere since we were growing up," he said mildly. "We can only keep an eye on her, make sure she doesn't go completely wild. And I'm sure she won't. Don't forget how much time she still spends with Mihail, and he's got his head screwed on right. You can't pretend his ideas would lead anybody off the straight and narrow."

*   *   *

"I wish you had something more dynamic in mind, that is all, Mihail," Andre was saying. "I can appreciate your love of clocks, the satisfaction you find in repairing them . . ."

"Then why won't you let me do that, as a job?" his son interrupted.

"You have not heard me out," Andre reproved. "As you tend not to hear me out on this. Clockmaking is hardly work which will make either your name or your fortune. You are young, too young for reaching decisions which may so limit your entire future."

"You're not saying anything, Mum," Mihail prompted. *She* knew how much he relished working at the bench they had set up at the back of her shop. Knew how good he was.

"You could still repair watches and clocks in your spare time," Pamela suggested. "At least until you've been to university."

"But what would I study if I did go there?"

"Languages perhaps, or literature?" suggested Andre. He'd always wanted his son to be considered cultured. But did that merely spring from his awareness of his own roots being so far away? Was he being selfish in expecting Mihail to prove that they were fully integrated here?

"You could do one year at least at university," his mother persisted. She hated to see Andre so disappointed by their son's obstinacy.

Mihail sighed exaggeratedly, returned to the half-hunter watch on which he was working. A few more days and he would have this one going again.

He had lost count now of the number of clocks and watches he'd repaired. His biggest thrill was listening to the eager ticking that emerged after all his hours of concentration; the second biggest when his mother sold one of the items he had restored.

Ever since he was fourteen he had known what he wished to do. No matter what anyone said, he could not view university as other than a waste of time.

"Maybe you couldn't take any clocks with you, but there'd always be a number of watches needing your attention," Pamela reminded him. "I'm sure you would find somewhere to keep them in your rooms."

Andre gave her a look, not certain that her suggestion was wise. If Mihail went to university, it should be in order to concentrate fully on his studies.

"Just give it a try, eh?" Pamela added. She would say no more. She only wanted Mihail to be happy and fulfilled. This was tearing her apart. Content though she was to support her husband's ideas, she didn't intend to see her son made miserable.

Andre ought to be satisfied that his own life, these days, was very full. He'd had plenty of bookings throughout this 1966/7 season. As solo violinist with orchestras up and down the country, he was performing a great deal. Pamela knew how good it was to have an interesting career; the antiques trade was even more rewarding than ever she'd imagined. They could afford to let their son choose work that wouldn't necessarily bring in massive profits, if that was what he wished.

Confronted for the first time with death since Kennedy's, Mihail was jolted out of the idea that when he left school he might spend the rest of his life doing the work he enjoyed.

He was listening to the radio one evening early in January when they announced that Donald Campbell had been killed when Bluebird had somersaulted at 300 mph. Campbell had been a hero since the day the family were staying near Coniston and happened to see him conducting trials with the boat.

He can't be dead! thought Mihail, shaken by being made to realise that it wasn't only old people who were lost. Perhaps there was something to be said for making your mark in the world while you still felt that you had aeons of time ahead of you.

Before that January was out further sudden deaths

set him thinking yet more seriously. Three American astronauts perished on the launch pad, trapped by fire inside their Apollo spacecraft. The fact that they were merely participating in a simulation of the forthcoming launch made their deaths all the more poignant.

A sensitive teenager, Mihail couldn't stop reflecting on how deeply this must have affected their families. Death was so dreadfully final. Considering all the members of his own family, he appreciated suddenly how greatly he would miss any one of them. Especially either of his parents. And his father so frequently seemed to him quite old. This year Andre would be fifty-nine and, no matter how energetically he pursued his musical career, his face was becoming lined, that glorious hair entirely silver. Although aware that his father's experiences while escaping from Russia had accelerated the ageing process, all signs of his advancing years made Andre seem vulnerable.

Mihail recognised now that he needed to do at least one thing to prove that he wasn't entirely driven by his own wishes.

"I'll do it, Dad, I'll go to Oxford," he told him after only another week of deliberating. No one would be left to wonder how differently events might have turned out. He would do all he could by taking up the place his excellent exam results warranted.

Twelve months at university would seem a long time, but he would tackle them with a will, as a kind of offering, which he hoped would contribute to his father's well-being.

Both Pamela and Andre were delighted by Mihail's decision, and that he'd made it without further intervention from them. Sonia was excited for him, and Tania congratulated him on being the first in the family to go to university. Pamela Anichka was absolutely furious.

She had been working for some time now in a trendy boutique in Manchester, driving herself there in the Mini bought for her by Tania. Travelling there each day from their home a few miles inside the Yorkshire border was well compensated by often seeing Mihail of an evening and always at weekends.

"How could you," she exclaimed. "How could you decide to go off like that for such a long time! You knew I took this job so that we'd never be parted."

Mihail knew nothing of the kind. PA had been determined to get work in the fashion industry, and this was the best she could find. The most enticing aspect of that boutique was the owner's interest in design, which meant that every year she produced a few in-house clothes for sale along with established brands.

"I'm sure she's going to teach me all I'll need to know," Pamela Anichka had enthused during the first week. "You'll see, Mihail – one day I'll be famous."

Already fame seemed to her to be a long time coming. At the end of six months she had been allowed to watch while her employer was drafting an outfit for the next season, but that was the extent of PA's creativity.

The prospect of Mihail's departure for Oxford in the autumn was the shock that hurtled the girl down to earth. Fun though the boutique was, with its lively clientele and the opportunity for trying on the more outrageous fashions, it had not produced the opportunities she needed.

"Give it time," Mihail told her now she was bemoaning its shortcomings. "Let's just enjoy these next few months, eh?"

The only way in which Pamela Anichka could enjoy the time they spent together was by blocking out the future. *Mihail wouldn't go away, not really*, she told herself.

She'd suggested as much to him shortly after hearing about his intention. "You'll change your mind, when it comes to it. You've always said you think university'd be a waste of time for you."

Mihail had simply looked at her, unable to explain. It wasn't at all cool, was it, to be spending a year of your life pleasing your parents? He couldn't imagine anyone else deciding on that. But not everyone had a father like Andre Malinowski.

He had heard the story so many times, yet it never became less moving to be reminded of how Andre had been in his mid-thirties when he had fled Communist Russia as the Second World War was ending. Seeing his wife shot hadn't prevented him from escaping, because his belief that he had got to reach England was over-whelming.

The home Andre had provided at Stonemoor for Tania must have felt terribly lonely until he was able to get his daughter out of their homeland, but he had endured. Meeting Pamela had been the best thing that could have happened for Andre, for all their sakes, but life since then hadn't all been easy.

His mother was the one who'd told Mihail how people who had misunderstood had taken Andre for a Communist spy, distressing them both by their false accusations. Mihail himself had seen while he was growing up the way that every mention of espionage reminded his parents of past antagonism.

The Profumo affair especially remained in his mind, making him aware of how hurt Andre would be by the suppositions that he might have become involved in similar duplicity.

By the time September came and Mihail went off to university he was beginning to look forward to this new experience. He was to study history, had realised that his life so far fitted him for enjoying that subject. Stonemoor House itself, which his mother had restored so effectively all those years ago, exuded the essence of its Regency period. And there were the antiques – not only within their home, but those that stocked Pamela's intriguing shop. If he gave his mind to all that he would be taught, he would return at the end of a year better equipped by far for being of use there. Clocks would always remain his deepest interest, but he might help his mother more widely once he had acquired additional background knowledge.

Actually leaving the West Riding was far more traumatic than Mihail had expected. He had been away innumerable times in the past, for holidays with family, more recently with friends. He had travelled abroad, relishing the freedom to laugh with his fellow students, to drink rather more than he should, and to chat up girls.

Pamela Anichka had punished him for that when she heard the family laughing over some of his escapades which had come to light, and she had punished him throughout the past week because he truly was about to go from Stonemoor.

PA's tactics were neither particularly original nor endearing. In a child it would have been called sulking, in a girl of seventeen it was a moodiness revealed in frigid silence.

She had refused to say goodbye. That was all right with him; Mihail's new maturity had not altered him so completely that he no longer felt awkward around her. But he would have preferred not to have this surprising distress exacerbated by PA's withdrawal.

It was raining on the day that Andre drove his son to the station in Halifax. Torrents of rain which tore across the valley around Stonemoor House, obliterating from view all but the meadows nearest to hand, their surrounding black drystone walls glossy with moisture.

Staring out of the car window, Mihail struggled to glimpse the hills which he had known and loved so well, longing quite desperately to imprint his mind with their wild beauty.

"You should find better weather, I think, while travelling south," said Andre, hoping to cheer. Awareness of that original reluctance to go there at all was dampening his own pleasure in Mihail's decision. Though not his pride in his son's achievement.

It was all too easy today to visualise the lad alone, dejected in rooms no more than adequate. Had Mihail made friends readily enough at school, or had the frequency of his outings with Pamela Anichka signalled some unease with other youngsters?

"You must let us know how you are."

"Of course, I will, Dad. I'll ring you later today."

"Not just to assure us of your safe arrival. You must keep in touch." Andre recalled an occasion years ago, while Mihail was tiny, when he had travelled to London trying to secure bookings to perform. He could feel right now the amazing pain created by being away from the infant. "We shall miss you, my son."

"You'll scarcely have time. If I know our Sonia, she'll make the most of being the only one at home. And there's Tania . . ."

"I have treated you all fairly, equally. Or I have tried . . ." Andre was not sorry to have the opportunity for saying this. He was as aware as anyone of undercurrents, the often silent reproaches from offspring dissatisfied. However brief their discontent.

"Come home whenever you can," said Andre later, seeing him onto the train while rain fell like rods of steel all about them. "You must always know you will be welcomed wholeheartedly."

Mihail had liked Oxford when he and his parents went there to see Magdalen, the college where he'd been accepted. He liked it even more today, surprising himself because the part of his nature that loved the open countryside around Stonemoor House could so easily have been uncomfortable among so many impressive buildings.

Here, though, lugging his suitcase along The High, he realised at once what a lovely place this was for studying history. Breathless from carrying the case plus a smaller bag, he arrived at the lodge and was immediately thrust into the life there. On the narrow winding stairway he met other young men, heard laughter and conversation coming from rooms to either side, all to him sounding excited.

His room was small by Stonemoor standards, but

pleasant enough, with substantial if ill-matched furniture which defeated Mihail's immediate attempts to date it. He was glad to see a table large enough to accommodate any watches for repair. Hurrying to the window, he smiled to himself, grateful for this view of the quad. He was thankful already that he hadn't held out any longer against the idea of studying here.

Unpacking and putting away the clothing and books which he had brought with him, he set beside his bed the silver-framed photograph of his parents with Sonia. He must phone them soon, let them know how well he was sure to settle in here.

He also found the box containing a Victorian watch which his mother had offered yesterday. "Do what you can with it, love. It certainly isn't working now, looks as if it hasn't for years!"

He would enjoy that challenge, but not before he had become acquainted with Oxford, and with his future companions. The college itself was imposing, of course, in keeping with all those that he'd passed on the way here from the station.

Before the meal that evening, he strolled towards Magdalen Bridge, then explored further, locating Radcliffe Square where he stood for a moment gazing about him.

While he was out Mihail found a call box and rang Stonemoor House. Andre answered, his voice eloquent with relief that their son had arrived quite safely and sounded happy.

"Yes, it's going to prove very interesting, I'm sure, Dad. Haven't met any of the other students yet; that'll begin tonight. Is Mum around?"

"Waiting to get a word in, yes."

Pamela needed to know that he'd eaten the sandwiches provided for his journey. And was that room of his warm? She imagined old buildings like that were full of draughts.

Mihail laughed. "But I've always lived in an old building, haven't I?" he teased. "I've been toughened up to endure any discomfort here!"

"Cheek! You've lived in luxury, my lad. And don't you go forgetting who made Stonemoor so comfortable . . ."

He would not forget, would never forget his home. But that fact wouldn't prevent him from relishing this new environment.

Sonia wanted to speak to him next, a Sonia who was trying hard to sound very grown-up and sophisticated. Now that her brother had gone away she would often rely on PA for company, and that young lady had matured rapidly since working in Manchester.

"Do they have lots of dances there?" Sonia wanted to know. "Or do you spend all your time in pubs?"

"I've scarcely had a chance to find that out, have I?" Mihail replied, and wondered what their parents must be thinking of Sonia's sudden interest in drinking. "I'll report back when I've tried them out. Are you thinking of coming up to Oxford when you finish school then?"

"No, but that doesn't mean I don't know what goes on away from this Godforsaken spot!"

Mihail smiled to himself again. Sonia was going through a phase when everything about home was considered boring. He supposed he had missed that phase himself, mainly due to occupying so much free time with his mother's clocks.

"Keep an eye on Mum and Dad for me," he said before ringing off. He suspected, though, that they might have quite a time restraining Sonia now. The question about dancing and pubs had reminded him that this young sister of his was trying to behave beyond her sixteen years.

Gradually absorbed into university life, Mihail soon became too busy to dwell on what his sister or anyone at home might be planning. Learning here was so different from school; just as enjoyable as he'd found most of his lessons in the past, but unnervingly strange. Not being obliged to conform to a timetable where every hour was filled took some adjusting.

61

From his earliest tutorials, Mihail recognised that he might respond well to methods here. And away from studying and his books, his love of rugby introduced him to a whole new set of companions.

The first real friend he made was Rupert Atherton-Ward, a young man taller even than Mihail himself, with the strong shoulders of a natural forward, dark hair, and brown eyes with a wicked glint.

By the second Sunday after term commenced Mihail had discovered that Rupert lived only a short distance away, near Chipping Norton. Invited to join the Atherton-Wards for tea, he was interested to find that their home closely resembled his own in size, but was constructed of the Cotswold stone which gave the exterior a mellow appearance.

Internally, the entrance hall even had similar oak panelling to Stonemoor's, although, he noted with a secret smile, in a somewhat neglected condition. The ground floor rooms were decorated in a more modern style than his home but, with the exception of a sitting room, they were furnished with antiques.

Noting Mihail's interest as soon as introductions were completed, Rupert's father smiled at him. "You have some knowledge of old furniture perhaps?"

"That's right. My mother's always been fascinated by history and old things. Actually, she's in the antiques business now, has been for years."

His hostess appeared surprised. "So, she doesn't find running the home keeps her completely occupied? Ru tells me you have a sister at home still."

"Mum has help in the house, a woman who's been there longer than she has. You see, my father was married before. His first wife died. And I have a half-sister Tania as well, but she has her own home. She's a lot older than me, her daughter's roughly my age."

"Sounds complicated . . ."

Before Mihail agreed that it was, Rupert's sister appeared in the doorway from the conservatory.

"Hi – I'm Annabel. I hope Rupert's told you I'm his twin?"

Rupert grimaced. "Why on earth should I? You always introduce yourself, anyway, to all my friends."

"And why not!" his sister exclaimed. "We share everything, always have."

Her words reminded Mihail of Pamela Anichka, but this girl's hand was reaching out, cool and smooth in his; her smile, lighting hazel eyes, seemed to penetrate into his head. He could not think for long about any other girl.

Annabel was almost as tall as her twin, but slender and quite small boned. The clothes she wore were unlike any Mihail was accustomed to seeing around home on either Sonia or PA. Her tan skirt and matching jacket were in leather that had been fringed at the hem, and they were worn with fringed boots, closely fitted to calves which made him mouth a silent whistle.

Even despite the affinity he'd already developed with her brother, Mihail could not deny that Annabel's presence made that visit to their home most exhilarating.

"Be sure and see me while you're there," he insisted when she arranged to come up to Oxford during the following weekend. Mihail could not imagine a more promising introduction to this new chapter of his life.

She was going to hate every moment of this year, Pamela Anichka knew. Unable to keep away from his home, she had been over to Stonemoor that Sunday afternoon. Everyone had appeared pleased to see her, and Sonia had been ecstatic when given a couple of skirts she'd discarded. But going there had been a mistake. Without Mihail, the place felt dead. A part of her, failing to accept that he had left, had expected to hear his voice, to see his wonderful smile which always widened when he found her in the room. Lonelier than ever in her life before, PA had lingered on, watching while Sonia tried on the skirts, commiserating with her about the failure of their parents to understand the latest fashion.

"Do you want to go dancing next Friday night?" Sonia suggested. "Mum and Dad would let me go to the Mecca if you were going."

Perhaps because of her barely acknowledged feeling that being with his sister might make her seem closer to Mihail, PA was preparing now for that Friday night. Taking care while making up her face and styling her short hair, because she would never go out without making an effort. She could not remember ever feeling less like going anywhere.

Sonia was excited, so excited that Pamela Anichka was annoyed. She was just like a little girl; who would be bothered to even talk to them at the Mecca? PA only hoped that people would be able to tell that they *weren't* the same age.

Whatever other dancers believed, both girls began attracting partners as soon as they emerged after the obligatory titivating of faces and hair in the cloakroom. They had only just arranged to meet regularly beside the counter where handbags were deposited when two young men approached them.

"Can you do this?" one of them asked PA while his friend was asking Sonia the same question.

The dance was the cha-cha-cha, and Sonia had learned the steps from her friends at school. Pamela Anichka didn't intend to admit that Sonia knew something that she didn't. Fortunately, the boy who had taken her onto the dance floor was the sort who enjoyed teaching someone, by the end of that number she had acquired the basic movements.

Out of the corner of her eye she had glimpsed Sonia and been surprised by her expertise. "You looked good," she congratulated her when they met up as arranged.

"I'll teach you if you want," Sonia offered, eager to please.

"Not here," said PA hastily.

Relieved that the next dance was a rock and roll, she persuaded Sonia to dance with her. Relaxing in something they both had done so often when they were together at Stonemoor, the girls fitted their steps energetically to the beat, and became conscious that they attracted quite a bit of attention.

Sure enough, they were surrounded by prospective partners the minute the next number started. Despite herself, PA was enjoying the evening, and Sonia looked thrilled with it all.

They had promised to be home by eleven-thirty, a promise which Pamela Anichka was happy to keep even when it meant leaving the Mecca before the end. She could be happy to dance with other young men, but there was nobody like Mihail. She wouldn't even want to go out for one date with anybody else.

Sonia was less content to go home. One youngster, who looked at least twenty but admitted to being seventeen, wanted to take her out.

"What do you think?" she asked PA before they went to collect their coats. "He seems ever so nice."

"Does he live near here?"

"Yes, only a mile away."

"Would your mum and dad like you coming on the bus by yourself?"

Sonia sighed. "I don't suppose they would. I wondered – well, his friend did say he fancied you . . ."

Pamela Anichka didn't even enquire which young man was his friend. "No, thank you. You can count me out, I'm afraid." Just because she had a car, she wasn't going to start driving Sonia all over the place.

Sonia grinned, and gave a tiny shrug. "It's all right, I'm not bothered really. I've had such a good time, I'll just look forward to coming dancing with you again."

The girls did return to the Mecca and go to other dance halls in different towns. They also went to the cinema whenever something appealed to them. PA found she didn't mind going around with Mihail's sister, while he was away.

When he came home for his first vacation from Oxford,

though, PA's attitude towards Sonia reverted to being quite wary. The girl did cling so to Mihail, to the degree that other people were being pushed out.

As soon as she got home from work on the day he arrived, Pamela Anichka dashed over to Stonemoor to suggest that she and Mihail should go to see *You Only Live Twice*. "We always see the James Bond films together, don't we?"

He smiled. "Actually, I'm taking our Sonia. You can come with us, of course. Why not?"

It was not the same, naturally. Somehow, Sonia contrived to sit between them; there was no chance now that Mihail would even hold PA's hand. And during the interval Sonia never stopped talking. She went on and on about the dances she and Pamela Anichka had been to, and how they'd had such a lot of partners.

"Did you meet somebody fabulous then, PA?" Mihail leaned across to enquire. "Got a regular boyfriend now?"

"No, I haven't," Pamela Anichka told him sharply. How could he even think that she would want to go out with anybody else?

The Sunday was no better. The whole family was invited to Stonemoor for Sunday lunch. PA wouldn't have minded that ordinarily – she liked to see Mildred Baker even though she wasn't strictly her grandmother. And Gwen and Tom were all right, the boys as well. Gwen had been quite kind since PA went to work in Manchester, asking her to the house occasionally, sometimes meeting her for tea in Kendal Milnes which had felt very sophisticated.

Pamela Anichka had silently warned herself not to get too excited about that Sunday; with so many folk around, Mihail's attention would have to be divided. Once again, though, Sonia appeared to be the one in favour with her brother. He laughed and joked with her so much that PA wondered what had transformed the girl into somebody suddenly so interesting. Hadn't he always in the past treated Sonia like the kid she was?

Walking back to the cottage with her mother and Ian afterwards, Pamela Anichka felt utterly deflated.

Neither Tania nor her husband were taking much notice of her. Ian had been talking to his sister. Everything would be different at work the following morning, and he really could not imagine how he would adapt to the changes.

Five

Ian had never really expected that Ted Burrows would return to work. It was so long now since he'd collapsed with that stroke, and Pamela had often said how concerned she was that their manager seemed to be making hardly any progress.

Canning's had continued paying Burrows something, Ian knew, although he hadn't known how much. Pamela had always maintained that keeping the man's position for him was providing an incentive to get better. The shock was enormous when she told her brother that Burrows was returning.

No one knew how much he would be able to do. Ian had listened while his sister explained that the responsibilities that went with the position should be well within the manager's capabilities now. She doubted if he would be up to tackling any of the physical work.

"I know I can rely on you to be good to him, Ian. There'll happen be times when you have to be a bit patient, like. But I know you'll be understanding. It was so awful for him, his family as well, when he had the stroke."

Pamela had gone on about how they must help them to get over this terrible time.

Ian appreciated all that, but he had a nasty feeling that his own terrible time was just beginning.

Ted Burrows arrived at the community hall which Canning's were refurbishing at five minutes to ten. Ian already had the other men working well and Eric, who had completed his apprenticeship now, was using the artistic talent he possessed to decorate the front of the platform.

"I always said that lad would make a fine artist," Burrows remarked after greeting them all.

Ian, aware that their manager had said nothing of the kind, simply nodded. "He's come on very well."

"Good, good. And are the other chaps the same as we've allus had; any new faces?"

Ian walked beside him as Burrows limped the length of that large main room to meet one newcomer. After a brief chat, the manager suggested they should let the man get on with the door he was painting.

Returning to the spot where Ian had left the cupboard he was sanding down, Burrows sighed. "I dare say you'll be glad I'm back to work again, Ian lad."

Ian flinched at the 'lad'; he was close to thirty-seven now.

Burrows smiled, and Ian willed himself not to stare at the side of his face which didn't quite match the other.

"Yes, you'll be relieved to hand on all the responsibility. Not everybody's suited for it, as you'll have found out. Any road, there we are. We'll soon have things back the way they were."

Before the week was over Ian realised that things would never become anything like they had been in the past. The situation was far worse than he had ever known at Canning's. Perhaps because he was so glad to be back in charge, Ted Burrows was issuing instructions when none were needed, countermanding Ian's directions over the simplest of tasks, until their workers became so confused that they were ready to rebel.

Determined never to mention problems regarding Burrows with his sister again, Ian decided that improving the atmosphere at work must be up to him. Travelling back and forth to the job, and on his own in the house one evening when Tania was singing in Leeds, he thought the matter through.

He's not going to leave, any more than I am, he reflected. And he's not going to change his way with everybody. I'm the one who will have to alter.

69

Could he become as understanding as Pamela supposed? Making allowance for the aftermath of that stroke, could he put up with the injustices, the slights that would continue to occur?

Had he been a religious man, that might have helped, but he was not. Thinking how unsuited he was to such an approach, though, Ian suddenly was reminded of the Good Samaritan. He'd always liked that story of the man who'd taken such trouble to care for someone he didn't know.

Happen I can do a bit of something for old Burrows, he decided. It wouldn't cost more than a little pride. Making the effort couldn't do any harm, might even do a great deal of good.

Putting the resolution into practice was far from easy. As he could have anticipated, Ted Burrows seemed to react scarcely at all to Ian's better grace. The other workers, though, did appear to appreciate there being less surrounding tension.

By the time he had schooled himself to put up with Ted Burrows's ways, Ian's home life was creating as much disturbance as ever his job had produced. Having had to put so much into his work, he hadn't noticed how worried Tania had become about Pamela Anichka.

Following Mihail's brief return to Stonemoor and PA's disappointment about his unenthusiastic response to her, she had begun going out more frequently, usually with Sonia.

The discount Pamela Anichka was given on clothes purchased in the boutique allowed her to buy new things quite often. Anything which she discarded was passed on to Sonia, and that was the chief reason why Tania became really annoyed with her daughter. For the first time in years she herself had been reprimanded. It soon became plain that she was held responsible for PA's recent shortcomings.

Invited for Sunday lunch at Stonemoor House Tania had initially felt delighted when Andre took her aside into another room for a quiet word. She couldn't remember how long it was since she and her father had had one of the chats which always reminded her of how special they were to each other.

"I need to talk to you about Pamela Anichka," he began.

Noticing that he was frowning and his grey eyes looked troubled, Tania felt her heart sink.

Andre didn't keep her waiting for the reason behind his concern. "Are you happy with the way Pamela Anichka dresses now? I am surprised if you are. Frankly, I am most perturbed by the way that Sonia looks when they go out together. And I believe most of the things she wears are inherited from your daughter."

"Oh, Dad, really! I am sure you have no need to be so upset. They are both young, it matters a lot to them that they should be fashionable."

Even while she was trying to reassure him, Tania was recalling how Ian had been equally perturbed by the skimpy little skirts PA delighted in wearing. Tania herself, accustomed to visiting large cities where such clothes were all the rage, now accepted them as normal.

Andre sighed. "Oh, well – if that is your attitude, I suppose I must allow you to make your own decisions about Pamela Anichka. You must be aware of the responsibility of letting her go out looking as she does. Regarding Sonia, however, her mother and I will judge what is best for her. I must insist, therefore, that Pamela Anichka ceases to hand down every item which she discards."

"Very good, Dad," Tania agreed wearily. Inwardly, she could have cried. This was anything but good! Andre's criticism of the way PA dressed was really a criticism of *her*. Believing he considered her an inadequate mother hurt her very deeply.

Naturally, as soon as Pamela Anichka and Sonia were told what had been said, they became all the more determined to continue dressing in the shortest miniskirts obtainable. Whispering and giggling whenever she saw

71

PA, Sonia conjured up ways of outwitting her father. Donning a longer skirt over a mini was no problem to her when she could take off the boring, respectable one in the cloakroom at the dance hall.

For some time this worked beautifully well, until one evening when a prefect from Sonia's school happened to be at the dance they were attending. Amused to see someone like that patronising one of her own favourite places, Sonia enjoyed pointing her out to PA, then forgot about her. But unfortunately for Sonia, even out of uniform their scholars were expected to behave well, and she was reported for appearing unseemly. Their headmistress, whom even most parents considered to be old-fashioned, thought she ought to discover if Sonia's mother was aware of her daughter's uninhibited behaviour.

Pamela was attending an auction; it was Andre who answered the telephone, Andre who was made to feel that he was failing to pay sufficient attention to the care of his younger daughter. Discussing the matter with Pamela as soon as she arrived home, he reminded her that he'd already complained to Tania about PA's influence on Sonia.

"It seems to have had no effect," he sighed. "Have you any suggestions? Obviously, we need to impress on both girls that they cannot continue to do exactly as they wish."

Realising, not for the first time, that her husband wasn't exactly up to date, Pamela tried to be fair. He was right to be concerned that the girls should come to no harm, but if he sided with the head now he might antagonise both of his daughters and PA along with them.

"I'll have a word with Sonia," said Pamela, although she wondered how she would effect a change drastic enough for Andre to approve.

"I think perhaps you might remind Tania also that she had agreed to keep an eye on things," he added.

Pamela never intended saying anything of the kind. For years now she had enjoyed a good relationship with her stepdaughter, one which had been achieved only after working carefully at winning Tania's trust.

On the day that she called at the cottage to see Ian, however, Tania chanced to mention Andre's anxiety about the girls' appearance.

"From what I see of your Sonia when she and PA go off together, Andre's got nothing to complain about now."

Awkwardly, Pamela cleared her throat. "Well, as a matter of fact, he isn't very happy about them." She told Tania all that she'd heard about the way Sonia had looked in that dance hall.

Tania frowned. "But surely *you* are the one who should be stopping Sonia from dressing in an inappropriate way. Why are you blaming me? And why make Pamela Anichka out to be a flighty piece who is leading your precious child astray!"

Pamela was appalled. "Eh, Tania love, I wasn't implying anything of the sort. We both know what kids are, especially when they're into their late teens and think they can do as they like. I'm not blaming you. I know our Sonia only too well. She's like lots of folk her age I'm afraid – will lie like heck to get herself out of trouble."

That, she was certain, was what Sonia had done that morning when tackled about wearing minis. Seeing how fruitless it was to embark on an argument with someone who would declare white was black, Pamela had examined the long skirt which Sonia admitted to wearing. Instead of insisting that she must be told the truth, she had left her daughter with the reminder that they were only concerned because wearing something so revealing gave the male of the species a wrong impression. She said as much now to Tania, and was rewarded with a glare.

"Do you think I do not understand that? You and Dad seem to imagine I have no idea what dangers my own daughter might encounter. You may be assured that I suffered enough myself through being incautious to leave me in no doubt!"

"How am I supposed to keep my temper?" Tania asked

Ian afterwards. "Between their opinions on what I should be doing, and PA's refusal to comply, I am being driven crazy. And you are not much help, are you? You never back me up."

Made to feel that he could never do enough to please anyone, Ian flared at his wife. "Why blame me just because you can't make her knuckle under? She's not going to listen to me, is she, not when I'm not her real father. In any case, she's getting old enough to look after herself, isn't she?"

"Not really, no. But you evidently want to free yourself from any responsibility for her upbringing. I thought we were partners, Ian – that I could rely on you . . ."

"As you can, you ought to know that by now. It's just – well, I don't want to upset PA by coming the stern parent. She's a grand lass, I think the world of her."

"And do you think I do not? Surely, that is all the more reason why I should continue to be concerned about everything she does."

The atmosphere between them grew tense, neither Ian nor Tania could bring themselves to smooth over the unease. Only after PA had come in from seeing *The Sound of Music* yet again and had gone to her room, did Tania approach her husband.

"Darling, forgive me," she said, sitting on the arm of his chair and hugging him. "I am a beast. Of course, PA is my responsibility. You are right to refuse to reprimand her. It is only that I feel unsure so often – unsure how to deal with her."

"I know, love, I know. And that's only natural. It's always difficult to know what to do for the best with youngsters their age."

Together, they went up to bed. Confirming the understanding which had kept them together through the years, they held each other close until confusion surrendered to their passion.

Wilful though her family might suppose Pamela Anichka

74

to be, her spirit was no more than a disguise, her refusal to show how miserable life was making her. Mihail came home again, this time for a longer holiday over Christmas. From the day that he arrived at Stonemoor, PA began to suspect that he really could be changing towards her.

Mihail was, in fact, changing a great deal although not especially in his affection for Pamela Anichka. The alteration was generated by the effect of university life. Everything about Oxford was so much more exhilarating than he had imagined it might be. Never afraid of putting his back into studying, he found the lectures and tutorials stimulating. And he was loving the company. He hadn't been short of friends at school, but the friends he had now shared more of his interests.

Rupert remained one of the closest, and from the day that his twin visited Oxford, Annabel proved to be surprisingly keen to know more about Mihail's favourite occupation.

Rupert had arranged to bring his sister along that evening and the three of them would go for a drink. Mihail was ready ten minutes before they were due to arrive, and could not resist taking another look at the watch he was repairing.

Even Pamela herself had known very little about the object when giving it to him, but he had discovered more when he began reading up in a book found in the library.

Nothing had prepared him for the wealth of volumes available in Oxford. He'd always loved frequenting the public library in Halifax, but there was so much more here. He became elated as soon as he located the book in which he was able to identify an illustration similar to the piece he was reconstructing. The engraved signature which Mihail had been trying to trace was not the watch's maker, as he had supposed, but its retailer. Reading on revealed that the movement was made by the company of a certain John Wycherley of Prescot in Lancashire.

Annabel and Rupert arrived while Mihail was re-examining the way that the balance wheel was recessed.

"Sorry, sorry," he said. "I am ready really, just having another look at this."

"It's an old watch, isn't it?" said Annabel, coming to the table to see what he was studying. "Grandfather used to collect them, and all kinds of chronometers. We loved to see him working on them."

"*You* did, you mean," Rupert corrected. "I always wanted to be out doing something more active."

"This seems to be dated around 1890," Mihail told her. "The old idea up to then was to have this balance wheel outside the plate. You can tell a lot by finding out when changes were introduced."

"I know. Gramps had masses of books explaining the differences. Is this the only watch you have? Does it work?"

Mihail grinned. "Not yet, but I should have it going soon. It's the only one here, but I've had a go at lots at home. Did I tell you my mother deals in clocks and watches, along with other antiques?"

Rupert insisted that if they were going out they ought to be on their way, but that was only the start of a special affinity between his twin and Mihail.

No one had said whether Annabel had always been a frequent visitor to Oxford, but she certainly started to make a habit of calling on them.

Mihail was pleased to see her, and particularly so when she turned up one Saturday afternoon when Rupert was playing rugby. Mihail had been disappointed that he was not picked for the team that day, but had reflected that he had plenty to occupy him. There was reading, and writing as well, to be completed before Monday. He spent the morning on that, and felt being conscientious justified his settling down to working on the watch. From past experience, he was pretty certain that he would have it going before the day was out, and was looking forward to telling his mother when he rang her in the morning.

Opening the door to Annabel's knock, Mihail grinned. "Nice surprise! Didn't you know Rupert's playing today?"

The girl shrugged. "Just wondered whether he was round here when I didn't get an answer at his rooms. I came to do some shopping so I thought . . ."

"Well, come in, come in." Standing aside, he gestured towards the table. "You see what I'm doing."

"Thought you'd be working on another by now!" Annabel teased.

"I might, if my tutor didn't expect other things from me. I have nearly finished this, though, as far as the movement goes. The case will still need some attention afterwards."

"Can I watch, if you'll forgive the pun, or don't you want any distractions?"

Mihail could not resist a distraction in such attractive form. But he made coffee for them first, well aware that all thought of providing refreshment of any kind might soon go out of his head.

"Don't know what time Rupert will be back," he warned Annabel while they drank their coffee. "It's an away game, and there is a tendency afterwards to . . ."

". . . Drink as much as they can? You don't have to tell me. And actually I'm not bothered, Mihail. This is much more interesting than boozing with my twin."

Mihail had never felt more contented as he returned to working on the watch while Annabel sat across the table from him. They spoke hardly at all, merely when he explained some detail of what he was attempting. He frequently was surprised when her response revealed how much she knew of the subject.

Beyond the window darkness had shrouded the quad, where any lights were hazed by a shower of rain, when Mihail finally exclaimed, "That's it," and held the time-piece for her to approve its steady ticking.

"There's no thrill like it, you know," he confided. Something in her glinting eyes and a twitching of her mouth made him qualify the statement. "Or nothing I've tried so far."

Taking the watch from him to press it more closely to her ear, Annabel regarded him challengingly. "Honest? Are you really as – as detached as you sometimes appear?"

"Detached, as in uninvolved with anyone, you mean?"

The faintest blush rose over her cheeks. "That kind of thing, yes."

"There's no one," Mihail told her. "No one special. I guess I was always surrounded by family. And the school I attended wasn't coeducational."

"I see. You make me feel better about not having much of a history of relationships. Being a twin did tend to make you feel you needn't make too much effort with friendships. Most of the boys I got to know at all well were Rupert's friends. And he did tend to ward off any who became too – well, too friendly."

Mihail smiled. "So, there we are. Just when I was beginning to feel unfashionable, rather out of step with the permissive sixties."

"Is your sister like you?"

"Which one – Tania, my half-sister, the one married now with a daughter?"

"You told me about her, but no, I meant the one nearer your age."

"Sonia? She's more the typical teenager than I ever was. She loves dancing; according to last week's phone-call she's in bother for wearing miniskirts that leave too little to the imagination."

Annabel laughed. "It is hard on parents, you know, having daughters. Mine used to go berserk. Luckily for them, I sort of – calmed down, I guess. The dancing scene gets a bit boring. Don't mind telling you I used to hate the feeling it was a market-place. You got all dressed up so's you'd get a better offer. I don't mean for sex," she added swiftly. "But you know – for a date with a terrific bloke."

"So, what do you do now? To try and meet someone terrific, I mean?"

Annabel smiled. "Early days yet. It's only a short while since I realised going to dances bored me."

"You must do something with your spare time, though? Tonight, for instance . . . ?"

"See a film perhaps, eat out somewhere. So long as it's cheap."

"Shall we do that together?" The suggestion was out before he could feel surprised at himself. Before she could have second thoughts perhaps?

"Good idea. *Camelot* is on, isn't it? Have you seen it?"

They enjoyed the film, despite some opinions that it was rather too lengthy, and came out afterwards with several tunes running through their minds.

"Do you like music?" Annabel enquired.

Mihail laughed. "Did I tell you my father's a musician – the solo violin? And Tania sings – usually classical these days, though she also used to appear with a popular band."

"And do you play or sing?"

"Neither. All having those two around ever proved to me was that I shan't make the grade."

"What are you going to do, what do you plan?"

"When I graduate? If I have my way, work on clocks and watches."

"Good for you! Not many people go for a career that's so different."

"And what about you? Don't think you've ever said . . ."

Annabel smiled. "So, Ru's not told you then? Career-wise, I'm afraid I'm the family disappointment. I want to paint, and no one believes I'm good enough to make a living at it. Dad's allowing me three years' make or break time."

"Are you at art school now?"

"Finished there in the summer." Annabel went on to explain that she was painting now, had actually sold one landscape already. "Although that doesn't really count – it was commissioned by friends of my parents."

"Commissioned, eh? Sounds very professional!"

Mihail was pleased to learn that he wasn't the only one who would prefer work which fulfilled an interest rather than guaranteed a vast, or even a steady, income. He sensed already that he and Annabel would have a great deal in common.

By the time that their long Christmas vacation was nearing, Mihail had begun to realise how much he would miss the Atherton-Ward twins, particularly Annabel, while he was away in Yorkshire.

The three of them generally met on a Saturday evening now, and either went to the cinema or to one of their favourite pubs. Never since that one occasion had he and Annabel spent any time alone together. Whenever Rupert was playing rugby so was Mihail himself.

Annabel remained interested in his work on the watch, just the same, and insisted he must show it to her when its case also finally was restored.

"That is so beautiful," she exclaimed, examining first the face and then the engine-turned back which had once been obscured by grime. Mihail had polished this to perfection.

I wish it was really mine, and not from my mother's stock, he thought, then I would give it to Annabel.

Two days before term ended Rupert came to him with their idea. "The parents have told me you'd be welcome to stay over Christmas, if you'd like. Annabel suggested it, but of course you may have plans of your own . . ."

Taken by surprise, Mihail didn't know how to reply. He would love nothing more than spending the vacation with these new friends. But he knew his own family were looking forward to seeing him again. His mother had always made such a thing of providing a good Christmas. He remembered her saying when he was quite small that Stonemoor House had needed a family like theirs to bring it alive.

"Perhaps another year," he told Rupert regretfully. "But do thank your parents for me – and tell Annabel

I'll look forward to seeing her again when we're back in Oxford."

In the train travelling home that December Mihail's emotions were confused. A part of him was longing to be in his home territory once more, to see everyone, yet he could not avoid wondering what the Atherton-Wards were doing now. He pictured their home so clearly, with its spacious rooms decorated for the season, most likely in a manner familiar in his own. And he pictured Annabel, brown hair gleaming in the firelight, her eyes glowing and alert as they so often appeared when they talked.

The journey seemed to take forever, and all the while Mihail felt as though he were being tugged apart. Still amazed by how much he was enjoying his new life, he was rather reluctant to step back into the old. He'd always been happy at Stonemoor, he reminded himself, couldn't have a better set of relations. He *would* have missed them had he indulged that impulse to go elsewhere.

Approaching his well-loved hills of Yorkshire, Mihail was thankful that it hadn't yet grown dark. He needed to feel the countryside drawing him in, yearned for the splendour of slopes which soared to craggy summits. Wanted to experience that dear, familiar contrast between sandstone communities and the greens of wood and meadow.

His mother met him at Halifax station, gave him a hug, and smiled. "I told your dad it was my turn. He's so often the one who meets family off trains."

"Did you close the shop then?" he asked when he had stowed his luggage and they were seated in the Ford Anglia that Pamela now preferred to Andre's larger car.

"Not likely!" she exclaimed. "Not as near as this to Christmas. I've been quite busy these past few weeks. No, I've left our Sonia and PA in charge."

Mihail wondered if everyone abbreviated Pamela Anichka's name now. Certainly, it was a mouthful otherwise.

"How is everybody?" he asked. "Is Gran okay?" The last time he was home there had been some concern about

Mildred Baker. She seemed to have become somewhat reluctant to join in family gatherings, and that wasn't at all like her.

"You'll see for yourself tomorrow. She's promised to come over. The rest of the family seem all right." She was not going to mention her own unease about Ian and the circumstances at Canning's. And as for the difficulties over Sonia and the way she dressed – Pamela could believe this son of hers was too near his sister's age to understand parental misgivings!

"PA can't wait to see you," she confided. And hoped that Mihail would not be so awkward in the poor girl's company. They had been such friends for as long as everyone could remember.

Pamela wasn't surprised that the shop was in darkness as they drove past. She had anticipated that the girls would be too eager to see Mihail to delay returning to Stonemoor.

As soon as she heard the car PA opened the door, and came running down the steps. She flung herself at Mihail, wound her arms around him and kissed him firmly on the lips.

"God, have I missed you," she exclaimed, then kissed him again more fervently when she saw that no one else was looking.

Shaken by the surge of attraction racing right through him, Mihail tried to ease away. "Just a sec," he said gently when he regained his mouth. "Got to take stuff out of the boot. You can help me carry it indoors."

Sonia was waiting in the hall, and his father behind her. In the kitchen doorway Mrs Singer was lingering.

By the time he had greeted them all Mihail was almost, if not quite, over the shock of PA's welcome. After taking his things up to his old room he returned to the sitting room, composure virtually intact.

This will need careful handling, he thought while Andre was offering a drink with a smile which indicated he was glad to have a son now considered mature.

The beer he chose was welcome. Sipping from the tankard aided the steadying process, and reminded him of Oxford, and the young lady who had become such an interesting companion.

Across the room PA was patting the sofa beside her, willing him to sit there, to resume their old relationship. That relationship, and more, Mihail reflected. How was he going to cope with this new, erotic, Pamela Anichka? How to cope, yet without destroying their well-founded affection?

Six

By Christmas morning Mihail was less perturbed by Pamela Anichka's behaviour. In fact, he was beginning to believe he might have imagined the sensuality of her kisses. Sonia had helped; this sister of his was one person around his own age whom he trusted entirely. Never less than enthusiastic about being with him, she had matured during his few months away in Oxford to become an interesting companion. Having heard him turning down PA's suggestion that they go dancing, Sonia was coming up with enough ideas to fill the hours for the first couple of weeks, at least, of the holiday.

Together, he and the two girls had tramped uphill over frosted tussocks of grass towards Stoodley Pike, from where they'd marvelled at the view across the valley to further hills surrounding Todmorden. Even on a wintry day like this with so many trees bare of leaves, the slopes for miles around remained green, contrasting with clusters of soot-darkened buildings, only altering to that bluish purple with distance.

On another fine day Sonia had insisted that Andre must accompany his son and younger daughter. Laughing and talking on the way, he had driven them over Blackstone Edge, then on to Hollingworth Lake. Well wrapped against the biting wind, the three of them had walked beside the water, pausing now and then to watch the birds who seemed the only other visitors.

In the evenings when Pamela was home from her shop, she and Sonia would discuss their plans for Christmas Day while the notes of Andre's violin drifted through the house on the scent of woodsmoke from their great fireplaces.

Absorbing these sounds and smells, Mihail relished his own favourite occupation. Delighted with the watch that he'd repaired, Pamela was displaying it in her shop window, and had returned to Stonemoor bearing a clock. Victorian, it was a 'skeleton' timepiece in the Gothic style and dated from 1860. The glass dome which had covered the clock had survived, but the mechanism and the intricate sections of its brass framework were in pieces.

His mother had smiled when handing it over. "The woman who sold me this admitted that her late husband could never resist the urge to discover how something was put together. Unfortunately, love, he didn't have your ability to reassemble things afterwards."

It was just what Mihail needed. Working on this he could be here, a part of his family, yet still have this intriguing problem to tackle. And as soon as he began laying out the bits in order to identify them he recalled the occasions when Annabel had taken such an interest in similar work that he was doing.

Although Mihail could not avoid wondering what it would have been like to share the festivities within that house near Chipping Norton, he felt content that he would see his friends early in the new year.

Again, it was Sonia who frequently increased his enjoyment by bringing him her own enthusiasms. In her last year at school, she suddenly was finding learning easier. Sharing her mother's and brother's interest in old things had increased her eagerness to study history. But geography had always been her best subject and, coupled with a recently discovered talent for languages, made her choice of career seem inevitable. To her, if to no one else.

"I'm going to become an air hostess," she confided to Mihail.

He concealed a rueful smile, willed himself not to mention the mundane tasks those supposedly glamorous creatures were obliged to carry out. "That'd certainly fulfil your urge to travel. And have them pay you for the privilege!"

Pamela was giving him a warning look. The next time that Sonia was out of the room he learned the reason. "Your father's trying to discourage the idea," his mother told him quietly. "He seems afraid that being half Russian might generate problems in some countries. Quite honestly, he'd much rather be assured that Sonia was safe in England."

"But she's been abroad in the past, we all have."

"For holidays, yes. With both of us."

"Not only with you, with friends from school."

"You have, Mihail, yes. Sonia hasn't, except on well-organised school trips."

"You mean Dad would worry that something might go wrong."

Pamela nodded. "We'll have to indulge him, if we can. You know what fathers are about their daughters."

If he's anything like he always was with Tania, our Sonia's going to find this a bit confining, thought Mihail. Wryly, he recalled how different he had been, with that original reluctance to move away even to go to Oxford. Was it always so difficult to equate young ambitions with the thinking of their parents?

"At least, he's well pleased with the way you're getting on," Pamela said. "I hope you realise that? I'm just very glad that you seem so happy at university."

"Oh, I am. Might even stay on a second year." He didn't add that this would depend very much upon his new friends, not least Annabel Atherton-Ward. If the frequency of her visits to Oxford continued, he would be reluctant to relinquish contact with her.

If Pamela Anichka had been aware of such ideas, she would have been even more disturbed than she felt already. The excitement of exchanging proper kisses with Mihail had waned all too swiftly. Even while still elated by seeing him again, she had felt slighted simply because he had neglected to sit beside her. Hadn't he known how much she needed to be near him?

That night when she went to bed she had lain awake for hours, feeling his mouth on hers, experiencing again the massive urgency pulsing deep within her. Why, oh why, had he chosen to be so *distant*? Some while later she had concluded that Mihail could perhaps merely have chosen to be discreet. He could be waiting for a time when they were alone, when he would reveal how deeply he was attracted to her. Loved her.

But they never were alone. And Sonia was an absolute bore. At Stonemoor, even out walking, she hung around Mihail for all the world as though she idolised him. Couldn't the girl understand that you didn't drool like that over your own brother?

Pamela Anichka refused to think about the complexity of her own relationship to Mihail. They'd always, always been special to each other, nothing else counted. She'd been terribly hurt that day later in the holiday when Sonia called and happened to mention that she and Mihail had been out with Andre. No one had thought to invite PA to go with them.

Christmas Day at Stonemoor House might perhaps be all right, PA supposed. It was good to see everyone. Gran Baker came with her nephew Charles and his wife Dorothy who was an old friend of Pamela's. They had a son and daughter, both appearing very grown-up now, the girl was roughly Mihail's age, the brother older still. Both had been working for years, and were talking of getting a flat together. Pamela Anichka envied them the freedom that such a move would create. Surely when Mihail finished at university next summer, he would find living with his parents stifling? Perhaps he would wish to share a flat with someone nearer his own age . . .

Tom and Gwen arrived with the boys, who came bursting into the house as though, within minutes, they would occupy the whole of every spacious room.

Ian rushed to greet his brother while Tania remained

seated on her father's chair arm, pausing only to nod across the room to the others before continuing their conversation. Watching them, PA swallowed, noticing afresh how fond her mum and Andre were of each other. Things would be so much better if *she* had a father she could talk to, one who understood. She must find out if her father was back in Yorkshire – he would be staying with the Thomases, wouldn't he?

Ian was all right; most of the time she didn't care too much that he was only her stepfather. On occasions, that was even an advantage – when he hesitated to become angry. Today he looked perturbed, though, not at all Christmassy. He was watching those young boys as they tore about, and his lovely sherry-brown eyes appeared haunted. PA liked him well enough to wish she knew what was wrong, to long to make him feel better.

They all ate too much, naturally, during the course of the day, and played charades, then a stupid game of bobbing for apples to please the little ones. Fortunately, Gwen was sensible and had brought along toys for the three lads, plus books which were better still as they kept them quiet.

Amid all the noise PA had scarcely exchanged more than a dozen private words with Mihail, and nothing he'd said had been what she wanted to hear. Sonia had been a pain, yet again, trying to arrange to go dancing one evening soon, when all the while she ought to have remembered that Mihail didn't fancy dancing now. Pamela Anichka wouldn't go there without him.

Mildred Baker was looking well, in a new Crimplene dress of a lovely sea-green shade. PA thought what a pity it was that she had no one special to admire what she wore. Although she so evidently relished being surrounded by family, she deserved someone just her own.

Sonia was the person today wishing with her entire being that *she* had a man who would gaze at her in the way that her Uncle Ian now was staring at Tania. Then there was the couple most important to her, Mum and

Dad – she had noticed before that when the house was full of family they often sought each other's eyes across the room, smiling just for each other.

She supposed Mihail would be the next to fall in love. He must meet so many exciting people in Oxford. That kind of opportunity was the need generating her own ideas for getting away from here.

These days, she couldn't get PA to go dancing very often. However did she believe they would meet someone? Glancing towards her now, Sonia thought she knew the answer. PA was looking fixedly at Mihail.

Was that still on? Did Pamela Anichka really believe it could come to anything? Sonia had seen that kiss, of course, on the day he came home. Couldn't have missed seeing it. She had wondered if their mouths had actually been open, like – well, like you saw on the television. Did PA truly not know that it wasn't right between them?

Sensing Sonia's critical gaze, Pamela Anichka frowned. What was wrong now? Nobody could claim she was monopolising Mihail. He'd spent most of his time with those other two, Jim and whatever they called the girl. PA couldn't see why, they weren't really friends; nobody would have known anything about them if Charles hadn't been Pamela's cousin, and Dorothy her friend. But then, Mildred Baker always had them under her wing, bless her; perhaps they weren't so bad.

New Year's Eve would be better, PA decided. Everyone would be coming to their cottage. Or not quite everyone. It was too far from Manchester for Tom and Gwen to keep the boys up late. And the relations so fascinating Mihail today were not invited. At last, at long last, she ought to have time alone with him. Time which she so desperately needed.

Sonia and her father were in the car already; Pamela was slipping on her coat when the telephone rang. The voice was beautiful, well-educated, feminine, and asking to speak with Mihail. Suppressing a smile, Pamela called to her son, watched his expression brighten as soon as he discovered who was at the other end of the line.

"Don't wait, Mum, I'll walk round there, it's no distance," he said, covering the receiver.

"Make sure you lock the door properly behind you when you leave," Pamela reminded him.

Normally, Mihail would have groaned. Tonight, he was too happy. "Good to hear from you," he told Annabel. "I hadn't dared to hope that you might ring."

She laughed. "Thank goodness! Didn't know what you'd make of my calling. Just wanted to wish you a happy New Year. And to ask how you were enjoying the holidays."

"Thanks – a happy New Year to you, as well. It's all right here, I suppose, quite good really. Some of us went walking one day, on another my father took us for a run into Lancashire. Christmas Day a mass of relations came to Stonemoor, as usual."

"And are you having a party tonight?"

"At Tania's – it's just down the road, did I ever tell you? And what about you, are your family entertaining?"

"The parents are – a lot of elderly aunts and so on. Boring. Ru and I have threatened to go out, but I suspect that will be overruled. We're supposed to help make everyone welcome."

"Which I'm sure you do in style."

"Depends who's coming. I still wish it was you . . ."

"Me too. Yes, I really do."

"We won't always have to put family first. I can understand how yours must feel, you know – you having been away for the first time, and that."

"So, what have you been doing since I saw you?"

"Seeing some of the girls from my old school. Riding most mornings with Rupert. A bit of painting. Oh – reminds me – what did your mother think of the watch?"

"She was pleased, put it right in the front of the window at the shop."

"Started working on anything else?"

"Have I! A skeleton clock, Victorian. D'you know the sort I mean?"

"Think so. Don't they have all the works showing?"

"And usually a lot of fiddly brasswork to support the mechanism. This one's in masses of bits."

"I'd love to see it."

Briefly, Mihail pictured Annabel at Stonemoor, longed to be showing her not just the clock but around the entire house. And then he thought of having to explain things at home, who she was, how much she mattered . . .

"I'll see if I can bring it back with me, depends how much else I have to carry. Or if it's finished. If I do get it going by then I imagine Mum will claim it back again."

They talked for a while longer then Annabel put her brother on. Glad though he was to hear his friend's voice, Mihail rather wished that he'd only chatted with Annabel. Knowing she had thought to phone him bestowed a sort of enchantment. He couldn't bear to have it diluted.

Walking along the road to Tania's the magic returned, enveloping him in a strange elation. He ran a few paces, gave a massive leap of sheer exhilaration.

Pamela Anichka met him in the hallway. Mihail sensed that she had been waiting there.

"At last!" she exclaimed, welcoming him with a hug, and a kiss which he manoeuvred onto his cheek. "Your mum said you were delayed by a phone call. Somebody nice?"

"Couple of friends from university, that's all. Is everybody else here then?" Mihail was hoping for PA's sake that his mother hadn't made too much of the call being from a girl. He wouldn't hurt PA for worlds, must make an effort tonight to be nice to her.

Delighted to have heard from Annabel, he put himself out to make everyone else just as happy. Tania and Ian had created a huge spread of food and drink and were inviting them all to take things from the buffet whenever they wished.

"It's always a bit funny with New Year," Ian explained. "It goes on so long, but some folk don't want to be eating right up to midnight."

As soon as Mihail had a beer on the table beside him Tania came across to join him on the sofa. "So, you've made some good friends at Oxford then?" she said.

"Marvellous."

"That's great, it evidently has helped you to settle. And do you still play rugby?"

"That's how I really got to know Rupert. One of the people who rang just now."

"But no more bashes on the head, I hope?" Tania enquired.

"Not so far. Maybe I'm a bit more careful now."

PA flopped onto the seat at his other side. "Aren't you listening? It's *All You Need Is Love!*"

Mihail grinned. He was no longer quite so keen on the Beatles, but he was in too good a mood to spoil things for Pamela Anichka.

"Don't you even want to dance to it here?" she persisted.

"Won't your mother mind, it's not very good for the carpet?"

Tania gave him a little push. "Go on – but in the hall perhaps."

The tiled floor was quite good for dancing, and being with PA not bad either. While he was here.

Her scent was sophisticated and her hair was freshly washed, gleaming, and in that style he'd liked in the pictures of Mary Quant. When he grew bored with dancing and went to sit on the carved oak settle PA continued to dance.

Her skirt was red, short enough to belie press claims that the era of the mini was over. Her top was black and long sleeved, silky, and it clung. Even away from her like this, his fingers seemed conscious of its texture. Pamela Anichka certainly was an amazing young lady.

"You're not wanting to go back in there, are you?"

she demanded, tossing her head in the direction of the sitting room. "If you're rather off the Beatles, I'll find something else."

While she was absent Mihail thought hard about PA. He wished he could fix her up with someone. Rupert perhaps, although he wondered whether they would get on. It would be good to see her content with a fellow who really cared for her.

The tune which emerged with her was slow and sensuous. Too late, he realised he'd been a fool to let her select the record. When she took his hand, tugging him to his feet, he couldn't refuse without seeming difficult.

Mihail wasn't that experienced a dancer. He could only hold her to him, accept the arms which clung, one around his shoulders, the other with fingers caressing the back of his neck. If this were Annabel though . . .

But it *was* Pamela Anichka, and everything ought to be all right, because they knew each other so well, had grown up like this, grown together.

She was singing softly against his neck, her breath warm, enticing. Deep within him the urge to take everything this young female was offering began insisting.

"Kiss me," she murmured, her voice husky.

A door opened. His father came out, crossing the hall to the cloakroom.

PA swore under her breath. "Later then," she promised.

Sonia looked towards them from the door left open, and remained there watching until Andre returned across the hall and closed the door behind them.

"Don't you think we ought to join the others?" Mihail suggested when that track ended.

"Nope. They know where we are. Why are you so reluctant now to be with me, Mihail? Am I boring since you've met all those new people?"

"Never that."

"Well, then. Just remember you'll soon be off to Oxford again. You used not to be so stingy with your company."

Sonia could no longer resist the urge to affect what was going on. They heard the music change to a rock and roll number, and she came dashing to join them.

"Three can do this," she asserted, and was satisfied that PA's annoyance was very evident in her livid eyes. Later, sometime at home, she was going to have a talk with Mihail. He might be older than her, but he was behaving incredibly stupidly. All PA wanted was a man; if Mihail got trapped by her there would be no end of trouble. He ought to be reminding himself that they were related, even if Pamela Anichka didn't believe that counted!

The others called the three of them to come and play cards and that, together with a quiz game bought during Tania's latest trip to sing in New York, kept them occupied until midnight.

The kissing and embracing became general then. Amid the good wishes and laughter, Mihail trusted that no one noticed how long and how intimately PA clung to him.

He wished quite seriously that he was away from here, away from Cragg Vale, the area of Yorkshire which he once thought he would always love more than anywhere in the world. He did care for PA; she was too much a part of his life for him to risk being cruel. But she was so alluring. The part of him which refused to acknowledge the complexity of their kinship was providing the most incessant longing.

"Promise we'll see in the New Year together always," she whispered, still pressing close. "In twelve months' time, and another twelve . . ."

Mihail had made laughing excuses rather than promises, and was thankful for that one year on. The family were all at Stonemoor on New Year's Eve. Pamela Anichka appeared, if anything, yet more determined to ensure that he was always around for her.

She had half explained her desperation months ago, in the summer, when she finally had realised he really did mean to spend that second year at university.

Nothing, least of all PA, would have altered his decision. Mihail had been only part-way through his first year when one of the happy chances that convince one of the existence of Fate, had introduced him to a new tutor.

Learning of Mihail's interest in timepieces, Jack Denham had delighted in explaining that he had studied horology. They had talked for hours, then afterwards prefaced many a meeting about Mihail's set work with a discussion of their shared interest.

Denham knew more about the history of clockmaking than his pupil had ever aspired to. The prospect of Mihail staying on at university swiftly changed from a possibility into something essential.

Andre and Pamela were delighted – she especially so when she heard that her son was to devote more time to his favourite subject. Andre was just very glad that further learning would better equip Mihail for a lucrative future.

Although still performing with good orchestras during each concert season, Andre was very conscious of becoming sixty. It was an age when even an optimist must accept that in his, often uncertain, profession there were no guarantees of extended employment. He must look ahead for his son now, and wished him to feel secure as well as satisfied in his work.

In other ways also Oxford was compelling Mihail to remain there. Rupert had continued to be one of his closest friends, and his twin just as appealing as when Mihail first met her. No one could have enthused more when Annabel was told about Jack Denham and his knowledge of the clocks and watches which were Mihail's greatest interest.

"I'm so pleased for you. This should help you to become truly professional."

"I know. And Mum is willing to put all her repair work my way when I finish here. She's also promised to recommend me within the trade – and she's made a lot of contacts who respect her."

Always unassuming, Pamela Malinowski had demonstrated during the past twenty years that she knew the antiques business. Her reputation had sprung from an eye for a good investment which was coupled with an innate fairness. People trusted her. For Mihail's future this promised to provide a good recommendation.

Andre had agreed, if only provisionally, that their son should have the opportunity to follow the one career he'd set his heart on. He would have space in the room behind Pamela's shop, and where better to learn of possible work?

There had been occasions, of course, when Andre had tried to insist that Mihail should aim for something more ambitious, more lucrative. No longer quite so reluctant to shrink from arguing with his father, Mihail had smiled wryly.

"Is that truly what you believe I ought to do, Dad? But surely when you began as a violinist there were no guarantees that you would become as successful as you are?"

Andre had laughed, his grey eyes rueful. "Do not expect me to answer that! Very well, Mihail, set out to show me how clever you are." He was pleased to have a son who could come up with a telling phrase, even against himself.

During those early months of 1969 Pamela Anichka decided to try to further her own ambitions. Working in someone else's boutique was beginning to pall. She knew she'd never be happy until she was running her own business. A year ago, efforts to see Gerald Thomas again to persuade him to invest in her, had failed abysmally. She had even gone over to the Thomas's house, but had found no one at home. A neighbour had told her that Gerald's parents were staying with him in London. Additional attempts to see him during the past twelve months had proved just as fruitless.

This time, PA had written to him at Christmas. He

hadn't replied. She was beginning to despair of ever seeing her father again when they met by chance in the centre of Halifax.

She had had a cough, so troublesome that her boss had insisted that she should take time off and visit the doctor. Their customers in the boutique did not want to be attended by someone who could scarcely speak for coughing.

After a few days at home responding to the doctor's medicine, PA was so utterly bored that she had driven as far as the town. In another few days Mihail would be on his way back to Oxford again. She meant to invest in a new outfit which would make him remember her looking extremely glamorous.

Gerald was crossing Commercial Street from the main post office just as she was doing the same in the opposite direction. After his initial surprise, he caught her arm, taking her with him to the footpath.

"How are you, my dear?" he enquired, and sounded as though he genuinely cared. PA's spirits rocketed – this was the moment that surely proved Fate was assisting her!

They chatted for a few moments and then he explained that he was about to go for lunch. "Why don't you join me? Or is Tania expecting you home?"

Pamela Anichka often relished asserting her maturity by not declaring when she might be expected back at the house. She was glad now that this freed her to have a meal with her father.

Seated in the dining room of one of the best hotels, she tried to give the occasion a good opening. She asked after his wife and family. Gerald seemed obliged then to enquire into her life.

PA sighed. "I'm not very happy at work, as a matter of fact. It's no longer very satisfying. Think I've been there too long. If only I had a bit of capital behind me, I'd set up on my own."

"And I take it your mother isn't being forthcoming? She can't help out?"

"Not really. She's not been doing as much singing these past two years." Pamela Anichka didn't know what was wrong. Dates were still being offered, but Tania was turning down many of them. She had asked her mother if she was unwell, but had learned nothing, yet she sensed that something was amiss.

She didn't mention this to Gerald, of course, and he seemed incurious about the reason why his former wife should be taking fewer opportunities to sing.

"Well, my dear, as you know I would help you, if only I could. Sadly, that simply is not possible at this moment. However, if I should happen to come up with an idea regarding finance, I'll be in touch."

PA had grown up enough by now to continue talking amiably throughout their meal, but she was so disappointed that she felt close to tears.

Saying goodbye on the steps of the hotel, she longed to hit out at him for being such a *useless* father. Why couldn't he do something for her for a change, instead of only thinking of his wretched new family!

That's it – *I'll* have to do something, PA resolved, have to find some means of making a better future for myself.

She needed something to make her feel better. So much in her life felt to be marking time. Mihail was away for most of the time, and would be until the summer, and things just were not the same without him.

The very next time she had an opportunity to get away from Yorkshire, she would take it. She would show everyone, most of all Mihail, what she was made of. Mouldering here was doing her absolutely no good at all.

Seven

M ihail's second year at university soon became even more interesting than his first. His friendship with Annabel was developing at exactly the pace that suited him, with moments of affection which promised a latent passion. They seemed to have an unspoken understanding that, because they both had so much to achieve yet, attraction would not overrule everything else.

Their restraint might make them seem unfashionable to many of their contemporaries, but neither of them cared overmuch about popular opinion. And they both were intelligent enough to have recognised all around them evidence that the sexual freedoms of the 1960s had resulted in too many relationships ruined by the sentiment of 'anything goes'.

As well as frequently being welcomed into the Atherton-Ward home, the hours when Mihail wasn't actually studying were often spent with Jack Denham.

The tutor's interest in Mihail's ability to restore old timepieces appeared to be developing into respect. After seeing him repair the skeleton clock, Denham had asked why he only tackled items from his mother's collection.

"She's the only one who's trusted me with anything, I suppose," he'd replied with a grin. "And she's kept me supplied with enough to keep me occupied."

"But if you took on work for people here in Oxford that'd get you known. You might soon be restoring clocks for some of the better antiques dealers."

"You can't seriously mean that. They'd want somebody fully trained, not just an amateur like me."

"You could give it a try – there's someone I know, has a shop just off The High."

Only being unsure how to refuse without seeming churlish had finally driven Mihail to go along with Jack Denham to meet this dealer.

The man's name was Ivor Smith and as soon as Mihail entered the cluttered shop and was introduced, they took to each other. Learning Mihail's surname, the middle-aged man behind the counter smiled.

"You are no more English than I am," he said, in a voice heavily-accented.

"My mother is English, my father's Russian – White Russian," Mihail added, never forgetting how Andre always emphasised the distinction.

"I thought so," Ivor Smith continued, his smile widening. "You may be surprised that, despite my adopted name, I also am Russian."

"I knew the two of you would get along," Denham exclaimed.

Mihail sensed fleetingly that the other two had been well aware already of this connection with his father's homeland. But Ivor was an engaging man, and soon was showing him so many of his vast collection of watches, clocks and chronometers that he could only surrender to indulging his chief interest.

Mihail had always thought his mother's shop was exciting, but this one was the most fascinating place he'd ever seen. Now that he was here, he realised that an antiques business developed more interest with every year after being established. And this, he learned, had been opened almost immediately after the end of the last war.

Every shelf and showcase within the window space and throughout the tiny shop was packed to overflowing with treasured items. Although the owner specialised in timepieces of every sort, he also displayed a quantity of jewellery and small collectibles. Framed miniatures occupied areas of wall where no shelves could be fitted;

carved jet necklaces and brooches were attached to dusty velvet suspended from the edge of a cupboard.

"It *is* the watches and the clocks that interest you?" Ivor prompted, eventually.

Mihail grinned, and halted his excited exploration of the shop.

"Jack tells me you enjoy restoring such things," Ivor continued. "Would you be willing to do this kind of work for me, on a regular basis?"

"But you don't know if I'm any good," Mihail protested cautiously.

The other two exchanged a glance before Ivor went on. "Do you suppose I would make such a suggestion without enquiring into your capabilities? I am a businessman, do not forget. I have heard you are skilled – do you not wish the opportunity to prove to me your worth?"

His accent and the word order he employed reminded Mihail of his father. Even if he hadn't been keen to try to restore some of the timepieces on the counter here, he would have found refusing difficult.

"Are you going to try me out with one of your less valuable watches perhaps?" he said tentatively. He could not risk failing to satisfy.

Ivor nodded. "But naturally. I shall select something today, to take with you and work on whenever you can. These things are not very saleable when they do not function. As you may realise from your mother's experience, a trade like this relies on clients who buy something in running order. Only rarely do they snap up an item with the idea of having it repaired themselves."

Mihail smiled in agreement and the man began sorting out which watch to give him. "This is the one, I think. I shall ask you to sign a receipt, then look forward to its being returned – whenever. I know that you must not neglect your studies."

It was agreed that Mihail would let him know if he happened to encounter any serious difficulties with the job. Otherwise, Ivor would be happy to have the watch returned in good condition as soon as possible. A price was agreed for the work – a sum which although not astronomical was considerably more than Pamela normally paid him.

When Mihail began tackling the watch he was nervous. Only ever working for his mother, he'd almost forgotten what it was like to feel he was being tested. Gradually, however, he became interested in putting the thing to rights and started to enjoy the challenge.

By the time he eventually completed that work satisfactorily and Ivor entrusted him with a second watch, Annabel was almost as delighted as Mihail himself.

During the past few months she had recognised that Mihail needed to prove his ability to repair the timepieces he loved just as much as she needed to paint. If most of his free time was to be spent in this way, she was happy to drive to Oxford in order to have his company.

Annabel's interest in art had always been something of a mystery to many of her friends – an occupation which inclined too much towards solitude for their liking. At one time in her early teens she had felt awkward about not conforming, but she'd always had her twin. Constantly being aware of the close bond between herself and Rupert prevented her from feeling alone, even when distance separated them.

And now there was Mihail. The fact that he was a friend of Rupert's as well seemed like a bonus, a reassurance that it was right they should feel so good together. They were young, optimistic, and more than a little in love. Neither Annabel nor Mihail had any reason to suppose that their happy situation might not continue.

"This can't go on. Look how many months it's been, years even. And I know what I'm like, Pam. I can't keep up this pretence of patience forever."

Ian and his sister had remained in the room at Stonemoor which she reserved for business. They had been discussing the situation at Canning's, a meeting to which Ted Burrows had, as always, been invited.

Outwardly, Burrows was still a decisive manager of the company, a man who knew what must be done and how that would be achieved. Below the surface, though, the reality was very different. Never since returning to work had Ted Burrows assumed true responsibility for running the firm. He came to wherever the men happened to be working, but it was on Ian that all responsibilities rested. And Ian, who had had more than enough before Ted returned to work following that stroke, was sick of being obliged to cope, especially without due recognition.

"I have tried, you know," he told his sister now. "But you could tell how it was while he was here just now. He doesn't fully comprehend what we need any longer."

Pamela nodded, quelled a sigh. "I do see that, Ian love. But our hands are tied, aren't they? We can't pull the rug from under him by kicking him out. Not when he has so little besides the job."

"I wouldn't mind so much about the pay he was getting for doing next to nothing, if he didn't have to be there. I wish we could just – oh, I don't know – pay him to stop away, I suppose."

"It'd destroy him, love."

"Happen so. And I sometimes think all this'll destroy *me*. He undermines me that often."

Ian began describing the trouble they'd had only the other day. Burrows had walked into the large house they were decorating, and immediately had begun telling the men what they should be doing. They were already working well, just as Ian had organised. For the rest of the day their team naturally had reacted to being instructed differently. Ian didn't like to see them discontented, and nor did he relish being obliged to try and smooth things over as soon as the manager was out of earshot. Picturing the disconsolate expressions which so often seemed to surround him, he tried to ensure that Pamela really understood the extent of their dissatisfaction.

"Before the week was out, Burrows had Eric spitting mad because he sent him off to start on one room when I'd just been discussing how he should tackle somewhere else." His sister knew as well as Ian himself that Eric had progressed through his apprenticeship to become a craftsman they would be reluctant to lose.

It wasn't only these problems between the manager and their employees, though. Ted Burrows resented Ian's ability to continue to participate in the physical work himself. This was revealed in smart remarks about whatever Ian happened to be doing. No matter how understandable the manager's sense of deprivation was, this attitude was making life even more difficult.

"Can you tolerate him just a little while longer?" Pamela asked. "I really will have a long think, and try and come up with some means of sorting this wretched business out."

Ian was heading towards the front door when his sister called him back.

"Just remembered – there's something else I meant to mention. Not about Canning's," she added, only too conscious that the firm was wearing Ian down. "Have you been in touch with Mum lately?"

"Not for a week or two, I must admit. Though I think Tania rang her up not long since. Why? She's not poorly or anything, is she?"

"That's what I wondered, at first. She seemed not to be answering the telephone. Now I know she's never liked the thing, wouldn't have dreamed of having one put in if it hadn't been for me starting to make a go of Canning's all those years ago."

"And now?" Ian prompted, his sherry-brown eyes worried. "*Is* it that she's taken against talking to folk over the phone?"

"Not according to her. I asked if she was having trouble hearing what we said, but she laughed at that idea. 'Happen I wasn't in when you tried', she said, still sounding amused."

104

"So maybe it's no more than that," said Ian. "We've been on at her for long enough, trying to get her to go out more."

"Let's hope so," Pamela said. "Any road – let us know if you or Tania find out anything, won't you? She's getting on now, perhaps we ought to keep a closer eye on her."

Only the next day Pamela had a call from Tania which reassured her about Mildred Baker.

"Ian told me what you'd asked him," her stepdaughter began. "And I didn't want you worrying unnecessarily. It was one day last week when I spoke to your mother, and she sounded perfectly well. Actually, she seemed very bright, and she has been going out more frequently as you supposed."

Pamela smiled. "Oh, that is a relief! I'm ever so pleased you've let me know, Tania love. I dare say I ought to see her more often, but it is difficult with the shop. And even with Mihail away there's always something to do in the evenings." Mrs Singer had lived in ever since her husband died, but she was ageing visibly and less able to cope.

The reassurance that her mother was well and content ended Pamela's concern about her, but as the summer of 1969 approached she and Andre made more of an effort to drive over to Halifax to see Mildred, on occasions to take her out. Both were agreeably surprised by how cheerful she always appeared. The old days when she had been disturbed by having no one to care for had evidently given way to this fresh contentment.

Contentment was, in the main, the mood which best described their own life now. Andre was looking forward to several bookings to play during the approaching concert season, while Pamela's shop continued to make a profit. She had found no solution to Ian's problems within Canning's but she'd had a discussion with Ted Burrows in which she'd suggested he might wish to retire early.

The manager needed time to reach a decision, but the possibility that he might choose to go was making Ian feel better. Pamela was sorry for her brother; he was trapped in an unenviable position. But so was Ted – and he, no less than Ian, had once put all he had got into making Canning's succeed.

"I wish sometimes that I'd sold out as soon as I stopped being able to do the actual work myself," Pamela confided to Andre one evening.

Her husband's smile was understanding. "But you would not have done so, would you? Building up the firm after the war had meant so much to you. Look at the way you transformed this place – anyone has only to see how spendid it still looks to realise how good you were."

"But there's been lots done to Stonemoor since, hasn't there, love?" she demurred.

He smiled again. "Oh, yes. Fresh paint here, new wall-paper there. Carpets to replace others that were ground to dust by young feet while the children were growing up. But always whatever was done has been to your taste and on your instructions."

"You make me sound a bit of a tartar – a martinet!"

Andre laughed. "You might have been, had you lived all these years with a different husband. As things are, you know and I know that you have only asserted yourself within certain boundaries."

Suddenly hugging each other, they realised yet again how well matched they were, in what once had seemed such an unlikely marriage.

Sonia happened to come into the room while they were embracing and hesitated, her emotions confused. She'd always been thankful that her parents got on so well together, that the love between them made the rest of the family feel more secure. During recent years, however, with Mihail away from Stonemoor she was conscious of being too much on her own. An odd one out.

She'd had friends at school, naturally, but her schooldays had ended last September. She was working now, although among people who were considerably older than herself and living several miles from her own Cragg Vale. Her job was not providing the fresh social life for which she was aching.

Unable to persuade Andre to agree to her choice of career as an air hostess, Sonia had been persuaded by her mother to have a go at what they supposed would be the next best thing.

Working as ground staff for one of the airlines flying out of Manchester airport had sounded all right. In fact, working that close to the job she really wanted was proving more tantalising than even Sonia had been afraid it might. Booking people in for flights which she yearned to take, and seeing cabin crew and pilots striding through the airport was not exactly comfortable.

With each week that passed, Sonia became more dissatisfied. So often it seemed that she was no more than a clerk who took in luggage, checked tickets, and issued boarding passes. Only rarely did she need her experience with European languages, and there was precious little time for doing more than dream about ever travelling abroad herself.

Away from the airport, life was no more exciting. She and Pamela Anichka still occasionally went out of an evening, but PA so often seemed in a strange mood. If the two of them ever felt to have something in common this usually sprang from parental disappoval of either the hours they kept or the clothing they wore. Both sets of parents were adept at stifling their enthusiasms, and it was all too easy for Tania and Ian to join Andre and Pamela in vetoing a particular scheme.

The girls' latest battle was against joint parental determination to confine them to what they apparently considered the relative safety of their own Pennine region.

PA was particularly annoyed by their refusal to grant permission for them to visit the Isle of Wight later this summer.

"I should never have let them know what was happening," PA complained to Sonia. "If I'd had the sense I'd have just said we'd like to go there for a holiday. They'd never have known then about the rock festival."

Sonia had been less eager to attend, but she wouldn't admit that to Pamela Anichka. She always was glad when the older girl was happy to go somewhere with her, and wasn't going to say anything now to ruin everything. Rock music wasn't her own particular fancy, at present. Ever since Mary Hopkin took *Those Were the Days, my Friend* to the top in 1968 Sonia had been a fan. And she still always bought each Beatles' record on the day it was released.

In many ways Sonia remained a dreamer, with a heart still set on meeting the man who would transform her life. Other girls could, and did, relish the sexual freedom introduced by the contraceptive pill and recent trends towards ignoring the constraints of marriage. She had different ideas. It seemed just now that she would never quite fit in. The only thing she was looking forward to was Mihail's return from Oxford. At least there would again be someone nearer her own age at Stonemoor.

Mihail was anticipating the end of his period at university with mixed emotions. He had felt so fulfilled throughout these months, and especially so since beginning to do work for Ivor Smith. Not only was he enjoying the restoration of watches and clocks for that shop, he was flourishing in the company of Ivor and his friend Jack Denham.

Quite often when he returned something to the antique dealer he would find Jack there, and the three of them would talk. Discussing all manner of subjects, ranging far beyond Oxford, beyond this country even, Mihail felt his outlook widening. So much of his earlier life had been narrowly confined. This was partly through his own character, which was never exactly extrovert; he'd always enjoyed one-to-one company rather than going around in a group. He now recognised also that Andre Malinowki's original wariness when arriving in Yorkshire had somehow conveyed itself to his son.

These days, it seemed all the more exciting to have in prospect a future that invited exploration. Mihail once had scoffed at his young sister's eagerness to have a career aboard aircraft; suddenly he could understand.

In April of that year when Concorde finally was completed, the feat set them all looking to days when travel throughout the world would be achieved so much more readily. But best of all, just as Mihail was experiencing misgivings about leaving his student days behind, Neil Armstrong landed on the moon. For a few weeks there was avid discussion between the three friends in that small shop in Oxford, reminders of the many stages which had led at last to this triumph. Both Ivor and Mihail were very conscious of the part Russian inventiveness had played in the early days of space flight. Who could ever forget that magnificent venture by Yuri Gagarin way back in 1961?

"You are proud then of your Russian heritage?" Jack Denham asked Mihail, with a knowing look towards their companion.

The young man nodded. "I suppose I am. Living in England has never prevented my father from remembering the things that are best about his homeland."

"And so," Denham continued carefully, "you would wish, I feel sure, to perpetuate those 'good things' created by his fellow countrymen?"

Suddenly inexplicably uneasy, Mihail hesitated. "I – I'm afraid I don't quite understand what you . . ."

Again, the other two exchanged a glance. This time it was Ivor who spoke. "We need educated young men like you, Mihail. Fearless individuals who would be willing to work to further the cause."

"What 'cause'?" He felt totally bewildered.

"Oh, come now, my friend. Between ourselves there is no need for euphemisms, disguising our intent. You cannot really pretend you are happy about the position of Russia in this modern world. This is a great opportunity for you, Mihail – the chance to bring Western skills to your father's native country." Denham sounded forceful, so forceful that Mihail was afraid.

"If you are suggesting what I believe you're suggesting," he responded, slowly, "I should need to consider the prospect very carefully before ever I could agree."

And that was merely an understatement to conceal his true reaction. He needed time to think out how best to refuse to cooperate in such an appalling scheme.

"Well, you may take a few hours to consider, I suppose," said Ivor calmly while Mihail read fury in his eyes. "But only hours. There must be no delaying while you play around, restoring timepieces, as though that were sufficient. This matter is much more important than that. I hope you understand fully – how greatly we are trusting you?"

Mihail hurried all the way back to his rooms, raced through to the bathroom and vomited. Nothing on this planet could have prepared him for the shock. For so many months now he'd considered Jack Denham a friend, his mentor. And Ivor Smith always seemed so genuinely to enjoy their mutual interests.

How had he remained so stupid? He'd not even suspected they might be trying to recruit him as a – as a . . . Mihail sighed. No matter how he tried, he could think of one word only. Spy.

Rupert arrived while Mihail was still seated by the window staring without seeing across the quad. The moment the door was opened to him Rupert recognised that something was wrong.

"Not had bad news, have you?" he asked.

"Suppose in a way I have. Certainly, an immense shock. If I tell you, you will keep this to yourself?"

"You shouldn't have to ask. We know each other well enough by now."

"Sit down then, it's quite a long tale." Mihail waited until his friend was seated on the sofa, sighed again, and continued. "You know Jack Denham, and how he introduced me to this chap who owns an antiques business? That I've been doing restoration work for his shop?"

"Sure. You told me ages ago. So?"

"They've really shattered me today, completely shattered. They're only trying to – well, to get me to work on their side. Did I ever tell you Ivor's real name isn't 'Smith'? Anyway, he's of Russian extraction; they've both known all along about my father."

"But Andre's White Russian, or so you've always said."

"He is, he is. Why else would he risk his life, and Tania's, to live over here? I thought Ivor was the same."

"Thought? You've never been sure?"

Mihail's laugh was grim. "Today, I'm so confused by the shock I feel I've never been sure of anything. Nor will be again!"

"What are you going to do?"

"Haven't had time to consider. Only just arrived back. Have to talk to someone, can't just leave it. But what about Jack Denham? Unless I'm gravely mistaken, he's involved in recruiting agents. Reporting this will mean he'll be out, won't it?"

"And good riddance, by the sound of it!"

"But he's a bloody good tutor."

"So long as he isn't inveigling students into becoming agents."

"Wish I knew who to talk to first."

"Why not my old man? We can be there in no time, ask his advice. He'll know who we ought to contact."

"God, I wish this had never happened! It's nightmarish – worse, because this one can't be dismissed as a dream."

Mihail fell silent in Rupert's car, too alarmed to converse during any of the journey towards Chipping Norton.

Annabel greeted them in the hall, hugging each in turn, then turning anxious eyes towards her brother. "Whatever's wrong? Something is, isn't it? No one's ill, are they? You've not been in an accident?"

"Nothing like that," they reassured her together.

111

"Dad's in, I hope?" said Rupert.

Lance Atherton-Ward took them both into his study. After a brief enquiry into their health, he invited them to sit. "So, what is it? You young people don't normally arrive looking as though the world has been hauled from beneath your feet."

"It's my problem, actually," Mihail announced. "Ru very kindly suggested you might know what to do. Who to tell . . ." The rest was less easy, the words seemed to be sticking somewhere below his throat.

"Tell what?" his host prompted, and Mihail was grateful for his gentleness.

"That one of the college tutors, together with a friend of his, has – have actually suggested I become a Communist spy."

"Are you sure? You can't have mistaken their meaning?"

"Wish to goodness I had! I thought he was my friend, that they both were. We liked the same things. History, of course, that's Jack Denham's subject, the clocks and watches that've always fascinated me."

"The other man is an antiques dealer, Dad. Just off The High," said Rupert.

"Who've you told so far?" Lance Atheron-Ward enquired.

"Ru. Haven't seen anyone else. He suggested we came straight here."

"Best you could do. Don't want you hanging round the university while they're at liberty."

Mihail frowned. "That sounds as if you think they'll have to be arrested." He didn't like to contemplate anything so drastic for two people who a few hours ago had been his close friends.

"What else? The authorities aren't going to want them around, especially somewhere like Oxford. Who can say how many others they've attempted to enrol?"

At that moment Mihail did not care how many, he just wished that *he* had not been involved.

112

"All right," said Rupert's father decisively. "I'll handle this. Just give me their names, the address as well for this fellow who isn't connected with the college. I'm afraid you'll be expected to swear to what you've just told me. Details, if you can recall them, of how the suggestion was put to you."

"It was – in the beginning it was sort of veiled. We were talking about space exploration; the moon landing, and so on, and how Gagarin was the first. My father and I were quite proud of that, I thought this Ivor Smith chap was the same as us – White Russian."

"Had he ever said he was?"

Mihail sighed. "Wish I could be sure. Might be that I just assumed . . ."

"Or that he wanted you to assume. He'd be unlikely to make his own allegiance plain until he believed he had the measure of your political affiliation. Right then. I'll do some telephoning."

The others waited while he spoke first to the local chief constable who appeared to be an acquaintance, and then to the man's opposite number in Oxford.

"I only hope that those two have tried this on with other students before," Mihail murmured to his friend. If that were so, it could be that the authorities had been alerted already. It might not be his evidence alone which was necessary to condemn the pair.

Whatever should emerge during the inevitable investigation, however, Mihail sensed that he would never feel the same. He had liked those two, had trusted them with his ambitions, his dreams.

Had his expertise ever really been of use to Ivor Smith, or was he no good at all? Had they endured, rather than enjoyed, all those conversations, simply to bring them to this situation? Was their interest from the start only kindled by their intention of enlisting him as a Communist agent?

Eight

The rest of that day and the night which followed became the worst in the whole of Mihail's life. With Lance Atherton-Ward and Rupert, who insisted on coming too, he went to the police in Oxford. At their request, he supplied full details of his acquaintance with Jack Denham and the man calling himself Ivor Smith.

All too soon it became evident that Mihail was the first person ever to report anything untoward about the two men. His heart plummeting while he sweated with anxiety, he explained about Jack Denham being his tutor and how he had done work for Ivor Smith. Feeling even worse, he tried to recall exactly how the approach about becoming an agent had been worded. He told the officer, as he had told Rupert's father, how the suggestion had been made while they were discussing space travel.

"All of a sudden, they came out with it – these hopes that I would be prepared to help the Communist cause. I couldn't dream of that, of course. My family is *White* Russian – my father's side, that is. My mother is English."

"One moment, if you please, Mr Malinowski. We must deal initially with what was actually said to you by these people. Then we may move on to your reaction." The man's smile was reassuring. "You can take your time . . ."

But taking time over this was the last thing Mihail wished; all he wanted was to have the wretched business finished with so he could get away from here.

Invited to write everything down, he struggled to form the phrases. This was condemning the people who for

114

months he'd believed were his friends. The actual words had so appalled him that they were imprinted on his memory, but that did not make sharing them any the easier.

' "You are proud of your Russian heritage?" Jack Denham asked me first, and I saw him look at Ivor Smith.

I think I nodded. "I suppose I am. Living in England never prevented my father from remembering the things that are best about his homeland."

Denham continued, "So you would wish to perpetuate those 'good things' created by his native people?"

I was so uneasy then that I hesitated. I told him I didn't really understand what he meant. Jack and Ivor Smith gave each other a funny look. I'm sure it was Ivor who spoke next.

"We need educated young men like you, Mihail. Individuals who are not afraid, who would work willingly to further the cause."

"What 'cause'?" I asked him. I was totally bewildered.

"Oh, come now, my friend." Denham was insisting there was no need to disguise our intentions from each other. He claimed that I couldn't be happy about the position of Russia in today's world. He made out this was a great opportunity for me. Something about the chance to bring Western skills to my father's homeland. He sounded so forceful that I was quite frightened.

I told him that if they were suggesting what I thought they were, I should need to consider the prospect very carefully before ever I could agree. That didn't begin to express the degree of my reservations. But I needed to get more time. I had to think how best to refuse to cooperate in such a dreadful idea.

It was Ivor Smith who said I could only have a few hours to consider. And I saw in his eyes how furious he was. He told me not to go playing around while I decided. Then he said something about how important this matter was, that I had to understand how greatly they were trusting me.'

Mihail felt miserable as he handed his statement to the officer. Before beginning to write, he'd been afraid that he would not recall enough, but he'd soon become acutely aware that he remembered more than sufficient to cause the police to investigate Jack Denham as well as Smith. Much as he had enjoyed working for the antiques dealer, Jack was the one he'd no desire to harm; Jack who'd been his tutor and had seemed such a true friend.

The police were pleased with the evidence he was providing, a fact which gave Mihail even deeper misgivings about what he was doing. When Rupert's father also commended him for issuing so forthright a statement, he felt even worse. However had such an innocent love of old timepieces involved him in this?

"I wouldn't have wanted to get them into trouble, not for worlds," Mihail said now. "But I could never agree. And I don't want them to go on working throughout Oxford, trying to enlist other students or graduates."

"And nor do we," the plain-clothes man assured him. "You know you have done what is right, we only hope that you will come to understand that doing right *can* be distressing. Especially when people whom we have trusted are the ones concerned."

Mihail nodded. "How much more do you need from me?" Something else was bothering him. "You do understand, don't you, that I'd never turn into some sort of spy?"

"You wouldn't be here, would you, if you'd even contemplated assisting them." The officer smiled again. "Your father may be proud of you, young man."

"I hope he will," said Mihail ruefully. "All I can

116

think just now is that he'll hate the way I've got into this mess."

Before facing his father, however, Mihail had other difficulties to endure. Term had not ended; until it did he would be obliged to remain in Oxford. The police were already on their way to arrest Smith and Denham. Not knowing who the pair might have as allies in the city, Mihail was afraid that he could face reprisals for his action.

His erstwhile friends would guess immediately who was responsible for informing the police; he couldn't imagine they would feel leniently towards him.

"You've done all you could," Rupert reminded him when he saw how perturbed Mihail was as the three of them left the police station.

"And acted courageously too," Lance Atherton-Ward added.

"But what now?" Mihail said dejectedly. "You can't seriously believe those two will do nothing? They'll know it was me."

Rupert's father grasped his shoulder as they walked along. "Take it from me, the police will keep those two in custody once they have them in for questioning. Espionage isn't treated lightly, you know."

"I hope you're right. At least – in one way, I do. Only I can't get used to the idea that Jack will lose his job."

Rupert grinned. "Cheer up, old chap. He must have known all along that he'd be suspended if he was found out."

"Then why do it? Why would he?"

Lance smiled. "Why did you refuse to participate in their scheme? It's all a matter of allegiance. He was determined to back his beliefs. He's not a child, Mihail, and he must have sufficient intelligence to be aware of the potential consequences."

The other two insisted that they go to Mihail's rooms, but only to pick up his things for an overnight stay. Rupert's father would run them both back to Oxford the following morning, by which time they could feel certain that Denham and Ivor Smith would have been apprehended.

In fact, as soon as they reached the house in the Cotswolds Lance telephoned through, and was assured that the police were holding both men.

"You may sleep soundly tonight," he told Mihail. "And if you wish, in the morning I will speak with your father."

Mihail thanked his host, but shook his head. "I'll tell him when I go home at the end of term, if you don't mind. There'll be time enough for thinking how best to put this across."

He could imagine only too clearly how disturbed Andre Malinowski would be, and needed to be there to try and explain how such a terrible thing had occurred.

The only good outcome of the incident was Annabel's reaction. She had waited up that night to learn what had transpired at the police station, but was too tired to say more than how glad she was that Mihail had had the guts to report those two.

In the morning, however, when everyone was about early because of the journey back to college, she came down to breakfast and flung her arms around Mihail.

"Thank God nothing went wrong," she exclaimed. "I was terrified that those two would be on to you, might try something. I'd never survive if anything happened to you."

Listening to her, reading in her eyes how earnest she was, Mihail understood afresh how important she was to him. He could no more contemplate life without her than she appeared able to without him.

"We've got to talk," he told her urgently. "Come up to Oxford as soon as you can."

He could not go back to Yorkshire without making sure that this lovely young woman understood he was committed to her.

*   *   *

118

Sonia was at Stonemoor House on the day her brother arrived after his final departure from Oxford. Flinging herself at him in an excited hug, she was disappointed that he didn't reciprocate with as much light-hearted affection.

"You're not turning into a fuddy-duddy, are you, I hope? Are you too wise and sensible to bother with your little sister now?"

"Of course not, love," Mihail asserted. "It's just – well, I've got rather a lot on my mind. Is Dad around?"

"You've just missed him. Tania wanted him to go over a score or something with her. Some brand new solo she's doing in London sometime."

But he knew I was arriving today, thought Mihail, and silently quelled his old familiar suspicions that Tania came first with Andre Malinowski.

"Mum won't be long," Sonia assured him. "She's closing the shop early, and we're going to have a special meal tonight. Mrs Singer's busy already."

Conscious that their housekeeper wasn't able to hear his arrival, Mihail set down his baggage in the hall and strode through to the kitchen. Mrs Singer looked thinner than he remembered, suddenly very old. He wanted to gather her to him, perhaps to convey some of the strength that he wished he might give her.

Her eyes were bright, though, when she sensed his approach and turned. Nodding and beaming at him, she fetched the pad she always used. 'Welcome home, Mihail love.'

He took the pen from her. 'Thank you. It's good to be here'

As she had years ago, the housekeeper showed him the treats she was preparing for him. There was fresh salmon to be baked in butter, then peas newly shelled, straight from their own garden, potatoes due for the scrubbing which would remove good Cragg Vale earth, other vegetables. Opening the fridge, she pointed to one of his favourite trifles. Mihail knew it would be enriched with the strawberries he adored.

Pamela came in from her shop while Sonia was watching from the kitchen doorway and Mihail had his back to them, his fingers sticky from clearing out the last of the mixture from one of Mrs Singer's bowls.

"Mihail!" Eager as a young girl, his mother came rushing to embrace him.

"Steady, Mum. I'm covered in goo."

Pamela laughed. "It's been too long for that to matter! Thought the last few days would never pass."

"You're glad I'm home then?"

"Don't you dare ask."

"You wanted me to go to Oxford," he teased.

Pamela shook her head. "Not deep down, no. But your father did. And it worked, didn't it? You'll have a good degree now behind you."

And a lot of trouble, if only you knew, thought her son, and yearned to talk with his father.

"I gather Dad's at Tania's. All right if I go round there?"

Pamela tried not to mind that her being there wasn't sufficient. "If you like, only he knows what time we're having dinner tonight. He'll be back in plenty of time."

Waiting was no good. He'd waited more than long enough already while the police revealed little of the situation regarding Ivor Smith and Jack. They had seemed of the opinion that having arrested the pair was enough, that Mihail had no reason to feel concern so long as they were detained.

Walking down the hill towards his sister's home, Mihail tried to decide how best to reveal the story to his father. Ever since the day that wretched suggestion had been put to him he had wrestled with how to explain events. He had reached no conclusion that satisfied him.

Tania greeted him at the door, kissed him on both cheeks, then asked if he'd had a good journey. Without waiting for his reply, she led the way into the sitting room.

"Dad and I are busy," she began, but Andre had heard

120

his son's voice and was abandoning the music stand and striding across to grasp his hand in greeting.

"Mihail, it is good to have you home. I am so proud that you have completed your studies. Congratulations."

"Thanks, Dad. There's something I have to tell you, though, something that's happened."

His ready smile was supplanted by a frown; Andre looked five years older in that moment. Mihail hated himself for doing this to him.

"What is it, son?"

Tania turned away. "I'll make some coffee."

"You remember my tutor – Jack Denham?"

"The one who encouraged your interest in clocks? Naturally."

"And how I told you of his friend – the dealer in Oxford who was entrusting me with watches for restoring?"

"Yes, yes. What of them?"

"A short while before I came away I found out why they were both so keen to be friendly. Oh, Dad, it's so awful—" Suddenly, Mihail could say no more.

Andre tried to manage an encouraging smile. "Do not forget that I have experienced several awful situations . . ."

"They only befriended me for a purpose – they wanted me to become some kind of agent."

"Agent? Not – you cannot mean for the Communists? Tell me that wasn't it."

"I'm afraid it was. I knew the man who called himself Ivor Smith was from Russia, but—"

"But you told me he was White Russian; we once discussed the coincidence of his having a background similar to my own."

"I know, I know. I can only think now that this was purely what he wished me to believe."

"You turned them down, of course. But where does this leave you? Who else has learned of their inclination, of your involvement?"

Andre remembered only too starkly those dreadful days roughly twenty years ago when people had thought *he*

121

might be a spy. He had suffered so deeply, on Pamela's behalf as much as his own, had been terrified that his nationality might cause her trouble.

"In addition to the police, it's only people I trust," Mihail was saying. "Sit down, Dad, I'll tell you all about it here. Don't want Mum upsetting."

He waited until Andre was seated in one of the armchairs, then went to stand with his back to the fireplace.

"Rupert happened to come to my rooms just after I'd left those two at the antiques shop. I suppose I was looking as shaken as I felt. Ru made me tell him, and that was the best thing I could have done. His father's a lawyer. Don't know if I ever told you. Anyway, we went to their house and Lance Atherton-Ward listened to it all. He told the police over the phone, then we went back to Oxford and I gave them a statement at the station."

"You would have hated that. Until then you always considered those men your friends."

Mihail nodded. "It was grim, yes. Can't say I felt any better for doing what I knew was right."

"Did the police locate this antiques dealer and Mr Denham?"

"Straight away. But again, I feel awful about it."

"Yet if you hadn't reported the incident they would have approached you again, might even have tried to force you into complying. People that determined resort to pressure – blackmail, and the like. Eventually, they would have made the suggestion to other graduates whom they believed could prove useful." Andre thought for a moment, nodded. "You have behaved admirably, Mihail. I cannot pretend I am not distressed by this situation, but you have handled it with great maturity."

"I thought – was afraid – you'd be angry that I'd got myself into it."

"You should not forget that I learned how readily one's birth may lead others to make all kinds of suppositions. And I hope you will always remember that whatever you may become involved in you can bring any problems to me."

Although greatly reassured by his father's reaction, and relieved to have spoken of the trouble which had hung like a physical burden upon him, Mihail remained perturbed. Andre was no longer a young man; he himself was the one now who ought to be protecting his father from difficulties, not providing cause for anxiety.

With her tray of coffee, Tania brought a distraction into the room, and soon was telling her brother about the piece she was rehearsing. New operatic arias were all too rare, and she was privileged to be giving this one its first performance.

Thankful for the opportunity to think about something so different from his own life, Mihail began to let the distress of the recent past slip away.

Ian came in from work, grinned as he shook Mihail by the hand, and congratulated him on completing his years at university. "Not something I ever wanted myself, mind, but I give credit where it's due. And I've allus thought you've studied with a will."

The four of them talked for a while longer, then Mihail suggested that he and his father should be heading back to Stonemoor.

They were in the bright hall, saying goodbye to Tania and Ian, when the door opened and Pamela Anichka came in. Initially, Mihail noticed how pale she looked, tired by her day in the boutique and the drive home through the early evening traffic. But then her eyes gleamed suddenly, and her mouth curved into a massive smile.

Rushing to him in much the same way as Sonia had earlier, PA flung both arms around him and squeezed. "God, am I glad to see you, love!" She kissed him hard, her lips firm on his. Only after several long seconds did she ease away slightly to speak again. "I thought this day would never come, you know – really couldn't believe you would ever be here. It'll be just like it always was."

She kissed him again, even more fervently. I'll have to

tell her about Annabel, he thought. Can't have her counting on my being around for ever; mustn't let her continue to bank on things being exactly as they used to be.

"We're going to be late for our meal," his father asserted, quite sternly. "Did you even see your mother before you came over here?"

They were walking briskly up the road through the drizzle that had started falling, when Andre revealed the source of his sharpness.

"I do not wish to add to your difficulties when you are only now recovering from the shock of events in Oxford. There is, though, something I must say. Now, today, while no one else is to hear. I have been concerned in the past, but hoped that time would alter the situation. It is about your relationship with Pamela Anichka. I believe you understand my meaning. While you both were so very young there did not seem too much harm in the affection between you. Now, though, you are a man. I cannot believe you are immune to attraction. And she is your half-sister's daughter, after all – my grandchild. You must know that there can be no other *relationship* between you."

Mihail smiled. "I do know, Dad. And you've no need to worry. In fact, I was going to tell you – there's this girl I've met. Annabel, Rupert's sister. His twin, actually. And – well, just before I left Oxford, I realised I've got to go on seeing her."

Relief warmed his father's grey eyes. "Ah, that is good. Very good, my son. So, you do not need for me to explain how unsuitable it would be for you to encourage Pamela Anichka."

"Not at all."

"You have made me very happy, do you know that, Mihail? Your mother and I shall have to meet this young lady, welcome her to Stonemoor House. Yes, I am very happy for you."

I just wish I thought for one moment that PA would come to accept the news so well, Mihail reflected. He would be obliged to tell her, but that prospect filled him entirely with dread.

The whole family were at Stonemoor House for lunch on the following Sunday. Immensely pleased to be surrounded by so many of them, so patently eager to see him, Mihail could feel his smile widening as they all sat around the large dining table.

He had told his mother about Annabel shortly after explaining to Andre, and had been unsurprised to learn that she already knew.

"Your dad said," Pamela had revealed, smiling. "He was that thrilled he didn't seem able to keep it to himself. And like me, he insists we must invite her to stay. Soon as you can arrange it."

Pamela had also told Sonia about her brother's girlfriend. Sonia so often appeared to feel she was the odd one out that her mother tried to involve her in everything happening within the family.

Sonia would never have said, but she'd been quite upset by the news. Hadn't she been counting on having Mihail around once more, the only other young person at home? Now he'd met someone he fancied she knew what it would be. Everybody was the same – couldn't wait to get a house of their own, start a family. Everybody but *her*. The only good thing about it was knowing that PA would have to face up to reality, have to accept that Mihail could never be hers.

During lunch on that Sunday Sonia watched them both. Mihail was savouring being home, answering questions from his uncles, teasing Tom and Gwen's boys, listening respectfully to Grandma Baker's advice concerning his future. Pamela Anichka was watching him, just as she always had, staring goggle-eyed, in the way she did at a dance when she was trying to will a chap to notice her. Mihail couldn't have said anything yet. And that wasn't right. It wasn't even fair to PA.

"When's Annabel coming to stay then, Mihail?" Sonia

125

asked. "You are inviting her soon to meet us all, aren't you?"

Sonia heard PA echo "Annabel?" under her breath, saw from his frown that Mihail wasn't ready yet for replying. He cleared his throat, gave his young sister a withering look, then began to speak.

"Very soon. I've written to her. So has Mum, to confirm that they're looking forward to getting to know her." Quelling a sigh, he faced Pamela Anichka. "I was going to tell you. I think you'll like her, you ought to be friends."

"Oh, really?" snapped PA, who sprang from her seat and ran out of the room.

They heard the front door open and slam shut again and footsteps hurrying down the drive. Tania half rose from the table, but Ian shook his head and she sank onto her chair again.

Wearily, Mihail placed his napkin on the table and stood up. "I'd better – if you'll excuse me."

Her head set admirably high as she stared straight ahead, PA was almost at the entrance to the drive when he caught her up. Only then did he see the tears rushing down her cheeks.

"I didn't mean you to find out like this," said Mihail, almost as emotional as she was. "I was only waiting for the right moment."

"There isn't one, is there, not for demolishing some-one's life."

He slid a hand into the crook of her elbow. Pamela Anichka wrenched free of his touch, walked more swiftly.

"Not in front of everyone, I meant," Mihail persisted, hastening along beside her. "That scene back there was the last thing I wanted."

"What did you want then, to keep it quiet until the day you marry your precious Annabel?"

"Don't be stupid. We're friends, aren't we, you and I? I wanted to explain . . ."

126

"Friends? You're the one who's stupid, Mihail. And you must have been blind for years. Don't you know how I feel about you, how I've always felt?"

"We've been close, agreed. But we've always known that – well, that it could only ever be friendship. You're my sister's child, for God's sake!"

"Somehow I've never believed that, if there is a God, he's had much of a hand in my feelings for you. Do you think I've *enjoyed* loving you these past two years while you've been all those miles away?"

"No one asked you to – to wait around or anything. Be fair, PA, I never said a word about . . ."

"And you think that makes it all right? That you can just take up with some female who turns you on, and drop me as if I don't exist."

"I'm not dropping you, I'm still just as fond of you as ever I was. But you must have known all along that we could never marry."

"That doesn't matter, does it. Not these days. It hasn't through most of the sixties. The 'swinging sixties' – which planet have you been living on?"

He sighed, glanced away from her, up the hill where they were walking in sunlight towards the moors. "You don't have to remind me of the permissiveness that seems to be the norm. University life wasn't exactly sheltered. I happen to want to be married, though, to have a family."

And so do I, thought Pamela Anichka, her heart like one of the black rocks on the hillside. And you're the only man I want to have children with.

She didn't, *couldn't* speak.

Walking on beside her, grimly, Mihail reached out, placed an arm about her shoulders.

"We'll always be special friends, PA – nothing'll change that, I promise."

"You might think that. I can hardly believe she will allow it. If by some miracle you were to be mine, I couldn't bring myself to share you."

127

"Wait till you meet Annabel, you'll see then. She is so different – I'm sure she would understand that you and I matter to each other."

Pamela Anichka shook her head. Turning towards him, she shrugged off his arm.

"She wouldn't understand. What's worse – *you* don't even begin to. Get back to Stonemoor; don't have everyone worrying about you."

"How can I? Not when you're like this. I can't leave you."

"But you did. It's too late. You left me on the day that you went after her. Go on, go back to the house. I need to be on my own."

The reservoir was miles away, near the crest of the hill where the road from Cragg Vale converged with the one leading over into Lancashire. Despite the heat of summer, the breeze here was strong, chilly. Gazing across at the waves it was stirring up, PA was tempted to swim. Or not to swim . . . just to walk into that water, to let it wash away all this hurt, and the blood that felt like it was draining out of her heart. He wasn't hers, he never would be.

She wished she could hide, in her room at home. Except that she never would be able to hide there. Her mother would pester and probe, until she learned the truth about this change in her. Ian would try with his kind questioning to ferret out what was causing her distress. Only Ian didn't count, he wasn't really her father. All he wanted was a child who was really his. She had heard them, heard them over the years longing for somebody else, somebody new.

Would anyone truly miss her?

Uncaring whether she lived or not, PA stared at the water.

She pictured them all, finding her, knowing what she had done. Imagined them thinking she had no guts, no ability to fight. There was a better way, wasn't there? She wasn't certain yet what it would be. While she was working that out, though, for once in her life she would do something that was *her* idea.

Nine

O nly when Annabel eventually came to stay at Stonemoor House did Mihail begin to feel better about Pamela Anichka's reaction on the day Sonia had revealed his plans.

He was feeling overwhelmed with happiness from the moment that he set out with his father to meet her train.

Annabel was wearing something he hadn't seen before, a summery dress which had a neat little jacket. They were in some kind of creamy coloured material and, with a skirt rather longer than she often wore, she looked so elegant that he wondered how he'd deserved her company.

Andre took to her at once. Seeing this in his careful opening of the car door for her, Mihail smiled. Accustomed over the years to youngsters who bounded in and out of vehicles and stormed into rooms, Andre was going to enjoy treating Annabel as the lady she so assuredly appeared.

As soon as they arrived at the house Pamela also became enchanted by Annabel's easy grace. In no time at all the girl was chatting as though she had known them for years, revealing in every word that she had absorbed everything that Mihail had told her about his family. From his father's violins to his mother's antiques she had something intelligent to say, and was ready to listen when they expanded on some aspect of their lives.

Sonia came in from her day at work, and was the one who asked most about Annabel's enthusiasm for painting. She'd never met an artist before, or not one who actually managed to sell her pictures.

"I wish I'd thought to bring you one, Sonia," Annabel said, with a smile. "I will next time I come. I'm always afraid I might bore people."

"You'd never do that," Mihail insisted.

They all laughed, content to see him so happy. During the meal that evening Sonia remarked that it must be great to be a twin. And wasn't Annabel missing her brother?

She grinned. "In a way, I do. But, of course, I got used to not having him around while he was at Oxford. At first, I quite enjoyed being an only one, but then the painting started to take off and I had to be so busy there was hardly time to think!"

"And how was Ru when you left?" Mihail enquired. Neither he nor his friend were much given to writing letters, and when he had phoned the Atherton-Wards he'd only wanted to speak with Annabel.

"He's fine, thinking of doing a PhD. Now he's away from Oxford he seems to be missing university. Did he tell you he was considering staying on there?"

"No. And it sounds like it was a surprise to you."

Annabel nodded. "Dad's rather torn. I think he's a bit afraid Ru will turn into one of those perpetual students. I don't believe he will. He's talking now of becoming a college lecturer eventually."

They all agreed he was to be commended for that ambition.

"So – how many clocks have you restored since you came home?" she asked Mihail.

His smile was rueful. "Do you know, I haven't touched any. The last few days of term were so traumatic that I arrived here exhausted."

"It is a holiday, after all," said his father.

Pamela winked at Annabel. "Don't you worry, love, I've got plenty of work lined up for him. Mihail might be determined to make a go of repair work for my shop; that's nothing to my determination to have him boost my profits!"

Annabel turned to her. "I hope you're going to show

me around your business while I'm staying. I've seen so much that Mihail has worked on, I can't help being interested."

"Just as well," said Sonia. "Once he starts on a watch or clock no one gets any sense out of him."

His work, nevertheless, continued to be set aside during the weeks which Annabel spent at Stonemoor House. Now that Mihail had at last got her here in his part of the world he was going to show her every one of his favourite places.

She had visited Yorkshire previously, but some time ago, and only some of the popular tourist areas. They explored those together, relishing the sunlight as they strolled about Bolton Abbey, marvelling at the splendour of Malham Cove, taking train and bus as far as Whitby.

Annabel was missing her car, but Mihail had been uneasy when she first suggested driving from the Cotswolds to Cragg Vale. Reluctant to disturb him and rather shaken by the depth of his anxiety for her safety, she had agreed to leaving the car behind.

"You don't drive, do you?" she remarked, surprised. So many young men now were learning as soon as their age permitted.

Slightly embarrassed, Mihail shrugged. "Don't know why not, really. Didn't want a car in Oxford; getting around without one was easy enough. Before that—"

"Yes?" Annabel prompted. She wanted to learn all there was to know about him.

Again, he shrugged. "Maybe I was too lazy. I don't know – or could be I never thought about learning. Didn't need transport to get to Mum's shop and my workbench."

There was also the question of how much running a car would cost, quite apart from the original outlay. His parents weren't ungenerous, but Andre's profession was unlike many which guaranteed a regular salary. Likewise, the takings of his mother's shop did tend to fluctuate.

"Once I seriously get down to work again, I think

I shall begin taking lessons. It'll give me an incentive to work harder. And then there's our future to consider."

"Ours?"

"I want you to marry me, Annabel. Haven't you realised that?"

She smiled. "I did wonder, but it's lovely to be asked."

"You will, won't you?"

"There's nothing I want more. I just hope you don't mind taking on an artist."

"But a successful one," he said lightly. "I was rather thinking that you would compensate for the insecurity of my own work!"

"I'm sure you'll be highly regarded in no time at all. You've plenty of experience already."

"You've no qualms then about our making a go of it together?"

Hugging him, Annabel beamed into his eyes. "I've been convinced all along that we're a very good pair. How soon shall we marry?"

"However quickly you can get everything together. I suspect I'm not going to be very good at being separated from you."

"Me neither. Shall we tell your parents tonight? Then if I could ring mine and put them in the picture. I suppose I'll have to go back before long; Mother will want to discuss wedding arrangements, and we'll have to book the church and everything."

Andre was somewhat uneasy about the alacrity with which Mihail had taken to the prospect of marriage. Newly home from university and with little to guarantee success in the career he wanted, his son seemed to be accepting responsibilities a shade too readily. But not wishing to spoil the excitement for the young couple, he mentioned his misgivings only to his wife.

After hearing him out, Pamela nodded. "I know what you mean, love. I was a bit alarmed as well, because he's not worked long enough to have something behind him. Only then I thought how lots of youngsters make the most of this permissive age."

Andre agreed. "At least they are not doing that. We should both hate it if they simply went off and lived together."

That same evening Sonia was asked to be a bridesmaid, and she began to feel that perhaps all these changes within their family life weren't necessarily bad.

"Do you mind, Annabel, if we also ask Pamela Anichka to be a bridesmaid?" Mihail suggested a few hours later when everyone else was in bed. "She's so near my age, and we've grown up together."

Annabel was too happy to raise any objections.

The person who did object was PA herself when Mihail took his fiancée along to the cottage the following evening.

The two young women had met earlier when Annabel was introduced to Tania and Ian as well. On that first occasion Pamela Anichka had been perfectly polite, though a touch frosty. Mihail's disappointment had lasted only until they were on their way back to Stonemoor House. With Annabel beside him, he couldn't dwell on any other girl's attitude.

Alone in his room afterwards, he had recalled PA's coolness, and worried for her sake as well as for the effect any future awkwardness might have on Annabel. That was when he'd come up with the idea of inviting her to participate in the ceremony.

The reaction when his fiancée made the suggestion shook everyone. "No, thank you," Pamela Anichka snapped, glowering at Annabel. "I don't even want to be there. If you want the reason, ask him!"

She stormed out of the room, leaving Ian looking acutely embarrassed as footsteps stomped up the stairs and across the floor above their heads. He apologised quite awkwardly, and wished that Tania hadn't had to go to London; he needed her to smooth things over.

"You mustn't worry about it," said Annabel, calmly. "I don't mind in the least."

Mihail minded a very great deal; he had set his heart on having his future wife and PA get on together. And this time as they walked back to Stonemoor House no one could take his thoughts away from PA's outburst.

Annabel was compelled to remark on how quiet he had become. "It's because of her, isn't it? I know you explained how complex some of your family relationships are, but I didn't expect someone who's been like a sister to have such a crush on you."

"Has it put you off? You don't think – haven't thought there was anything, well, vaguely incestuous between PA and me?"

Annabel shook her head. "I know you, don't I, darling. You're not the sort who'd go in for anything of the kind."

"We were just pals, that was all."

On your side perhaps, she thought. I'm not at all certain what has been going on in Pamela Anichka's head.

Two days later Ian came home from work quite late. He'd been determined Canning's men would finish the job on which they were working. Ted Burrows had taken the day off, something he did quite frequently now. Their team seemed to cooperate more smoothly whenever Burrows was absent, and Ian wanted to see the task completed without any adverse comments from their manager to mar his satisfaction.

Tired, longing for his shower and perhaps a drink before their meal, he got out of the car and frowned when he noticed PA's mini was missing from its usual spot outside the cottage.

Tania was away rehearsing, but only last night he and Pamela Anichka had been discussing what they would eat this evening. She was good about being in to cook most of the times when her mother was away. In fact, PA and Ian relished eating some of the dishes which Tania's fitness regime would ban. Having to keep well in order to remain in good voice did tend to make her very particular about consuming the right things.

Ian wondered if Pamela Anichka could be having trouble with the car and have been obliged to use public transport. He called her name as he unlocked the door and came into the hall, but unsurprisingly there was no answer. There was a possibility that she might have dropped in at Stonemoor House, of course; feeling ridiculously alarmed, Ian rang through there.

Pamela answered, sounding almost as tired as he was, but quite cheerful. In the background he could hear Andre's violin and the young people talking.

"Is PA there by any chance, Pamela?"

"No, sorry. You are at the house, I suppose? She's not turned up there, I take it?"

"That's right. And with Tania away – well, PA's normally reliable. I'm beginning to get quite worried in case the car's broken down."

"She's in the AA, anyway, if it has, isn't she? They'll look after her, see she gets home. Why don't you come to us for something to eat? There's plenty. Save you cooking."

"Thanks, but I'd better not. Got to stick around in case PA phones."

Pamela Anichka did not contact him. When Tania rang from her London hotel for a chat Ian tried hard to sound as though everything was quite normal. But Tania knew her husband well enough to read the unease in his voice. "What is wrong, Ian? More trouble at Canning's?"

He sighed. "Oh. Didn't mean you to know. No, it isn't to do with work. It may be nothing, actually, but PA hasn't arrived back yet."

"And she did not say she was going out after the shop closed?"

"Don't think so." Ian became aware that he mustn't spell out the fact that he and his stepdaughter had planned what they should eat together and everything.

135

"Oh, well – you know how she loves to assert herself occasionally. I expect she is relishing the idea of a night on the town, and a sudden rebellion against keeping us informed."

Still sounding unconcerned, Tania chatted for a while before promising to call him first thing next morning to check what time her daughter finally reappeared.

Tania's call came while Ian was placing the breakfast dishes in the sink. Glancing at the clock, he registered that he would be late if he spent much time on the telephone. If PA was the person on the other end of the line he would have to delay reprimanding her for being inconsiderate.

"It's me. Thought I'd better ring before taking a shower, or you'd be off to work. What time did Pamela Anichka arrive home, Ian?"

"Actually, I'm afraid she didn't, love. Must admit she's got me in a bit of a panic by now. Don't quite know where to start checking." He had spent the night resisting urges to ring hospitals or the police to check about possible accidents.

"You could phone the boutique for a start," Tania suggested. "But not before nine, of course. Or I will ring them, if you wish."

"Could you? We're starting at this new place today, and I'll be late as it is. Don't want Burrows coming the heavy boss if I haven't got all the men organised. If you can contact the shop and ask there, I'll give you a ring later on. You do have a number where I can reach you?"

There was nothing she would be able to tell him. Tania learned from the owner of the boutique that Pamela Anichka wasn't there. What was more, she'd been absent for the whole of the previous day.

From being mildly concerned because her daughter seemed to be asserting her freedom to do as she liked, Tania felt her emotions churning up into panic. *Had* PA had an accident, or had something else horrible happened to her? She ought to go straight home to Yorkshire, but how could she? The first night of the new opera was this evening. She had a major role, how could she let everyone down? Opting out and having her understudy go on in her place would be most unprofessional.

When Ian got through to her within an hour Tania was thankful to be able to share her anxiety. The only trouble was that his evident alarm confirmed how serious PA's disappearance could be.

"I do not know what on earth to do," she confessed as soon as she had told him that Pamela Anichka had not been at work the previous day. "As you know, we have our first performance tonight. I feel so torn, darling – I ought to be up there, searching. But they are all relying on me at the theatre."

"Steady on a minute," said Ian gently. "You couldn't go searching, not really. Where would any of us begin? You go ahead with tonight, leave everything to me. I'll contact the police now, get them to check that – that nothing's happened. And I'll speak to the woman at the boutique, ask if she remembers anything from the last time she saw PA. She might even have heard her making arrangements to meet one of her friends . . ."

After checking that the men were getting down to work on the new offices they were decorating, Ian telephoned the police. While explaining the situation he asked if they might be able to check with the force over in Manchester as well as locally, to find out if Pamela Anichka had been involved in an accident.

They were helpful, promising to check up as he requested. Since he was out at work and couldn't be reached by telephone, they asked him to give them an hour or two before ringing back to enquire if anything had been learned.

Scarcely able to concentrate on the job, Ian next rang through to Stonemoor House. Andre answered and, hearing that PA still appeared to be missing, sounded just as troubled as Ian himself.

"If you need me to, I can start looking or something," he promised immediately. "What about Tania, does she know Pamela Anichka has not arrived home yet?"

"Yes. I've just been talking to her. She'd spoken to the woman who owns the shop. Did I say PA wasn't there yesterday?"

"And it is Tania's first night, isn't it. We shall have to try and solve this without her. But did Pamela Anichka give no hint that she might be going somewhere?"

"Not one word."

"And nothing has upset her?"

"Mihail's engagement, of course. She's been very quiet since she heard the news."

"Oh." Andre would have felt better without that reminder. For years now he had been troubled about Pamela Anichka's very evident affection for his son. He had cautioned Mihail against letting feelings between them become too unrestrained, but he suspected now that he should have done so much earlier. He quelled a sigh. "Well, keep in touch, Ian. I shall be here all day; let me know at once if there is any way I can help."

"Is Sonia there by any chance?"

"Afraid not. She's on duty."

"I only wondered if she might have some idea what PA is up to."

"I have a number where we may contact her, if you think she might help."

Reaching Sonia at the airport took some long while, and was just as unproductive as every other call they had made. Ian returned to work utterly depressed.

Had PA disappeared at any time he would have felt dreadful; having her vanish while he was the only other person at the cottage left him feeling he was somehow responsible.

The police reported that there had been no accident locally, nor in Manchester or any place in between where a young woman of his stepdaughter's description had been involved. They also reminded him that at nineteen she was well able to live away from home.

Although of course relieved that there was no account of her being injured, Ian felt totally bewildered. What in the world should he do next in order to try and locate her?

The traffic in London was rather alarming. Being used to other cities seemed to make no difference while she waited to cross the road near St Martin-in-the Fields. There seemed so many of those huge red buses belching out diesel from noisy engines, while black taxis sped around corners to get ahead of other motorists.

Oxford Street yesterday had been no better, but she had turned off towards Liberty's and then had found her destination, Carnaby Street. Every bit as exciting as she had anticipated, she had spent hours there, browsing in every shop. She hadn't bought a thing, a fact which showed how strong her willpower could be.

Pamela Anichka was proud of her ability to resist such massive temptation. No matter who had disapproved of some of her behaviour in the past, they would be obliged to admit now that she'd acquired plenty of good Yorkshire sense.

Being thrifty might be uncharacteristic, but it was an intrinsic part of her plan. Entrance to this gathering of rock fans where she was heading was supposed to be less than three pounds, but she needed money for the journey to the Isle of Wight. And she would have to eat throughout her stay there.

Her one indulgence since arriving in London had been the ticket for tonight. Accommodation last night had been modest indeed, provided by the YWCA. If some of her friends could have seen her they would have been astonished, but it had served. And she'd only been a little disappointed that her first night in London hadn't been enhanced by a glittering major hotel.

The theatre was quite full already when PA entered the foyer. Hundreds of glamorous women with their stylish escorts increased the excitement surging all around her amid the murmur of polished voices.

The only place she'd been able to secure was standing at the back of the stalls. Her feet were aching now from all the walking during the day. But she was wearing low-heeled shoes, bought especially for coping outdoors at that rock festival.

Gazing around, she felt the atmosphere increasing her anticipation. This theatre with its velvet upholstery and gilded embellishments made the perfect setting for any first night.

The orchestra began tuning up; she felt her pulse rate increasing. The cast would be nervous; new operas so rarely appeared in England. She had heard Tania Malinowski sing many times over the years, but only occasionally in something of this kind. Her own taste for pop music had meant she more often attended when the event was a concert of some of the more accessible classics. Further back in the past, so long ago that she could hardly remember the venues, she'd heard Tania indulge her affection for songs from the 1940s. It had been good to recognise then that singing professionally hadn't induced any prejudice against more modern pieces.

Today, she didn't have long to wait for Tania's first appearance. Slender, exquisite in an ankle-length gown of palest aquamarine, the singer looked so young that she brought emotion surging to throat and eyes.

Immaculately-pitched, Tania's voice was as beautiful as ever in the past, charged with the richness that only genuine feeling expresses.

Listening enraptured, PA silently thanked heaven for prompting her to linger here in the capital long enough to hear her mother sing. No connoisseur of opera herself, PA still appreciated the high quality of singing from all the principals, and whenever the chorus appeared she thrilled to the power and the range of their voices.

It was Tania most of all, naturally, who engaged her fervent attention. Tania who during a final aria moved her so deeply she found tears on her cheeks.

Head down, she slunk into the YWCA for her last night

140

there; was glad now that she knew no one in the entire building.

Twenty-four hours ago she had wished from the depths of her heart that there had been someone here with whom to chat, to share this first visit alone to London. All she wanted tonight was to find enough seclusion in which to recover some composure.

Waiting at Waterloo station next morning, Pamela Anichka still felt overwhelmed by the emotions which had troubled her since those hours in that theatre.

Inwardly, she still was weeping. I'm sorry, I'm sorry, something inside her cried while she set her face, raised her chin, and resolved to look forward to her journey. But she was sorry for the distress which she knew she must be causing to her mother, and to Ian.

He was a good father, always had been as far back as she could recall. He could not help not being her real father, any more than she could help the insecurities inherited as Gerald Thomas's daughter.

Even without Gerald's refusal to help her financially, she had understood enough to realise that Ian Baker was worth ten of him. She could telephone him perhaps, from the Isle of Wight. Stop him worrying, have him feel better about being obliged to tell Tania about her disappearance.

After PA had left her car at the station and caught the train for London she had been preoccupied with travelling and looking ahead to what she would do in the capital. She'd heard about the YWCA place quite by chance, and had been glad that the charges there were modest.

Only since getting off the train that had brought her south had she begun to imagine how her family would feel about her sudden departure. And not only Tania and Ian would be hurt and confused. Andre Malinowski was the kindest grandfather imaginable, his wife had never once implied that PA was anything but her blood relation.

There would be trouble, she knew, when she did eventually go home. And she was certain already that

141

she *would* go back there. This trip was no more than that, something she simply had to do. Proving she had a mind of her own plus the ability to carry out her plans alone was only a part of it. She wanted to participate in this rock festival, yes, but she needed most of all to get away from a life obsessed with Mihail. PA willed herself to start on that by noticing what was going on around her. Coming away would only work if she could begin to relinquish the ties keeping the past with her.

The young man now sitting across from her in the train speeding towards Portsmouth Harbour was nothing like any man she had ever seen. His hair was long and dark brown, he had a beard, his eyes too were brown, challenging. At first glance, from behind, she had taken him for a girl, because of the hair, and the brightly patterned scarf that he'd tied around it, low on the forehead. His jeans were worn at the knees, but reasonably clean; over them the garish red shirt and knitted purple jacket clashed disturbingly.

"You're not making for the festival, are you?" he enquired, glancing at her new black maxiskirt which had come into the boutique just the day before she left. The only other colour she wore was the light blue of her sweater.

"I am actually, yes. Been staying in London, couldn't miss the festival, though."

"You're from the north, aren't you?"

"How could you tell?"

"The accent, of course, darling. I'm an actor, see. Accents are my speciality. So – why don't you go along there with me. This is your first time, I'll bet; need somebody to show you the ropes."

His eyes were glittering with enjoyment; just looking at him made her feel happier. Pamela Anichka suspected she amused him, yet something in his glance conveyed that he would be pleased to have her company. There also lingered in his smile more than a hint of daring her to agree.

"Why not," she said in her jauntiest voice. "At least until you've shown me where it is."

"I'll show you everything, sweetheart. And show you a good time, as they say."

Ten

Tania had been compelled to come home. Somehow, she had got through the first three nights of the show, but then realised she couldn't endure being so far away. Ian had been magnificent, phoning her several times a day, trying to reasure her that all would be well, that Pamela Anichka was safe and would turn up once more. Staying away any longer wouldn't have been fair to Ian, even if she herself had been able to survive in London. He was PA's stepfather, after all, shouldn't be expected to cope with everything.

She had wondered yesterday if she ought to contact Gerald, let him know their daughter was missing. Her own reluctance to admit that she had let this occur wasn't the only reason preventing her from calling him. She had tried to forgive Gerald Thomas years ago – for his brutality to her, his failure to be interested in the girl, his original seduction. Forgiving might have been achieved but Tania had been unable to forget. And the strongest memory of all was of his assertion that she was completely inept. Gerald surely would be tempted to use what had happened now to reinforce that assertion. The intervening years might have convinced her that he was the one unprepared for responsibility, the one who lashed out when balked, who took every mean advantage, but today she felt too vulnerable to withstand his criticism.

"Do *you* think I ought to tell Gerald, darling?" Tania asked Ian nevertheless.

They had talked for hours over the dinner she had cooked. She had tried to make light of the need to surrender her role in London, emphasising how delighted her understudy was, convincing Ian – if not herself – that she felt satisfied because she had performed for those few nights.

"Gerald knows," Ian told her carefully, watching her grey eyes for signs of annoyance. "I thought it best, and that informing him would take less out of me than it would of you." Mentioning that he'd been afraid Pamela Anichka might have run to her father wouldn't help Tania.

"Bless you, Ian. You're a lovely man. You have been wonderful always, but especially during these dreadful days."

"Only wish I could have done more. That it could've – well, you know . . ."

His beautiful sherry-brown eyes were glossy with tears. Tania rose from the table, hurried round to hug him.

"She is like my own daughter, you know," he admitted. "Don't know why I've ever felt that I needed another youngster."

They cleared the dishes together, stood side by side at the sink, silent yet never closer to each other.

"I am so tired," she said when everything was tidied away. "I'll just give Dad a ring, let him know I'm home. They've both been so good, everyone has."

"We'll have an early night then, love." Ian had seen how exhausted she was, so drained that it hurt him. He felt no better himself, but was used to that. He always felt tired whenever Tania was away, as though wherever he was the lighting had dimmed. His brain was merely functioning, on inadequate power.

"I can't unpack tonight," she said forlornly walking into their bedroom like someone in a trance. "Don't even want to look for a nightgown."

There was one on her pillow, a favourite purchased that time they were in the States together. Pale peach chiffon with an under layer the brown of dark chocolate.

"You've found that for me," she exclaimed, and smiled. Ian shook his head, a rare blush darkened his cheek.

"Found it the other night, when I couldn't bear being here without you."

Tears spilled from her tired eyes, ran down her face, and suddenly her sobs were beyond control.

"I know," said Ian. "I know."

His arms warm around her, they sat on the edge of the bed; he sighed when Tania pressed her face into his neck. She wept while minutes passed, massive gulping tears that shook her body.

"I just wish we knew something," she said at last. "At one time, during the first night actually, I had the strangest feeling that Pamela Anichka hadn't really gone away. That it would be all right. Since then – I haven't the slightest idea what might have happened."

The only comfort he could give was in his embrace, in the bed which they had shared through good times as well as bad. Holding her he gave thanks, silently from a full heart, that she was here now, that they would face whatever, together.

Despite their weariness, neither of them could sleep. The antique clock which Pamela had given them chimed out the hours from the hall below.

"I wish that thing would stop!" Tania exclaimed at two o'clock.

Ian pulled her close against him, kissed her hair, a cheek, the lips which for so many years now had expressed her love of him.

"I'd do anything, anything in the world if it could bring her back for you," he said huskily.

"Just hold me." If only something would obliterate this dreadful, gnawing fear.

Holding and kissing, longing to use his love for her, Ian was surprised to find he possessed the energy to experience this urgent attraction. Gently, a little afraid that she might protest, he began to caress her dear, familiar body.

Tania stirred, kissed him more fervently, clung. And convinced him that only like this might they recover some

146

semblance of peace. Slowly, tenderly, he drew closer still, sensed her readiness, and pressed into the warmth and eagerness he needed so passionately.

"Oh, love," she sighed. And excluded words along with all emotions beyond the pair of them.

For this little while even concern for Pamela Anichka no longer seared into them. Tomorrow, the desperation to trace her would begin again, but they could be strengthened by this private renewal.

The young man offered to carry her bag when the train was drawing towards the harbour. PA hadn't brought much with her; not knowing exactly how or when she was travelling had convinced her to be practical.

She was tired still from that emotional night at the opera. She also was glad• to avoid tackling the ferry crossing alone. He bought her a drink on board, a shandy because she daren't risk anything stronger until she was more sure of her bearings. And feeling less exhausted. His name was Tony, he said. She told him hers was Anichka, the entirety was such a mouthful.

Tony smiled. "Is that Polish, or something?" He had several friends of Polish extraction, from families who'd come to England during the war.

PA grinned. "Russian actually, my father's side of the family."

"Don't know many Russians. Makes you seem all exotic!"

She wasn't going to argue with that. Feeling dreadfully ordinary wasn't an experience she enjoyed; she welcomed anything that suggested that she – that this entire occasion – could be special.

After their drinks they went up on deck, leaned on the rail to watch the sun glinting on surrounding waves. Portsmouth and Southsea were hazy in the distance. Ahead the island glowed in the August light, looked small enough to be a friendly place.

"Have you been here before?" she asked him.

Tony placed an arm about her shoulders. "Of course. You stick with me, you'll be fine."

"I'm not worried, you know," PA said hastily. "I go around a lot on my own."

"Sure, sure. Only thought you might enjoy it more – not wasting time learning your way about."

She had sounded ungrateful, stand-offish even, and she was sorry. He'd tried to help ever since they met up in the train. She smiled.

"I didn't mean – you mustn't think I'm giving you the brush-off. Just—"

"Give you time to get to know me, that it? There'll be plenty of time, once we get there."

Without Tony, she might not even have reached the massive site where the festival was being held. At his side, the rest of the journey had been uneventful, yet quite entertaining.

Tony's claim to be an expert on accents appeared genuine enough. And he had an immense horde of stories. From his days on stage; at drama school; on the set of some obscure film in which he'd appeared.

The site as they approached was enormous, rendered alarming by the gigantic mass of people already assembled. Entering the edge of the area, Pamela Anichka reached instinctively for his arm.

Tony raised one eyebrow, then laughed at her. "Changing your mind, are you? Ready to admit you'd prefer to have me around?"

"I never said I wouldn't."

"Okay, okay. Pact. We won't quibble over that. Tell you what, we'll fix a spot where we can always meet up. Side of that sandwich bar there. Just hope he doesn't pack up and move along somewhere."

More relieved than ever she would admit, PA started to enjoy herself. Privately acknowledging she was fortunate to have met up with someone so accommodating, she made a mental note to stick close to Tony.

He found a small space among the ranks of music

enthusiasts. "Put your groundsheet down, here – next to mine."

PA was looking confused.

Tony grinned, one eyebrow soaring again. "Don't tell me. You haven't brought one."

"I didn't know." There had been no one to advise her.

"So, you will have to stick by me. Sit down then. Best stow your things with mine, between us. And keep an eye on your gear. Remember you don't know anybody. Except me, of course."

He was enjoying this. The festival had been worth a visit in the past, this time picking up a bird had been easy, a bonus already. And with three days to go – he didn't believe he'd require much ingenuity.

PA was hungry, hadn't eaten all that well yesterday, and with the journey and everything was beginning to feel light-headed. Tony sympathised when she told him, offered to fetch them some food. *This time.* Her turn would come afterwards.

Alone in the crowd, she grew aware of the noise; none of the officially arranged bands was playing yet, but other instrumentalists were giving their own impromptu interpretations of the latest pop tunes. Loudest of all, though, was the thrum of chattering humanity, a pulsing clangour – or was that in her own ears, perhaps? The unnerving effect of paying meals scant attention?

Smoke was drifting over nearby heads, from cigarettes and substances other than tobacco. She'd never tried drugs herself – or only once years ago, one 'purple heart' from a girl at school. PA recognised the smell of cannabis, though; no one who frequented nightclubs could remain ignorant of its existence.

Tony was absent for ages, so long that she needed the reassurance of his possessions as witness to his eventual return. Hungrier than ever, she scanned the middle distance, stood up briefly to try and see further.

He startled her, returning from the rear, and thrusting a

stack of sandwiches over her shoulder. "Grab that. There's this as well." He handed her canned beer.

"Thanks, and for going. What do I owe you?"

Tony shook his head. "We'll pool our resources. Best that way. Sort it out when we've finished eating."

He seemed more intent on drinking his beer than on food. PA wondered if he'd eaten something on the way through the crowd, dismissed the thought as unworthy. He said they were sharing.

Tony must have been queuing next to someone smoking dope. As he settled more comfortably on the groundsheet beside her she noticed the smell suddenly was stronger.

Her hunger satisfied, she immediately felt better. She was drinking the beer, but only slowly, sip by sip.

Tony was on his second can. "Couldn't carry more. D'you want me to save you half of this?"

"No, thanks. It's all right. Plenty with this." PA was desperate to relieve herself. She hadn't liked to excuse herself and go off and find the toilet in the train, not when she hardly knew him. And on the ferry he'd stayed at her side.

She hadn't spotted a Ladies anywhere here. She couldn't ask Tony, but there was a girl sitting in front of them. PA touched her shoulder.

"'Ere what do you think you're on?" the girl demanded, swinging round.

"I only wanted to ask you something. Do you know where the toilets are?"

The girl pointed in the general direction of the perimeter. "Over there somewhere. If there's too many folk waiting, there's always behind the trees."

Tony was laughing.

Picking up her shoulder bag, Pamela Anichka set out. She would worry on the way back about finding him again; right now only one thing mattered.

There was a queue, and the facilities were primitive but, this early in the proceedings, bearable. She refused to consider what the situation might be after a further two days.

Tony's brilliantly hued scarf made him identifiable; if not readily, at least when she was twenty-odd yards away.

"Better now?" he asked.

PA didn't answer. Instead, she plonked down beside him, and opened up her wallet. Away from him, she had recognised how guilty she would feel if they became separated before she settled with him for their food.

"How much are we putting in the kitty then?"

He shrugged. "Ten each, for starters, eh?"

Ten pounds sounded a lot for somewhere like this where the food would hardly be cordon bleu. But they were here for quite a time, of course.

Tony took her ten pounds, tucked it in a pocket. "Best if I keep it, got to wise up yet, haven't you, on looking after yourself in a crowd like this."

Once the groups booked to play there began the whole atmosphere intensified. The sound and the beat grew so insistent that everyone around them seemed to be moving in time to the music; even the earth beneath them was thumping.

On and on the rhythm went, long after darkness fell; Pamela Anichka became tired in spite of her elation. Beside her, Tony had a habit of strumming one hand against a knee, sometimes on *her* knee. She wished he would stop, but was reluctant to annoy him by criticising. If only she hadn't found yesterday so exhausting she might have been ready to relish all these sounds for as long as they continued on every side of her.

They had eaten again, though not very much, so little in fact that she was surprised when Tony, who again fetched their food asked her for another ten pounds. Very aware that she had come here extremely ill-prepared, she handed it over and wondered if the savings she had brought would last throughout her stay.

Still feeling rather empty, Pamela Anichka felt her attention wavering from the entertainment which seemed to be riveting everyone else. When her eyelids drooped and her head slumped towards Tony's shoulder, she came to suddenly and sat upright.

Smiling, he pressed her head back onto his shoulder again. "You're not shy with me, then? Not now."

He adjusted his position slightly until his arm was around her. As soon as he kissed her PA realised he had misinterpreted her move as encouraging him. Silently, she rationalised what was happening.

She'd been dancing often enough to know that most boys wanted a kiss or two at the end of an evening. This was perfectly safe. It was anything but private here amid more people than she'd ever seen together in her life before. There must be nowhere where she'd be more adequately protected. And having Tony's arm about her was more comfortable than sitting up straight on ground that felt so hard.

Amazingly, she slept, no longer disturbed by the noise or by movements in the crowds surrounding them. Once or twice during the night she awakened, grew conscious of Tony's arms and that they had somehow found enough room to be lying down.

PA came fully awake in the chilly dawn. Tony wasn't at her side, and once again she was desperate to relieve herself. By the time he returned she was wondering how she would hold on, and if she dared risk asking someone nearby to keep an eye on their belongings.

He hadn't brought any food with him, but handed her a can of beer. His own appeared to be almost empty, and he was smoking a cigarette. PA didn't believe it only contained tobacco. In too great a hurry to say much, she indicated that she needed to dash off. "Was there a long queue, or something, for breakfast?" she asked, prepared to provide opportunity for him to explain.

"I don't eat it. Better get yourself something, if that's what you want."

PA couldn't wait while she initiated an argument about money, but she had handed over quite an amount to him yesterday. She might have slept, but that hadn't obliterated her memory.

Once her more urgent mission was completed, she began seriously to consider severing the arrangement with Tony. He might have been amusing originally, even helpful, but her increasing impression was that he was more intent on looking after himself. Unfortunately, ever since seeing the extent of the gathering here, she'd become alarmed by the prospect of coping on her own.

Nothing was quite as she had pictured when planning the trip. Aware that it was held outdoors, the venue hadn't surprised her, but the limited organisation of its facilities had. Most of all, though, she was intimidated by the number and the variety of these other participants.

Waiting in a queue for food, PA began talking to the girl ahead of her who looked about her own age. If perhaps she made a friend of someone like this, she could dispense with Tony. She wasn't entirely helpless, all she required was company at her side.

Having heard all manner of voices and accents since she got here, PA was unperturbed by the uneducated tone of the girl she'd spoken to. And conditioned by Tony's outfit she was unfazed by the assortment of garments which the girl had strung about her. The things that finally put her off were the scornful glance as her own clothing was assessed, and the comment that followed.

"You're not one of us, are you? Not a traveller. What you doin' here, 'aven't you got no place of your own, without tryin' to crowd us out?"

So much for new friendships, thought PA wryly. She would have to collect her belongings from where she'd left Tony. Maybe she would decide to stick with what she had. At least he provided company until she felt more au fait with the system here.

There wasn't much of a system, of course. That fact alone ensured that PA settled for spending that day at least where she was. When she had finished eating, though, she explained that she was going to tidy her possessions.

There was no need to tell Tony she intended to have everything ready in case she had to move on elsewhere.

As the morning progressed he became more cheerful. Forgetting her suspicion that he could have been on drugs, she guessed he just wasn't a 'morning' person. Not everyone was. And he had consumed more than a few cans of beer since they'd arrived. Enough to produce a bit of a hangover.

Affable now, Tony was chatting to several people around them. Losing the self-consciousness induced by such an unfamiliar situation, PA began joining in, and genuinely enjoyed herself. Feeling truly a part of the throng, she relished the music even more, was less troubled by the vibrating crowd, and gave herself up to the excitement.

The thrill of it all reached a zenith for her when Bob Dylan started to perform. His first concert after the motorcycle accident three years ago that had threatened his career, the welcome here was overwhelming. Tunes like *Subterranean Homesick Blues* and *Tambourine Man* soon dispelled memories of his semi-retirement, and generated ecstatic applause.

By the time that darkness enveloped the crowd on the last night of the festival Pamela Anichka was still on a high created of sheer excitement. Alarmed though she had been at times, out of her depth and uneasy, she wouldn't have missed this experience for anything.

They had eaten quite well that night, sharing the food they bought with the group where they were sitting, and enjoying the chance to sample what others had purchased.

PA had grown more accustomed to beer; the quantity she'd drunk had dispersed any lingering misgivings. She had learned so much, and in the process was realising that her old impressions that she'd enjoyed rebelling were merely illusion. Here, she'd become accustomed to other people's total lack of inhibitions. Those whose eccentric dress, make-up, or hair colour astounded her appeared

154

quite normal set among others who discarded every scrap of clothing to display themselves unashamedly.

Laughing and talking with these new friends, PA relished the sensation that she now belonged in a more liberal world; she finally had discovered the importance of these swinging sixties.

Unafraid of Tony now, she had no reason to dissuade him when he pulled her against him for a protracted session of necking.

The music gradually had altered, quietening just a little, though with the continuing beat which seemed now to echo throughout her own senses. Virtually unnoticed by her, people were beginning to leave. As the throng around them thinned, she simply was thankful to be able to stretch out on the ground. Three days of sitting on the earth and with no support for her back had produced more aches than she'd believed possible.

Smiling, Tony lay beside her; his mouth moved yet again towards hers, slowly he leaned across her. He was pressing close, his jeans rough against her legs where the shorts she'd worn since yesterday to save her maxiskirt provided little protection. The music encompassing the area was haunting, more subtle than most that she had heard here, as rhythmical as the stirring of the man now stretched out on top of her.

Deep down inside her a pulse answered, its insistence delicious and scary enough to increase her excitement. Tony's kisses grew deeper, more prolonged, his hands beneath her T-shirt renewed the intensity. Inebriated by her own longing, PA hardly noticed when his hand moved downwards between them. Only when his fingers began tugging at her shorts did she suspect what he intended.

"No, Tony," she said, quite gently; she didn't want to sound prudish or to provoke a scene. She must keep her voice low, no one must discover how far she had let him go already.

He might not have heard her. His hand continued its

onslaught, his touch on her skin affecting her so acutely that a part of her willed him to go on.

"I said no," she insisted, reminding herself as much as him that this must cease.

Dragging at her shorts, Tony stripped them from her. His breath was hot on her neck, sharp teeth sank into her throat, she felt his hips grinding against her own. The scratching of the open zip of his jeans warned of the urgent need for action.

"Oh, no, you don't!" she snapped, her hushed voice determined. Exerting all her strength, she pushed him sideways away from her.

"You're not a virgin, are you?" Tony demanded scornfully.

"What if I am? You're not going to change that, certainly not while I hardly know you."

"I can't believe I'm hearing this! Where else did you think all the petting would lead? You must know what it's doing to me."

PA could hardly deny that she knew. Even the surrounding darkness failed to conceal the gaping jeans, some garment beneath, the only too potent evidence . . .

"Come on, Anichka, come on," he wheedled, bending to kiss her again. "There's a horrible name for girls who do this; I can't believe you're a tease."

To her, teasing had always meant young, innocent games; nothing at all like these alarming fumblings. Before he could thrust himself onto her again, PA rolled right away. She heard his face slap into the groundsheet as her head slid out of range of his kisses.

"All right, darling, all right," said Tony, raising his head while he attempted to redeem something from the situation. "Never meant to scare you. I can be reasonable."

Pamela Anichka had located her shoulder bag which she'd kept close by her since the day she left home. Stuffing her shorts into the larger bag, she glanced about her, was thankful she hadn't left any belongings strewn around.

Tony was watching. "You've made me bloody uncomfortable, you can't just walk away."

PA didn't walk, she ran. All the way as far as the hedge at the perimeter of the ground. She glanced back across the heads of the crowd. No one was running after her. She hadn't thought that he would. Tony hadn't really wanted *her*. He'd wanted a girl, any girl. But he wasn't following.

She paused long enough to pull the rolled-up skirt from her bag and put it on. At least that covered her. No matter what she felt like inside, she would look decent. Wherever she went no one else would be disgusted. But where on this earth would she go?

Eleven

Tania blamed the anxiety concerning her daughter. She had felt queasy for hours, for so long now that she couldn't recall precisely when she'd begun to feel so unwell.

Ian had gone to work. She understood, he had no choice. The men from Canning's had only recently started on this particular job, they needed their foreman present. Pamela had asked if he could possibly arrange to be there. Somewhere beyond this all-consuming worry, Tania had heard them saying that Ted Burrows finally had retired as manager. If they hadn't been so utterly taken up with all this concern for PA, they would have been glad that Ian would at last be promoted to running the firm.

The cottage felt terribly empty. It seemed years rather than days since they'd badgered Pamela Anichka about leaving her possessions around the place. Tania couldn't stand this.

At Stonemoor House the quiet equalled that of her own home. Her father was out; Tania wondered if he was playing somewhere that night, and could remember no mention of any concert. But she could recall very little of substance about the events that constituted their normal lives.

Emerging from the kitchen, Mrs Singer jumped, startled to find Tania motionless at the doorway of the sitting room. Unable to hear either door or footsteps, let alone voices, the housekeeper relied on the family to inform her of their comings and goings.

Seeing Tania's evident distress, she collected her own wits, turned aside to pick up pen and paper from just within the kitchen. 'Have you heard anything, Tania love? What do you want me to do?'

Tania looked hard at her, at the kindly face with lines etched by the effort of years spent striving to comprehend. From the day that she had arrived from Russia this woman had done everything in her power to look after her. For some time before that she had cared for Andre Malinowski.

"Oh, Mrs Singer!" She took the pad from gnarled fingers. 'I want her back. God, how I want her back.'

Tania wept, they both did. Holding each other, their desperation and grief made them cling like mother and daughter.

Some long while afterwards the housekeeper slipped back into her accustomed role and made a pot of tea. Later Tania walked as far as the shop. In her usual composed way, Pamela glanced up as her stepdaughter came in. A couple of clients had left as Tania was approaching; both women were thankful that, for the present, there were no other customers.

From the room beyond a clock chimed. Pamela smiled, though her blue eyes remained shadowed with worry. "Your brother's got it going! Do you want to go and look?"

Tania didn't want to do anything, or nothing that could be managed here. But Pamela was kind, she always had been, she couldn't hurt her. And Mihail needed a bit of reassurance.

Tania hadn't been blind to her brother's distress which she knew was increasing with every day of Pamela Anichka's absence. He was blaming himself. No one spoke of the responsibility weighing so heavily, least of Mihail himself, but nor could Tania ignore it. She had never liked to look too closely at the bond which had always existed between Pamela Anichka and Mihail. A childhood affection, almost a conspiracy which had tended to exclude others, she saw it now for a relationship too potent of dangers.

"Hello, Mihail. Mum says you have got that clock to work."

"Any news?" he enquired, before nodding. "Yes. Just thankful for something to do really." And yet this clock was different from all the others that he'd ever tackled. In any other circumstances, he would have been totally exhilarated.

He showed her the work he'd been doing. He'd suspected it was awareness of his desperation for a distraction that had prompted his mother to entrust it to him.

"It's called a mystery clock, you see," he explained to his sister. "The mystery being how the mechanism functions. This one's French, most of them are."

Tania was admiring the female figure holding the clock. "Is she in bronze?"

"That's right. Can you guess how it operates?"

"I have no clue at all. Show me."

"She's the one who moves with each impulse from the escapement. The action is barely perceptible, but it activates the pendulum she's holding."

"And it really was not working until you had a go at it?"

Mihail grinned. "True! Must admit, though, this one wasn't as terribly difficult as I expected. Mostly needed cleaning, adjusting a bit, that kind of thing." He was wondering already what he could tackle to occupy the rest of the day, and the hours stretching beyond that.

Pamela had considered that already, came through from the shop and crossed to unlock the safe.

"There's a watch here, Mihail, like to look?"

He hadn't worked on a watch since returning from Oxford. Hadn't most of his work for that little shop been on watches? Nothing had gone right since the day he first met Ivor Smith. And now, with PA going missing, he felt that all joy was drained from everything. He had tried to explain to Annabel, had prayed she would understand about suspending wedding plans. Until Pamela Anichka was found again.

Over the telephone his fiancée had sounded dreadfully disappointed. And also rather insecure. Mihail wasn't a fool – he could guess that Annabel must be afraid that he could care more about PA than he really did for her.

"Darling, all the family are terribly anxious. If we were to get married as soon as we'd planned, they simply wouldn't be able to put much heart into it."

"All right, Mihail, all right. Don't worry. I'll explain to Mummy and Dad." The trouble was that from the moment that she'd come home from Yorkshire with an engagement ring on her finger they had put their hearts into commencing arrangements.

"Perhaps it's for the best," Lance Atherton-Ward said when Annabel told him. "Give you a bit of time to sort things."

While he had been happy to encourage his daughter in something which made her so ecstatic, he had retained one almighty reservation. None of them had known young Malinowski's background. All that bother concerning his potential as a Russian agent hadn't yet been cleared up. If this delay meant that the court case against those two men in Oxford would go ahead first, he'd feel more content about Annabel's future. And the young man to whom he would entrust her.

Mihail wasn't sorry when Tania remained at the shop. Watching as he began repairing the old timepiece, she seemed glad that the two of them were together. Occasionally they shared a slight smile, listening to his mother whenever clients came into the shop.

Pamela was a wonderful saleswoman, Tania discovered. She left people to look around when they wished, but offered authoritative advice where it was needed. She also had a way of listening to her potential customers. Her respect for their knowledge – which often was quite wide – emerged in questions which even someone outside the antiques business recognised as educated.

"You're a clever lady, did I ever tell you?" Tania observed when the shop was empty. "I used to think

161

so when I'd only to look around Stonemoor House to see how skilfully you'd restored the place. Then you had to go one better, and tackle a different career. And make a success of it like this!"

Her stepmother smiled. "This wasn't so difficult, though; becoming informed about antiques was gradual. And surviving no longer depended on making my work pay."

"But it has got to, for me," Mihail put in. "I need to be sure that the amount you're paying me is justified by the work I do." Since becoming engaged he had thought very seriously about this job. He had to feel certain that he could support Annabel in a home of their own.

Pamela turned to him, her blue eyes narrowing. "You can stop worrying, my lad – don't forget I'm Yorkshire through and through, not like you lot! I'm not going to pay you more than you've earned."

The three of them laughed, but each of them remained aware that there was no real light-heartedness in even the briefest humour.

Ian arrived home to find the cottage empty, and felt annoyance overtaking his earlier satsifaction. The working situation was infinitely better now that Ted Burrows was no longer on his back. And although he knew that until PA returned none of the family would feel much like discussing future plans, he knew his sister. Their Pamela would give him the position he had coveted for so long, and would ensure that the rest of the board would accept him as manager of Canning's.

Tania hadn't said she was going out. Indeed, since her daughter's disappearance she had insisted on remaining at home in case PA was trying to contact them. He supposed she would be at Stonemoor House, or otherwise the shop. All the family knew that someone was always around if they needed to get in touch.

When the telephone rang Ian supposed it would be Tania to explain that she was on her way. This wouldn't be the first occasion that she'd become so involved in conversation with her father that she'd overlooked the time.

162

"Dad? It's me. Don't be cross . . ."

"PA! Where the hell are you? Don't you realise we've been out of our minds with worry."

"I'm sorry, I really am. I didn't do this to make you anxious."

"But you should have thought. Your mother is making herself ill, wondering what's happened to you. She had to come home, couldn't continue in the show."

"Oh. And she was so good . . ."

"You saw it? So that's where you are, in London." He would go there, fetch her back.

"Not now, no. I came to the Isle of Wight."

"For that bloody rock festival, I'll bet."

"I knew you wouldn't approve."

"So you didn't tell us! You really are the limit, PA. Well, when will you be home? How are you going to get here?" He imagined her without money, camping somewhere even.

"I shall come back, before very long. But I've got a job."

"Doing what?" His wife would need to know every detail. "You'd better give me your address," he added swiftly, realising that Pamela Anichka was capable of ringing off.

"It's in a boutique, just for the rest of the summer. And they're letting me use the flat above." It was little more than just one room, actually, but it served.

"Tell me the address then," Ian persisted.

"Is Mum there?" PA asked, after he had written down the details.

"Not just now, no. You'd better ring again or give us your number."

"This is a call box, sorry. They don't let us have private calls."

Ian heard the door opening, turned to see Tania putting away her keys. "It's PA!" he exclaimed. "Quick!"

Tania sped along the hall to snatch the receiver. "Hello, love, hello," she said into the telephone, her eyes awash

163

with tears. The only sound from the other end of the line was of the number disconnecting. "She has hung up on me! Oh, Ian – how could she?"

"She's pretty scared, I expect. Of what you'd say."

"And not without justification. After all she has put us though." She was weeping copiously, handed the receiver to her husband. "Call her back, please, love. I have got to speak to her."

"I only wish I could, darling. She says there's nowhere we can ring her. That was a kiosk."

"But there must be. Where is she staying – with friends?"

Ian shook his head. "No, but . . ."

"Do not tell me. She is with her father now, yes?" They had been obliged to inform Gerald when Pamela Anichka had been missing for more than the odd day, hadn't they? "He might have let us know. He must realise how desperate we are."

"She's not with him, love. She's on the Isle of Wight."

"What on earth is there for her over there?"

"There was a festival – rock, or some such. Think it's finished now."

Tania walked slowly into the sitting room, sank onto the nearest chair.

Ian poured brandy, handed her a glass. "She is working, sounds all right. In a boutique. We can write to her, I've got the address."

"I shall go there tomorrow."

"We'll talk about that," her husband said. "Decide what's best."

"Best for whom?" Tania demanded, her accent strong. "For her? She does not deserve any consideration. She did not give any to anyone else."

"I was thinking more of what might be best for you. We've got to think this through, love. Suppose you go storming over there, and she refuses to come home with you – you'll be more upset than ever."

Tania sighed. "Not than ever. The worst part ever was

not knowing whether she was alive or dead. At least now we have been assured she is all right. Today." She needed to know this daughter of hers would remain all right. She still believed she would have to go after PA. Could not imagine just staying here.

If her daughter hadn't telephoned again, Tania would have set out for the Isle of Wight the following morning. But Pamela Anichka did ring later that night, when she had gathered courage enough for speaking to her mother. Contrite and tearful, she repeated much of the conversation that she'd had with Ian.

Massively relieved to be hearing her voice, Tania began to understand a little, to believe that she would eventually forgive her.

They had told the rest of the family, of course, and they all had gathered at the cottage. Tom and Gwen had left the children with a baby-sitter, and brought Mildred Baker who had been staying at their house in Manchester.

Tania went to lie down for half an hour after speaking with Pamela Anichka. She had expected to be entirely well again as soon as she learned where her daughter was; instead of that she felt quite nauseated. It could be excitement creating this inner turmoil, she supposed.

Her father came into the room after hesitating in the doorway to check that she wasn't sleeping. Sitting beside the bed, Andre smiled down at her. "So – you now know that girl of yours is quite safe, that even while she is away from home you need not remain extremely anxious. I do understand, you know, better than most." When Tania said nothing, he continued. "When I first arrived in England and you were so far away, and in a country where your mother had been murdered, I knew no peace."

"Poor you. But you got me out. You brought me back. Do you not think I am right to want to go after Pamela Anichka?"

"Not necessarily. You were much younger than she is now, you needed care. I think perhaps your PA is in a situation more like my sister. She can look after herself, make her own decisions. Although," he hesitated, smiled, "actually, your Aunt Irena is reaching the other end of the scale now – nearing the age when she would benefit from the care of others, of family."

"But Irena writes of being happy, doesn't she?"

"And of missing me, her only living relative now. I have in mind to try to persuade her to come to England."

"To live with you at Stonemoor?"

"But naturally, where else? And besides, in a short while when Mihail has a home of his own, we shall have yet more empty rooms there."

"How shall you get her out of Russia? You would not go there again?"

Andre seemed quite elderly to her now, and she did love him so deeply. Tania felt as though she'd never endure being separated from another person who mattered so much to her.

He smiled. "I am hoping that I shall not have to return there. We still have friends in that area, you know. People with whom I have remained in contact. And I believe the authorities are no longer quite so difficult about allowing their citizens to leave."

Tania was surprised that her father had said nothing of his renewed desire to bring Irena Malinowski to England. And Pamela certainly hadn't mentioned it. Perhaps she did not know.

"I have not troubled your stepmother with discussion of this," he told her carefully. He might have read her thoughts. "She would worry."

And might not appreciate having a sister-in-law whom she'd never met living at Stonemoor House, thought Tania. She said nothing. She and Ian had problems enough without trying to solve anyone else's.

Unable to sleep, and feeling a little less sickly, Tania went downstairs when her father joined the others. Mihail and Sonia had just arrived at the cottage. She had been working late at the airport and their brother had suggested hanging on at the house to explain to her about PA.

He also had taken the opportunity to phone Annabel while the others were out. He had no wish to upset anyone. But his relief that Pamela Anichka was located was greatest because of his own plans now being likely to go ahead.

"Is it too late to rearrange the wedding for the date we'd set originally?" he asked his fiancée. "PA is on the Isle of Wight; seems she went to the rock festival and decided to stay on for a while."

"I'll speak to Mummy, and let you know," Annabel promised. "It will depend on whether the bookings for the church and reception have been snapped up by anyone else. And whether Dad's made some other arrangement for that day, of course." Glad though she was that they should be able to revert to marrying on their first choice of day, she didn't mean to let Mihail keep changing things that they had fixed.

"Annabel thinks we might be able to have the wedding sooner, now that we know PA is all right," he told everyone at the cottage after listening to Tania's account of what her daughter had said. "It'll give us all an occasion to look forward to, a time when we'll be together enjoying ourselves."

Mildred Baker seemed to have listened particularly intently. When she spoke after clearing her throat, her voice sounded rather unlike her usual one, quite forceful.

"Actually, Mihail, you won't be the first of us to gather the family together. I've got something I've been waiting to tell you. And this is about a wedding, an' all. Mine."

"Yours?" Pamela asked, incredulously.

"Aye. You're not the only one who had enough of being a widow. Even if I have stuck being on my own for years. I met Cedric a while back, playing whist. We've allus got on fair champion, it's been a right tonic for us both having somebody to go out with. And to sit at home with as well; we don't always have to be gadding about."

"So, where does he live?" Andre enquired. "You must tell us all about him."

"I'll say you'd better!" Pamela exclaimed. She might be pleased that her mother wouldn't spend the rest of her life alone, but she would have preferred to have been told something a little earlier in the relationship.

"He's retired now, of course. Used to be an overlooker in the mill, a loom tuner, you know. And he has a nice little house near Birdcage Lane. That's where we're going to live. Don't think he fancied our street."

"Is he about your age, Mum?" Pamela asked.

Mildred laughed. "Eh, I don't know. I weren't for telling him how old I am, so I suppose he has a right to his secrets."

"Good for you, Grandma!" Sonia exclaimed, and rushed across to hug her.

"When is this wedding to be then?" Mihail wanted to know. He'd no desire for it to clash with his own revised date.

"Oh, a week on Saturday. At St Paul's; three o'clock. It won't be posh, but I shall expect all you lasses to turn up in new frocks."

"And hats as well," Tania insisted. "I am so delighted for you."

"It's all right for Tania to be so delighted about it," Pamela said to Andre while Ian and Mihail were sorting out drinks for a toast. "She's not *her* mother. I'd have needed to know more about this chap, if I'd been given the opportunity. Does she plan on only letting us catch our first sight of him in the church?"

Mildred had heard her, and laughed. "Got you into a right tizzy, have I, love? Didn't think your old mother could spring summat like this on you, did you?"

It was Andre who responded. "We are simply just a little concerned for you, that is all, Mother. But I am sure that we wish you well. And we shall be reassured when we do meet this Cedric."

"Aye, well – we have that all worked out. We're

holding open house this Sunday. At my place, since you know where that is, and you mightn't easily find his. There'll be other folk as well, not just family. We've got them from the whist drive coming."

"But how will you fit everyone in?" her daughter asked.

"We'll manage. I'm organising a buffet – it'll go on all day. It isn't as if everybody will come at once. I thought you lot might arrive first, if that suits. You can come and go as you please. Them from the whist will most likely make it afternoon. Some of 'em are getting on a bit, aren't up and about so soon."

"Do you want to borrow Mrs Singer for the day?" Pamela suggested. "She could help organise, keep the washing-up bowl going."

"Thank you, love, but no. A lot of my neighbours have offered to help. It'll be like that party we had for the end of the war."

"Only indoors, in your house," Pamela remarked, still sceptical about the potential success of such an occasion.

"Aye – it'll be all right if it pours," her mother retorted.

Gwen and Tom were saying nothing. Pamela had an idea that they were in the picture already. Their mother had been staying with them, hadn't she.

Ian had glasses assembled on a tray, and bottles of sparkling wine opened. "It's not champagne, I'm afraid. Even when it was simply news about our PA we were celebrating, I'd no time to get any. But we do wish you every happiness, Mum. You and – er, Cedric."

Following the toast, and another to the absent Pamela Anichka, Ian spoke to them again. "I want to thank you all tonight, for being such a lovely lot of folk. I know I speak for Tania as well, when I tell you we'd never have survived this awful time if it hadn't been for having you all behind us." He turned to Andre. "I know she's your granddaughter, and you naturally were deeply concerned, but it has been that *good* to know you were there for us at Stonemoor. When I had to go to work, it was a great comfort to me to be sure that Tania always had you to turn to."

Mildred was not going back with Tom and Gwen to Manchester. She wanted to be in her own home to finalise preparations for the party she was giving, and for her wedding. The three of them left together, nevertheless, Tom insisting that no one else need turn out except for covering the short distance to Stonemoor.

"You've all had that much anxiety over Pamela Anichka, you'll need what rest you can get from now on."

Andre only wished that he could rest that night. Pamela had been deeply shaken by Mildred Baker's failure to confide in them earlier about planning such a massive change in her life. From the moment that they left to walk up the hill to Stonemoor she'd exclaimed repeatedly upon all aspects of the forthcoming marriage.

Andre had insisted that they should go to bed, and leave such concerns until tomorrow. There was excitement enough about Pamela Anichka being located, and good news could often be just as exhausting as bad.

"Are you calling my mother's decision good ncws?" his wife demanded when their heads were side by side on their pillows.

"We may be justified in hoping that it is," he said. "You have been saying for some time that she needed somebody to care for . . ."

"Somebody to care for her, more like," Pamela snapped.

Andre disagreed. "No, I meant what I said. We all are aware that since Tom married and moved away, she has missed the need to be looking after those dear to her."

Pamela was beginning to see that her husband's assessment was true, but that made her no less agitated about her mother's plans.

Conscious that his wife was still lying awake, Andre was finding sleep equally elusive. The conversation with Tania today had set him thinking again. Remaining in touch with his sister Irena, although easier than it had been at any time since the end of the war, was no longer so reassuring. From the tone of her letters, she seemed to be suffering the fate common to many Russian women: she was ageing far beyond her years. He himself, at sixty-one, had benefited from escaping to England and only occasionally really believed how old he was. Irena, although a few years younger, sounded so often to have become an elderly lady.

Andre wanted to give her an easier life for her remaining years, a life where she might enjoy being part of a family. The enquiries he'd made some time ago had convinced him that the friends he still had behind the Iron Curtain could assist in getting Irena away to Britain. Her coming to Stonemoor House would, of course, alter their own way of life, and the person most affected would be Pamela. Tania had made him recognise that he was rather afraid of suggesting to his wife that their household should be increased in this way. Not normally cowardly, he liked himself less for being to reluctant to broach the matter.

His reasons for not doing so earlier remained the same as ever. Pamela's life was busy already, running the business as well as their home, and continuing to keep an eye on Canning's. Her responsibilities regarding that company might lessen now that Ian would be appointed manager, but it was still the firm that she had built up. Andre couldn't picture her relinquishing it entirely. At home, old Mrs Singer grew increasingly frail, unable to shoulder quite so many of a housekeeper's duties – yet more weight on Pamela.

Torn between concern for his sister and for his wife, Andre sighed. He wouldn't burden Pamela for worlds, but nor could he leave Irena to cope without him all those miles beyond the Iron Curtain.

By morning he thought that he had reached a satisfactory conclusion. If he should succeed in bringing his sister here, she was the very last woman to wish to be idle. She would help Pamela run the house, thus providing herself with a fresh purpose, and her sister-in-law with additional assistance.

The concept was so vivid in his mind that Andre banished all doubts and mentioned the matter during breakfast. Explaining first that he had noticed how tired Mrs Singer was becoming, he added that he knew of a means of lightening the load for Pamela.

"I know how much you enjoy the antiques trade, my love, and wish to ensure that you have time enough to continue in it. We could have more help around the house, you know, and in such a way that we should be doing someone else a great deal of good."

Pamela waited, wondering if Andre was about to suggest that they take on some musician who was having difficulty in securing enough bookings to play in concerts. Years ago, Andre had suffered that bad period when suspicions that he could be a Communist denied him work; since then he often sympathised with those in worse circumstances.

"You have seen Irena's letters," he continued now. "And know as well as I do that she seems to have become quite old. I fear that if she stays over there, that sort of life will hasten her death. I am thinking of getting her out, bringing her home. And then, my love, you will have someone always to hand, ready to help you."

Always to hand. *Always* to hand! God, no! With her own work taking her away from Stonemoor, and in the concert season Andre's absences, they had little enough time on their own now. And as for having Irena round her neck in the kitchen, or elsewhere about the house, whatever she was doing . . .

Pamela felt her teeth clenching, willed herself not to disagree with Andre immediately. She could understand his concern for his sister, applauded the fact that he had never forgotten Irena, but she had never met the woman and did not want now to have to put herself out to accommodate anyone, least of all someone who

172

probably knew very little English, and certainly would be totally unfamiliar with their ways.

I can't say no, she thought, and felt trapped in her own home with the prospect of nothing at Stonemoor ever being the same.

Twelve

M ildred's small house in Halifax was uncomfortably full. Despite the fact that, so far, only family had arrived, they were crammed into the living room and kitchen, and spilling out into the yard. Tom's three boys were romping around on the settee. Pamela's fingers itched to spank them. No one else appeared to notice.

Gwen wasn't feeling well, one of her rare migraine attacks had developed in the car on the way from Manchester. Instead of going upstairs to lie down as Mildred suggested, she was determinedly sitting in a chair, but with closed eyes and flinching at every sound.

Tom, apparently oblivious to his wife's distress, or perhaps because of it, was out by the front gate, chatting to Ian. About to be fully installed as manager, Ian was starting a fresh campaign to advertise Canning's. Willing to let him have his head, Pamela had consented to the company being publicised as far afield as Lancashire. She just hoped Ian knew what he was about, and would be able to lay on enough men to cope should the scheme bring in massive amounts of new business.

As far as she was concerned, this wasn't the time for getting herself involved any more deeply in Canning's affairs. Mihail's wedding and now the prospect of her mother's had been occupying her thoughts quite sufficiently. And then the other morning had brought Andre's bombshell. How could he even imagine that she would acquiesce without one word of protest when he suggested that she should share her home, *share her kitchen*, with his sister. That the poor woman had a plight, Pamela would

174

agree; she sympathised with anyone who had no family close by them. But surely Irena's circumstances had been generated by the life they led over there, a life to which she was well accustomed. If she had really wanted to get away, Irena might have done so years ago, while she was of an age to create her own existence here. Not invade someone else's.

Peggy Kemp from across the street edged her way between those who were standing out in the yard, and stomped up the front steps carrying her massive teapot.

"Eh, hello love," she called to Pamela across Tania and Andre who were talking with Sonia near the door. "I've still got my old teapot that we used for them street parties."

"Good, good," said Pamela, managing a smile. Did Peggy mean when they were kids? She couldn't recall parties then. How old was Peggy anyway, would she have been dishing out tea? The Kemps had never been known for their smartness; Pamela couldn't remember her looking much different from the way she did today. Although she supposed her hair hadn't always been quite so grey.

"I don't think you should do that, boys," Pamela told her young nephews. "Your gran's sofa isn't one of them trampolines, you know. And folk will want to sit down in a minute, won't they?"

The lads giggled, gradually slowed the bounce to an irritating vibration. As she turned her back, she glimpsed the eldest making an extremely rude gesture. Not my kids, thank goodness, she thought, and headed towards the kitchen. Every surface, including the top of the cooker, had been laid out with plates of food. Sandwiches and sausage rolls, bowls of salad, tinned salmon and every imaginable type of cooked meat. There was ham on the bone, a joint of cold beef, and thickly sliced chicken. Three large dishes of trifle stood on the wide marble sill of the window, with what looked like a week's product of Mildred's home baking nearby.

"Nobody'll starve, any road," Peggy Kemp observed, and grinned at Pamela. "Aren't you so well, love, you're looking right peaky?"

"Just a bit tired."

"Thought you'd be full of the joys now. Tania's lass has turned up, hasn't she?"

"That's right. It's all been a bit of a strain." I just wish that had been the only problem, Pamela thought, struggling not to sigh. This was their mother's day.

Cedric arrived in a smart car; not large, but shinier than any which regularly rumbled along the setts of this street. He was smaller than she had anticipated, Pamela noticed, as he strode through the gap that parted for him in the yard. She could bet Mildred must be a head taller. He was pleasant-faced, though, had quite a bit of hair for his age, sandy in colour encircling a pate that had seen too much sun. He wore sideburns which increased the geniality of heavy features.

In the open doorway, Cedric turned and faced those who were standing outdoors. "Well, I'm here – thought I'd introduce myself to all on you at once, like. Cedric Vickers, and very happy to be nearing the time when I'll become one of your family."

Ian and Tom smiled together and said, "How do you do?" in unison. Everyone else remaining in the yard murmured the phrase after them.

"How do you do, how do you do?" yelled Tom's boys as they simultaneously jumped off the settee. The smallest one fell over, whacking his knee against the tiled hearth. Too excited to cry, he got up again, rubbed the knee with chubby fingers, checked a quivering lip and grinned.

Cedric hurried towards the lad, grasped his shoulder. "And you're one of Tom's plucky boys, eh? I've heard all about you three. And is this your ma?"

Advancing on Gwen, he seized her right hand in his before she could even offer it. "How do you do, lass?" he bellowed, his grip on her fingers making her cringe.

"Nice to meet you, Mr Vick—"

176

"Cedric," he boomed, correcting her.

Mildred had appeared in the kitchen doorway. "Hello, Cedric love. Are you all right?"

"Never better. Now which one's your Pamela?"

Pamela emerged by her mother's shoulder, and had her hand squeezed.

"Your husband's Russian, I hear. Has he come with you?"

"Oh, yes." Pamela came back into the living room to lead her mother's fiancé towards Andre.

Tania and Sonia were next in line, then Pamela's cousin Charles, and Dorothy his wife. When he met Mihail, Cedric remembered that the young man had been to university, and congratulated him.

"There aren't so many folk from round here achieve that, think on. And there were fewer still in my day."

Cedric was enjoying himself, Pamela could tell; apparently a sociable man he was relishing this opportunity to meet so many people. She wondered how large his own family was.

"Cedric never had any children, you know." Mildred was at her side, explaining. "And he only has one sister. Her and her husband went to Australia with that scheme where you only pay ten pounds for your passage."

"How long has he been a widower?" Pamela couldn't remember if her mother had said.

"Eh, donkey's years. Though not as long as it is since I lost your dad."

"Well, he seems pleasant enough. And he has a nice smile."

Mildred raised her eyebrows at her. "Is that all? Don't you think he's good-looking?"

"So long as you do, that's all that matters."

Her mother chuckled. "I'm pulling your leg, can't you tell? He's kind and considerate; that means a lot more to me than looks. You want to stop worriting, you know. Me and him's going to get on like a house on fire."

177

The party was very successful. Gwen's migraine gradually eased, and she was able to make tentative attempts at sampling the splendid array of food. Most of the family had finished eating when the crowd from the whist drives began to arrive.

"I think we ought to be going now," Pamela suggested to Andre. "There's little enough room without us hanging on when we've had our turn." Unsurprisingly, she found her mother in the kitchen. "This is your celebration," she reminded her. "You shouldn't be doing all the work."

"I'm not. I were just having a word with Peggy, like."

Peggy turned from organising clean cups with another neighbour whom Pamela hadn't met. "You're looking a bit better than when you arrived, love. I dare say you were worrying about your ma's plans, weren't you?"

Pamela couldn't deny that, but nor could she tell anyone the cause of her greater agitation.

"We shall miss her round here, you know," Peggy went on. "She's allus been a good neighbour. A valiant woman, an' all. The way she brought you three up on her own. Mind you, you're a chip off the old block, as well. I haven't forgotten the way you helped at the party for the kids when the war ended. And never a word that your first husband had just died."

Sobered by the reminder and the familiar sympathetic smile on Peggy Kemp's lips, Pamela grew pensive. "I don't know about me," she admitted. "All I felt that day was lost." Utterly lost.

All the way home in the car Pamela was quiet. Andre often said very little while driving, but Mihail and Sonia were arguing in the back. She had needed Peggy Kemp's reminder. Deserved it. Until meeting and marrying Andre, her life had been nothing, empty. Oh, she had worked, had even relished teaching herself to do that bit more than just decorating homes for people, but inside she had felt dead.

"I'm sorry, love," she said to Andre as soon as they were indoors at Stonemoor House. "I was being thoroughly mean about your sister. Of course she must come

178

here if she wants. We've plenty of room. And happen it will be good to have a bit more help an' all."

She had made herself say that last sentence. It wasn't true. She would hate having another woman doing things in her kitchen. But that poor Irena seemed to have nobody else. They would have to make her feel that she belonged.

St Paul's church always looked rather austere, Sonia thought, with its stone walls, and so many plain windows. Today, though, for her grandmother's wedding, the altar wore its bright embroidered frontal of cream and gold. Someone had filled the place with cream-coloured flowers – on the altar itself, along the choir stalls, beside the lectern and pulpit.

Entering on Ian's arm, Mildred suddenly looked beautiful, and the bright touches around the church linked with what she was wearing. Her neat pale cream hat and a toning dress and jacket seemed to be emphasising that this was the start of a new way of life for her. No longer obliged to always wear sensible clothes which would last, without showing the dirt, Mildred was heading towards future enjoyment.

Cedric Vickers had seemed equally happy when he'd walked down the aisle with Tom at his side. In fact, he'd glanced sideways as he'd reached the end of the pew and had given Sonia a wink. No one else had noticed. Mihail was studying the prayer book. His own wedding had been fixed for the original date. Sonia knew how seriously he took life, was sure he was thinking very hard about his future. She only hoped that he didn't get so enmeshed in the solemnity of marriage that he forget to make life fun for Annabel.

Sonia had liked Annabel from the start and was looking forward to the time when she would be her sister-in-law and living in Yorkshire. She would enjoy having another girl of similar age around again. At least, until she met somebody herself and had a home of her own.

179

The organ stopped playing. Grandma Baker was standing beside Cedric now, had given him a smile that made Sonia afraid that she might cry. It *was* lovely that two old people like that were going to be happy again.

Behind them high-heeled shoes made a frenetic clattering as some latecomer came walking down the aisle. There was a gasp from Tania in the oak pew behind her, and then the sound of shuffling as Dorothy and Charles and their family slid along. Unable to endure the suspense, Sonia turned round when the vicar began speaking. It was! It was Pamela Anichka. They would have such a lot to talk about when the service was over.

Everyone was assembling in front of the cloisters that linked the church to the building used for the Sunday School. Watching while the photographer arranged first one combination of participants and then some other variation, Sonia made sure of standing next to PA.

"It's great to see you again! Did you have a good time on the Isle of Wight?"

"Really, really fab! You wouldn't believe how marvellous it is to get away and do your own thing, like that. You want to try it."

"Are you going back there, PA?"

Pamela Anichka glanced around to see where her mother was before responding. "I might, only it is a bit quiet now the rock festival's over. And it'll soon be the end of the season. Actually, I have other ideas. Tell you later." She had seen her stepfather looking her way.

PA had no intention of having anyone intervene before her plans materialised. She had arrived late today only because of stopping off in London. Determined on what she must do, she had walked the length of Carnaby Street. It had taken ages but in the end she had found one boutique willing to interview her, if no more, as a candidate for working there. They were going to let her know within the next week. If she got that job, she would be off to London immediately. Meanwhile, she must prevent her mother from guessing that she wasn't home to stay.

180

Not that she would cause her parents any anxiety this time. She had been shaken by how deeply distressed they had been when she had disappeared. From now on, she would tell them what she meant to do and where she would go. When it was too late for them to prevent her.

Eager to impress on her family how accommodating she could be, Pamela Anichka made an effort to go and chat to Gwen Baker where she was trying to amuse the three lads. As best man Tom was occupied with several tasks at once, and it seemed that Gwen was not coping terribly well with their energetic offspring. PA could sympathise, in a way, three so near in ages must be the proverbial handful. Not that she had any knowledge of mastering children, and no likelihood either of that coming her way. Not now.

Annabel was here today, of course, on Mihail's arm. And no doubt her whispering to him now concerned their own imminent wedding.

I shall not be around then, Pamela Anichka vowed silently, and widened her smile for her mother and Ian who were approaching. She was done with the years when she had permitted people to see how much she cared about Mihail Malinowski.

"I'm that glad that you managed to get here, PA love," her stepfather exclaimed. "We were afraid you might not be able to make it."

"Just delayed a bit, that was all. But this is such a surprise, I wouldn't have a missed it for worlds."

"We are all fond of Gran Baker, I always have been," said Tania. "Even before I married Ian." Smiling, she hesitated, gazing at her daughter. "I am pleased we have got a few minutes like this, away from the others."

She hesitated again, glanced at Ian who nodded. "We have got a surprise as well, Pamela Anichka, one that we wish to share with you before your dad tells the rest of the family. You are going to have a small brother or sister next year . . ."

"What? *You can't be!*" shrieked PA.

Not recognising the extent of her daughter's horror,

181

Tania giggled. "Yes, we also were afraid that I would never become pregnant. And your dad has longed for this for years."

He's not my dad, thought Pamela Anichka rather inconsequentially. But the shock was nothing at all to do with Ian being her stepfather. It was this whole idea of them *doing it*. At their age. They were so embarrassingly old.

"Well, if it's what you want," she muttered. "Personally, I think it's disgusting."

"Hey, hang on a sec, PA love," Ian began.

Tania frowned. "It should hardly affect you, sweetheart. You have your own life."

Precisely, thought PA. Thank God! And I am close on twenty. I shall certainly make sure now that I don't hang around in Yorkshire.

When Ian made the announcement towards the end of his mother's reception Sonia thought it was terribly romantic. Naturally, she had heard people talking over the years and understood how much Ian and Tania longed for a baby. She wondered if they might ask her to be a godmother. She would love that. And PA wouldn't be living anywhere near Cragg Vale when it arrived; she had confided that much when they met in the Ladies just now. Evidently Pamela Anichka was all but guaranteed some job in London, in Carnaby Street. Briefly, Sonia had wondered if there also might be work for her. But she wanted more than a position in some boutique, however trendy the place.

Working at Manchester airport had only strengthened her determination to travel. Organising flights for other people had done no more than whet her appetite for escorting them abroad while exercising her ability with languages. If *she* were ever to spend much time in London it would merely be as a stepping-off point for travelling further.

By the time Mildred and Cedric Vickers were waved off on their way to a honeymoon in Scotland, Tania was

182

longing to have a talk with her father and stepmother. But Pamela was chatting with Dorothy whom, despite being an old friend and married to her own cousin, she saw all too rarely. Andre was speaking with Mihail and his fiancée, and looking so earnest that Tania believed they must be discussing further details of the next family wedding. She went across to them, nevertheless, and was relieved when Andre saw her and excused himself from the other two. She needed someone to be pleased for herself and Ian. Hearing their news, everybody had applauded. But PA's awful reaction had made her wonder how much that public response had owed to courtesy.

"What do you think, Dad – really, I mean – about our having a baby?"

Andre smiled. "It is what you want, presumably, and Ian also?"

"Ian even more so," she said emphatically.

"Then what could be better? It will affect your career, of course, but that may be continued afterwards; provided you do not neglect your voice. You succeeded once in resuming your singing, after taking time out for a baby."

"A long time ago, though." And her own daughter had made her acutely conscious that she was growing older.

"You are not yet forty, surely, my sweet?"

"But it is looming over the horizon!"

Andre laughed, but Tania remained perturbed. To hear Pamela Anichka, you would believe thirty-nine was ancient, and the prospect of childbearing ludicrous.

Her father was watching the grey eyes so like the ones he saw each morning in the mirror. Tania was more distressed than he liked, and at a time when she should have been rejoicing.

"Is not everyone as pleased for you as we would hope?" he enquired, his thickening accent witnessing his concern. But then he smiled. "You should not expect too much perhaps. You must give people time. I know how you tried so very hard to be happy for us, when a small brother was to change our lives for ever. Not

183

everyone has your capacity for trying to be generous in such a way."

"And I am sure I did not succeed in concealing the occasions when I felt just that bit neglected!" Tania exclaimed ruefully. Her father was right, of course, and *he* was being generous in overlooking the tears which she had shed all those years ago when young Mihail was receiving masses of attention. But there was a difference in today's circumstances. When Mihail was on the way it hadn't been her own mother who was expecting. And had young people in those days been quite so preoccupied with the act which preceded pregnancy? It seemed strange to her that sex could obsess them so frequently while the thought of others indulging appeared to be embarrassing.

Determined to make a friend of Pamela Anichka, Annabel had hurried over at Mihail's side to greet her. "You went to the rock festival, didn't you?" she exclaimed. "That must have been exciting."

PA nodded, but merely glanced towards the girl, and without releasing Mihail from a hug she couldn't resist giving him. "Oh, it was. And I've been working on the island since it finished." Speaking of her job there was fine, preferable to dwelling on the shocking way in which the festival had ended for her.

"We're going to a club or something tonight," Annabel continued. "Why don't you come with us. Mihail's asked Sonia as well."

Hastily, PA disengaged herself from Mihail, shook her head. "Can't, sorry. First night home, and all that." Was Annabel Atherton-Ward thick or something? Couldn't she realise when she was expecting too much? How could she imagine I would enjoy sharing Mihail with her, even for one evening?

In the car Ian tried hard to lighten the atmosphere. Whatever Pamela had thought about their mother's remarriage, he believed it was ideal. Cedric was a nice enough chap, and he had sufficient means to prevent Mum from having to worry about the future.

184

He'd enjoyed today, and most of all because at long last they'd been able to announce that Tania was expecting their child. He would have preferred it if PA had been as delighted as they were themselves, but he was hardly surprised. The girl was nineteen, after all, might feel a bit ridiculous to have such a gap between herself and a brother or sister.

From what he'd heard whispered around today, he understood that Pamela Anichka was already planning to go off again. At least, they would have no cause to worry in case she felt her nose was being pushed out. Dearly though he loved the girl, he couldn't feel sorry that he and Tania wouldn't always be obliged to spend every day skating around PA's delicate emotions.

Ian wasn't sorry either that Tania had asked her father and Pamela back to the cottage for the evening. Between them, they might somehow cheer his stepdaughter up a bit. He had seen her talking to Annabel and Mihail, had witnessed the unrestrained hug which she had given the lad. His heart ached for PA at times, but she'd never have listened years ago if he'd insisted that she was becoming unhealthily attached to Mihail.

"I shan't be here when they get married, you know," PA stated from the back of the car. "I shall be working away, probably in London."

Beside him, his wife flinched. She opened her mouth to speak, but evidently thought better of it. That's wisest, thought Ian; we have to let her go, they all want to do their own thing these days. He would be here for Tania, and they had the baby to look forward to. This time, they would know where PA was; it could never be as bad as enduring her disappearance.

Ian was surprised that the atmosphere in their cottage became altogether more relaxed than he'd anticipated. Pamela Anichka had always been very fond of her grandfather and his wife, and seemed now to be content to listen to what they were revealing about their plans.

Tania was the only other person who'd had any inkling

that Andre intended to try and bring his sister over to England. The rest of them seemed surprised when he first explained, but Ian soon recognised that it was perhaps inevitable. Andre Malinowski had taken Yorkshire to his heart, and in turn had loved being accepted by the people here who had become his own. He wasn't a man who would ever neglect family; gathering this last remaining member of his clan to him was something he needed to achieve.

To concerned questions from Pamela and Tania as well, Andre confirmed that he was not planning on visiting Russia himself.

"I still have friends there," he reminded them. "Some of whom have considerable influence today. Irena writes to me that, at last, she is willing to come. All we do now is await that wonderful day when we shall be notified of the arrangements."

Thirteen

S onia was finally studying towards the work which she really wanted. Not quite certain how, she had persuaded her father that she wouldn't be happy until she had trained to become an air hostess.

They had tried to talk her out of the idea. Her mother's smile had been wry while she insisted that Sonia had better be sure about this.

"You could find that the job's a cross between a waitress and a nanny – and even with bits of cleaning thrown in!"

More seriously, Andre had resurrected old arguments. "My main concern is the matter of your future safety, if you should travel to certain parts of the world."

"Like Russia, you mean. But you say your attempts to bring Aunt Irena out from behind the iron curtain are likely to succeed now. Surely that suggests that they wouldn't be interested in detaining me, even if I did happen to land there."

"And Sonia has a British passport, don't forget, love," Pamela had continued. "Despite her name, there'd be no reason for anyone over there to think of questioning her nationality."

But I wanted all my children to be proud of the part of them that is Russian, Andre had thought, then silently reproached himself for possessing such a mass of conflicting sentiments.

Once her parents had agreed, albeit reluctantly, the only difficulty was that Sonia was obliged to wait until she was twenty-one before any airline would accept her. But they had given sufficient advice to convince her that being too young was the only problem. Explaining that any experience she might gain would be to her advantage, they had recommended that she acquire some knowledge of nursing and perhaps catering also.

She was assisting now, whenever she could, as a volunteer in the children's ward of a local hospital. The work was hard, but it also was fun, even when she began to understand that her mother's assessment of her future role might be pretty accurate. Sonia was surprised that, tired though she frequently was after her hours at the airport, she enjoyed these tasks, however tenuous their connection with the lust for travel and using foreign languages.

Through her position as ground staff, she knew that children quite often travelled without a parent or other adult. Learning how to care for these hospitalised children now was preparing her for looking after any, travelling unaccompanied. It also endorsed her long-standing hopes that she would marry and have a family. Until she met the right man, however, she'd be content to do as much as she could to secure work caring for people when they were airborne.

Her more immediate ambition was to look truly glamorous for Mihail's wedding in December. She had been elated when Annabel asked her to be a bridesmaid, and ecstatic when allowed to choose her own dress for the occasion.

Annabel's twin brother was to be the best man, and when he'd visited Stonemoor House Sonia had been enchanted. Rupert Atherton-Ward looked so strong, with his rugby-player's physique. And he had such an attractive smile. Best of all, though, he gave no hint that Sonia – still barely nineteen – seemed to him too young to be interesting.

The twins and Mihail had included Sonia while they dashed around exploring Yorkshire, and spent their evenings alternating earnest discussions with a lot of laughter while they sat in picturesque country pubs. Throughout it all, Rupert had seemed fascinated by Sonia's ambition to travel, listening intently while the other two had eyes only for each other.

Any girl would be forgiven for entertaining wishful dreams; Sonia Malinowski had dreamed for so long of her ultimate ideal as a partner that meeting him epitomised was disturbingly heady.

For once, her mother was quite understanding even while insisting that they shopped together for that bridesmaid's dress. Pamela herself was to wear blue, Andre's favourite colour, and one which would not conflict with the bride's mother's outfit in dove grey.

Blue was the colour she suggested also for her daughter, but Sonia wanted something pale. Secretly, she meant to have Rupert associate her with all things bridal. It could not be white, of course, but she chose a delicate shade of peach. The material was quite heavy, its weave the effect of brocade which enhanced the cloth far more than any additional colour might. The style, though, was the feature which sold the dress to her. Simply cut, with a wide boatline neck and long sleeves, it was semi-fitted to the waist where the seam descended in a V-shape. A similar V at the back culminated in a neat bow which she knew would draw attention to the slender curves of which she privately was proud. The skirt was long, virtually straight and brushed her ankles. When she wore the dress for future events she would only need to shorten the skirt slightly to comply with the current maxi fashion.

Thankful that no one had tried to influence her against her own first choice, Sonia smiled to herself. She was beginning to see that she could not blame her mother for the years of attempting to curb some of her notions. It seemed ages now since she and PA had been in trouble for their determination to wear miniskirts. Although she still had several in her wardrobe, they rarely emerged when she was going out. The people she met since she and Pamela Anichka ceased to see as much of each other, dressed rather more modestly. The boyfriends she had

– and there had been a few, although none were serious – wore casual clothes, and nothing that would raise too many maternal eyebrows. Obliged to wear uniform at the airport, Sonia tended to go for comfortable gear off-duty. Trousers, or skirts that didn't reveal too much leg when she was helping at the hospital. For dancing her favourite was a maxiskirt which made her feel romantic.

"If only Irena could have been with us today, she would have loved to see Mihail married."

Pamela glanced sideways at her husband, rather puzzled. They were in the car driving towards Chipping Norton. It was early December, and she wondered how Andre might have even hoped that his sister could be in England this soon. It seemed such a short while since he'd first mentioned the possibility of organising Irena's departure from his homeland. Surely, the necessary arrangements and acquiring all the documents which must be produced would take a long time. Pamela began to wonder if Andre had perhaps begun to set things in motion before putting the idea to her.

If that could be so, she wasn't best pleased. However, this weekend was for Mihail and his bride; she would keep silent on any matter that could cause contention, at least until they were back at Stonemoor.

Pamela had never seen Mihail more excited. Normally quite a serious young man, and especially so since that trouble in Oxford, he rarely revealed any elation. Yesterday, when he set out with Annabel for her home, Pamela had been thankful that the girl was driving.

Mihail had passed his test during the summer, at the first attempt, after applying himself most conscientiously to learning. Evidently, visualising him at the wheel while he was in this highly charged state had been no more appealing to his fiancée than it was to the family.

Sonia was travelling in the car behind theirs, willing to take over from Ian if he grew tired. Although she hadn't yet taken her test, Sonia loved driving and was seizing every opportunity to practise. Tania, whose pregnancy was still making her feel unwell, was only too glad to have someone else around to deputise as the driver; she was also thankful to have another person there who would chat and take her mind off the fact that her own daughter had stood by her decision to keep away from Mihail's wedding.

The only consolation about Pamela Anichka remaining in London was knowing that she was happy there. She rang home fairly regularly now, always enthusing about her Carnaby Street job.

Tania had wanted to continue on as far as London this weekend, but Ian had refused to take her. Now the manager of Canning's, he treated the responsibility extremely seriously, and took time off only when absolutely necessary.

He was right, of course, and his wife would have loved him rather less had he been given to considering the position lightly. To her, Ian's work had always seemed demanding rather than in any way glamorous. But, as Pamela had done all those years ago, he put in hours of painstaking work which produced beautiful results to the satisfaction of all the firm's clients.

Tania had been surprised when she visited the offices which Canning's had recently decorated. Light and airy, they had been turned into attractive places where pastel-tinted walls and white-painted woodwork contributed a pleasing ambience.

Most effective of all, though, was Ian's skill when enhancing their own cottage. Whenever she had persuaded him to make the time to refurbish a room there, Tania had noticed that he really did emulate the craftsmanship first employed by his sister at Stonemoor.

Their two cars drew in only minutes apart outside the Atherton-Wards' home. Annabel and her mother were greeting Andre and Pamela on the steps, when Sonia carefully negotiated the drive and halted. She had driven only the last twenty or so miles, but was flushed with elation as she turned off the engine.

Meeting the Atherton-Wards, Tania was surprised that they seemed to know a great deal about her, including her pregnancy, as well as the fact that she was a professional singer.

Ian had expected to feel somewhat ill-at-ease. Despite the long years of having his sister live in a house the size of Stonemoor, he frequently hesitated on the threshold of other large homes. Would he always feel comfortable in such places only if he were to work on them? On this occasion, however, he was permitted no such moment of misgivings. Their hostess was drawing them inside the hall as soon as she had shaken their hands.

Her husband began pouring and offering drinks when all introductions were completed. And then Mihail came running down the staircase.

"Rupert is late, I'm afraid," Mrs Atherton-Ward announced. "He left Oxford this morning, but was calling on a friend on the way here. We shall begin our meal without him if he hasn't arrived when we're ready."

The whole family were dining with the Atherton-Wards that evening before taking up the rooms reserved for them at one of the lovely stone hotels for which the Cotswolds were famous.

Rupert arrived just as they were filing into the dining room. He was looking well pleased, if somewhat breathless. Sonia smiled in his direction, feeling suddenly speechless. With colour in his cheeks, and his brown hair slightly windswept, he appeared so glamorous.

There was less opportunity to talk than she had hoped, only a few words were exchanged between them amid the general conversation passing across the table. Tomorrow, she resolved. It has got to be tomorrow that I make the big impression. She could only thank heaven for that glorious dress, and pray that it would give her the confidence to really sparkle.

Getting ready as a family was fun, Sonia thought. Her

mother was less certain of that, but she wasn't in a mood to give herself up entirely to enjoyment. Despite her resolve, Pamela remained troubled by the suspicion that Andre's desire to have his sister live at Stonemoor had not been declared as soon as it might.

Mihail was more nervous than excited today, and feeling quite sick with apprehension when Rupert arrived at the hotel to drive him to church. Although still completely sure that he was right to be marrying Annabel, he was beginning to doubt his own maturity. How was he to cope with ensuring that they would have a home of their own, how provide all the thousands of things which seemed to be essential within it?

They were starting off less well than he had intended, sharing a room at Stonemoor House. Deciding to marry without delay had left no time in which to find a house or flat, and to get together the deposit that would secure it. For the first time in his life, Mihail understood how unreliable his own income might become. Annabel was earning, of course; her paintings continued to sell, but he was reluctant to rely too greatly on her. Annabel, being the modern young woman she was, declared this attitude quite ridiculous, but they had reached a stalemate on the subject and, for the present, were discussing it no further.

Glad though she was of this reason to keep her son at home, Pamela intended to broach one idea with which she had been toying. While Mihail loved renovating any clocks and watches needing attention, she could see that as he worked more quickly on those which she acquired her supply would dwindle. Rather than have him grow short of work, she would prefer to have Mihail extend the scope of what he did in the shop; she could then pay him for covering for her.

These days, although she admitted this to no one, Pamela tired more easily. The leg that she had fractured so badly all those years ago ached quite fiercely when she had been standing for hours. But there was another reason – if Irena Malinowski was to become a member of

193

their household, Pamela had no intention of being absent from the house for such long periods. Always wanting a career in addition to running a home didn't prevent her from being reluctant to delegate her household duties.

Sonia looked stunning in her bridesmaid's dress, so sophisticated that both Pamela and Andre experienced a surge of emotion. Exchanging a glance, they smiled.

"You look beautiful, my sweet," Andre exclaimed, and crossed the room to hug her.

"Careful, Dad, don't crush my frock. And try not to dislodge my headdress."

She was wearing her blonde hair rather longer now, and had chosen an ornamental comb from her mother's shop. Gold-coloured and fan-shaped it was almost like a tiara, gleaming amid her glossy tresses.

Entering the church at last those few paces behind Annabel, Sonia gazed immediately towards Rupert. Looking more comfortable than her brother in the morning coats chosen for the day, he appeared more attractive than even she had imagined him.

Mihail, Sonia noticed, saw no one but his bride. And he might be justified in that, she supposed. In a long white gown which had a bodice encrusted with seed pearls, Annabel was enchanting.

Hardly able to haul her attention away from Rupert's face, Sonia found the service hastening by while all the words that she had meant to savour floated about her. Only towards the end of the ceremony did she focus on the significance of the promises witnessed, and sense the total commitment in which the principal participants were engaging.

How wonderful it must be to know you were secure for all time in such eloquent devotion! One day, she promised herself once again, one day she would be the woman to have such happy assurance. Leaving the church on the arm that Rupert offered while he smiled down at her, Sonia allowed herself to pretend that this was *their* day, that his family and hers were joining to celebrate their union.

The party halted in the porch while photographs of bride and groom were taken. Sonia smiled up at Rupert, inhaling deeply yet so ridiculously tongue-tied that she could do no more than ask how he was today.

"Fine, fine," he told her, and she suddenly believed that her presence had more than a small connection with his well-being.

And now they were the ones central to the camera lens, for a picture she knew she would treasure until their relationship became more than her dream with only a photo to sustain it.

The groom and his bride had moved down the steps, were smiling now into each other's eyes, oblivious to all. The photographer again took charge, marshalling both sets of parents and Sonia and Rupert, assembling them to either side of Annabel and her new husband.

Sonia's hand was warm still from contact with Rupert's sleeve; even now that they stood barely touching, she could feel the heat which had spread through the fine cloth of his coat. I shan't need a thing to drink at the reception, she thought and contained a giggle. She wouldn't have credited that any person could make one so intoxicated.

The wedding party regrouped; further members from both families came to join them. Sonia was reminded of her gran's wedding those few weeks ago, realised how very different she felt today, and knew that Rupert was responsible.

The voice was attractive, well modulated, just behind her. "Rupert darling, here's the confetti we bought. Don't let them get away without . . ."

Turning, expecting to see some girl with the Atherton-Ward colouring, a cousin perhaps? Sonia was stunned. This young woman was tall, almost as tall as Rupert himself, and her exquisite brown skin revealed her Indian connections. The sari she wore was the green of the sea, embellished with gold embroidery. When Rupert's gaze met hers it blatantly conveyed a kiss – a kiss no relative would receive.

Feeling physically sick, Sonia instantly recognised the truth and what an utter fool she had been. The look in Rupert's eyes couldn't have been more eloquent. This magnificent female was the woman who had transformed life for him, the woman he loved.

The reception was complete perfection, exquisitely presented in a major hotel where the decor was equalled only by the food. Sonia loathed every minute. Pleading a headache when Pamela remarked on her miserable expression did no good. Her suggestion that she might be excused to return to her room was met with a frown.

"You can't do that, love," her mother protested. "This is your own brother's wedding, don't forget. Look how Tania is managing to smile at everybody, and be genuinely interested in what's going on – and you know she's been feeling unwell for weeks."

The reason behind her half-sister's indisposition was anything but a consolation, especially when today's bombshell seemed to confirm that Sonia wouldn't ever have the family for which she had longed so consistently.

Although her parents alone seemed aware that Sonia was upset, she privately admitted that everyone else was terribly kind to her throughout the rest of that weekend. Rupert was kindest of all during the following morning, but the fact that his ravishing girlfriend did not appear didn't prevent Sonia from being aware of her. Nothing Rupert might say or do now would make things come right.

Pamela and Andre had been talking late last night, discussing Rupert's thoughtfulness. Hadn't he delayed announcing his own engagement purely because he refused to steal even a little of his twin sister's limelight on her wedding day.

"The Atherton-Wards are delighted, of course," Pamela had said. "Apparently, the girl's father is a lawyer as well. They have known them for years."

The family arrived back in Yorkshire, driving through fog which had made the journey long and exhausting. By the time they drew up outside Stonemoor House, neither parent seemed to care that Sonia intended going straight up to bed.

Pamela herself was tired, but she was still contemplating Andre's remark concerning his sister. Was there a substantial reason why he might have hoped to have Irena attend Mihail's wedding?

Having waited and wondered, for so many hours, Pamela knew she would not rest until she heard the truth. And Andre provided the opening as they sat in the kitchen over a light supper.

"You have always made each Christmas here so special – what ideas have you about this year, my love?"

"Why do you ask? You're usually content to leave everything to me."

Was his smile when he replied slightly embarrassed, not quite so open? "I – actually, I am hoping for news of Irena any day now. She could even be on her way here."

"I wondered if that was it," Pamela said, and considered suggesting that he might have confided in her more closely. But then she saw the anxiety in his grey eyes, and recalled how he had yearned for so many years to bring his sister over to England. To his home. Had yearned to know that Irena was safe at Stonemoor House.

"I have hardly dared to speak of the details," he continued. "There might be less cause now to fear that Irena would be prevented from joining us, but I am superstitious about counting the days."

"You do hope it might be in time for Christmas, though?"

"Oh, yes. From what I hear, she has set out already."

Andre explained that friends of his in Russia had been fortunate in learning that a young man destined for a position in their London embassy might accompany Irena.

I hope we have a bit of warning before she arrives, thought Pamela. As well as the necessary preparing of a room for her sister-in-law, she needed to prepare herself. Life would never be the same once this woman she had never met was included in their household. I've thought this all along, she reflected. And I've known since that first time that the feeling was utterly selfish. I must never do or say anything to make Andre feel I'm at all reluctant to welcome Irena.

Mustering a smile, she willed herself to tackle the prospect as a reality, one which she would accept. "Which room do you wish her to have, Andre?" she asked.

"I shall leave that decision to you. I know I can rely on you to choose one that will accommodate her comfortably." And, he added silently, from what I recall of Irena's Russian home, Stonemoor House will seem extremely elegant.

Preparing for Christmas in addition to getting everything ready for Irena's arrival created days of frenetic activity. Pamela also was busy at the shop, where the name she had made for herself as an antiques expert brought numerous clients to her door.

With Mihail away on honeymoon, she experienced the kind of pressure which had been unremarkable in the days when he was at university. Only now was Pamela beginning to appreciate how just having her son around had provided moments of relief. If simply between customers when they were able to chat. At least this confirms that I must try to persuade Mihail to take a more active role here, she thought, looking forward to the day when he would bring Annabel home to Stonemoor.

It was in the home, though, where Pamela found her work the more demanding. Obliging though their housekeeper was, Mrs Singer had aged rapidly during the past year, and seemed exhausted as she struggled to work an eight-hour day, coping with routine washing, ironing, and cooking along with extra jobs ahead of the festive season. Pamela was thankful that the woman had lived in since being widowed and didn't have a journey home when she was so tired.

Elated by the prospect of reunion with his sister and in the midst of a well-booked concert season, Andre was the only one who seemed entirely happy.

Sonia was causing her mother anxiety, particularly as she appeared determined to avoid confiding the reason for her bleak despair. Aware that Sonia's withdrawal dated from Mihail's wedding, Pamela could only assume that she was missing him quite terribly, although as her daughter had coped so well during the years while he was at Oxford this reaction now did perhaps seem rather unlikely.

Too preoccupied with tasks demanding her attention for dwelling on Sonia's state of mind, Pamela decided that letting the girl work out her disturbance would have to suffice. They were always here for her if she decided to confide. She was glad that the voluntary hospital work combined with Sonia's regular job to keep her busy. When the holiday came Pamela would have more time to help her to overcome this dejection.

They had heard now that Irena definitely would be in England by Christmas. Mihail and Annabel were due to return from their honeymoon in Tenerife before then, on 20 December. Their flight was due to touch down during the late evening, and they planned to drive from Heathrow to her parents' home where they would spend a night before travelling north.

Throughout that Sunday, the 21st, while continuing with the chores still to be tackled, Pamela kept looking out and listening, eager for the young couple's arrival. She and Andre were sitting down to supper when the telephone rang.

"That could be news of Irena," Andre exclaimed and hurried to take the call.

Smiling to herself, Pamela reflected on her husband's excitement. Even Mihail's imminent return was overshadowed by Irena's coming.

He strode back into the room with a shrug. "Mihail. They are going to be late. The flight was delayed, and they are only now setting out from the Atherton-Ward's home. He said not to wait up."

Sonia came in from the hospital an hour or so later, and reported that her duty at the airport earlier that day had confirmed that her brother's was not the only flight suffering hold-ups.

"From the sound of it, Heathrow has come off rather worse than Manchester. Is Aunt Irena coming by air as well?" she asked her father.

Andre did not know. Even after all these years his respect for differences between the situations here and in Russia had prevented him from enquiring too closely. He would never forget friends and family who had suffered as a result of too many questions asked.

"Much as I would have liked to have known every detail of her proposed journey, I thought it wiser to remain in ignorance. The fewer people who are aware of her plans, the safer she may be."

Pamela thought that he was being a shade too melodramatic about the business, but she refrained from commenting. In another few days she would need to watch what she said to, and in front of, Irena; beginning now to restrain her tongue would do no harm.

Sonia had eaten with the children at the hospital, and took herself off to bed ten minutes after arriving home. Andre, disappointed that he had another day to wait before seeing his sister, went upstairs shortly afterwards.

Pamela had hoped that the three of them might have decorated the Christmas tree, which had stood in its pot in the hall since the previous day. She could have begun the task herself, but the decorations were still in their boxes in the attic. Disturbing the other two was unneccesary; the job could wait until tomorrow.

Instead, she went into the kitchen where Mrs Singer was adding finishing touches to the cake she was icing. Aware suddenly of the mutual frustration engendered by the housekeeper's inability to converse, Pamela watched her for only a few moments before turning to the notepad.

'I am going up to bed now. You should not be too long, you're looking tired. And there's always another day.'

Mrs Singer smiled and nodded, and glanced from the pad back to her cake. She was tired, but she was no less determined than ever in the past. This cake was to be special; a welcome home for Mihail and his bride more than a celebration of Christmas. Carefully, she chose the nozzle with which she would complete the entwined A and M, the feature of its centre.

They entered, breathless and giggling, into the silent house, Annabel protesting that he must put her down, for Mihail had insisted on carrying her over the doorstep.

"Perhaps I should carry you up to my room," he suggested.

"Perhaps you shouldn't!" his bride exclaimed. "You might spend the rest of the week incapacitated."

Laughing, Mihail set her on her feet and drew her against him for a kiss.

"I'd better bring in all our luggage," he said eventually.

"Leave it till morning," Annabel suggested. "We don't want to disturb the whole house, they're obviously in bed."

"But our overnight stuff . . ." Mihail persisted.

"Haven't noticed you wearing pyjamas yet."

Grinning, he locked the front door behind them. "Well, I need a bite to eat, and a hot drink," he said, striding along the hall towards the kitchen.

Until that moment the kitchen light being on while everyone was sleeping hadn't registered as odd. Coupled with the fact that the door to the larder was standing open, it made Mihail pause now, looking around.

He saw her then, lying between the sink and the island unit with its worktop still bearing an array of icing nozzles and tubes, a basin with congealing sugar. Her silver-grey hair gleamed against the dark tiling of the floor, and increased the abnormal pallor of the face transfixed in a final smile.

"God! It's Mrs Singer. Quick, Annabel."

His wife could do no more than he could. Mihail recognised that even before he dropped to his knees beside the old housekeeper.

"I liked her such a lot," he said gravely, closing the woman's sightless eyes as he slowly struggled to his feet.

Watching, Annabel saw the tears sliding down her husband's cheeks.

"I know," she said. "I know, darling."

"We'll have to waken them all, tell them." And he didn't know how. From being a man proudly showing his young wife the world, he'd become a boy again suddenly unable to surrender a vital feature of his childhood, the familiar presence of this trusted woman.

Fourteen

M ihail wakened his father and mother, after taking a few minutes to contain his own emotions. With Annabel at his side, he stood by their bed, absorbing their excited greetings, their fervent welcome. And then he steeled himself for the explanation.

"Actually, we wouldn't have bothered you tonight. We know it's late. But we've had rather a nasty shock."

"Not an accident?" Pamela exclaimed, sitting upright in the bed.

"Are you both sure you are all right?" Andre demanded.

"It's neither of us," Annabel assured them gently.

"I'm afraid it's Mrs Singer," Mihail continued. "We found her in the kitchen."

"She's ill?" asked Pamela, already out of bed, reaching for a housecoat.

"Worse than that, Mum. A lot worse."

Calling in the doctor was obligatory, even though he could do nothing for her. The words he had for them increased everyone's distress. He had not been treating Mrs Singer during the past few months; this meant a post mortem must be held.

No one slept very much during the remainder of the night. Sonia had been wakened in the early hours, and came running downstairs, bleary-eyed, to hug her brother and Annabel. Andre had told her the news, and was moved by his daughter's tears.

"She was such a love," Sonia had exclaimed. "Stonemoor won't be the same without her."

Long before daylight those sentiments brought them

203

all from their rooms again. They were up and dressed, awaiting the undertaker who would arrive to make what arrangements he could. Most of the organising would be merely provisional: until the cause of the house-keeper's death was ascertained no death certificate would be issued.

"The funeral won't be till long after Christmas," said Pamela. "I can't imagine what sort of a time we shall have now that this will be hanging over us."

The hearse was in the drive and the undertaker and his assistant were carrying the coffin towards it when the car drew in behind the vehicle. A black car with darkened glass in its windows, it might have been a part of the cortège. But the young man who sprang from the nearside door to the rear wore a brightly coloured sweater, his trousers a pale shade of cream. He glanced curiously towards the hearse and frowned, but went then to open the car door for a second passenger.

The woman was grey-haired, smartly dressed though quite dismally in a grey shades darker than her hair. Looking towards the coffin, she gasped.

"*Nyet*," she exclaimed, shaking her head, appalled. "*Nyet* Andre?"

"Irena?"

From the far side of the hearse, Andre heard and appeared, running. Seizing his sister by both hands, he gazed and gazed at her. After all these years he could scarcely believe that she had finally arrived in Yorkshire.

Watching, listening from the undertaker's side, Pamela waited until the flow of Russian questioning ceased. Andre sought her then, drew her forward to be introduced to Irena.

"I have explained about Mrs Singer. Would you take Irena indoors perhaps, show her to her room. I must see if we need to do anything further before – before the body is taken from here. And then there is Nikolai – this young man has been so kind bringing my sister to us."

Mihail had taken over and continued sorting out everything necessary regarding Mrs Singer. The car which had brought Irena to Stonemoor was moved and the hearse drove slowly away.

The young man who'd introduced himself as Nikolai Trepliov was already addressing Andre in Russian when Pamela led her sister-in-law towards the house.

"As Andre has told you, our housekeeper died last night, it was very sudden, like." She looked into eyes very like Andre's, smiled as she gave a tiny shrug. "Eh, I'm that confused with all that's been going on. I haven't asked – do you understand English?"

Smiling back, Irena nodded. "So long as people do not speak very quick. And I am sad to learn of your – your dead person. You say she is your . . . ?"

"Housekeeper. She looked after us, cooked and cleaned, did the washing. Oh – and so much more!"

Mihail had followed them into the house and smiled as he was introduced to his aunt. He delighted her with a few words of her native language; then Annabel emerged from the sitting room and further introductions were made.

Andre brought Nikolai indoors with him, and told Pamela that the young man had nowhere to stay. She heard herself saying that they would find him a room, and knew that this was what Andre expected from her. How she would cope, Pamela could not imagine. Losing Mrs Singer was bad enough; having a full house and Christmas all but upon them daunted her completely.

It didn't feel like Monday morning, but she would have to open the shop today. Several regular customers had reserved pieces which they particularly wanted for Christmas and would be coming in for them. A delivery was due too, of items she had purchased at a recent sale.

"You must not worry," Irena was saying as they walked side by side up the staircase. "I am here now, I shall help you, no?"

No, thought Pamela quite firmly, and recognised that she must alter that opinion. She would be grateful for her sister-in-law's assistance before this day was out, never mind during the ensuing week.

Annabel offered help also. Following them upstairs, she caught Pamela by the arm when she'd left Irena exploring her new bedroom.

"I'm quite domesticated really, you know," the girl confided eagerly. "And I was feeling rather disappointed because I didn't expect to be cooking for Mihail just yet."

"Thanks, love – well, we'll have to see. I shall need to have a look round that kitchen; I'm not sure what Mrs Singer had done." The shock of the housekeeper's death had driven all sensible thought from Pamela's head. And time was moving on, inexorably. "Do you think you could cope for a few hours?" she asked her daughter-in-law. "Mihail knows where everything's kept. In fact, he was always Mrs Singer's favourite, spent a lot of time with her."

Sonia had heard most of this from the bathroom where she was getting ready to set out for work. Opening the door, she glanced across the landing to where the aunt whom she'd never met was looking around the bedroom she'd been given.

"Hello, I'm Sonia," she greeted her from the doorway. "I'm ever so glad that you've got here at last, but I can't talk properly. I'm late already for the airport."

"The airport?" Irena enquired slowly. "You are going on a journey perhaps? When shall I see you again?"

Sonia shook her head and grinned as they grasped each other's hands. "No – I work there, that's all. I'll be home tonight. We'll have a nice long chat."

Noting how bewildered the woman appeared, she leaned forward and kissed her cheek before calling "See you!" as she turned to run down the stairs.

She saw him then, a strange young man with brown hair whose dark eyes lent drama to his pleasant face. He was talking with her father, and she noticed immediately how alike they were – in their stance as much as in their build. Perhaps that was a part of being Russian.

Turning, the young man's smile lit those compelling eyes while he walked smartly towards her. "You are Sonia, I feel sure. Your father only now was telling me about you."

"And I'm in a fearful rush," she declared ruefully. "I hope I'll see you again."

"Oh, you shall, you shall."

Sonia couldn't think how. Now that this young man had delivered her aunt to Stonemoor, he would return to London. If not to Russia.

Her disappointment was only slight, surely? Sonia thought as she ran for the bus. Her love for Rupert, however hopeless, prevented her from even really noticing any other man. This *was* what she had concluded only those few days ago wasn't it?

Pamela went back to the house at lunchtime. As soon as she arrived at the shop she had realised that she couldn't keep away from Stonemoor throughout the whole day as usual. There had been no time for even checking what food poor Mrs Singer had bought in; she couldn't leave Mihail and Annabel to cope with providing a meal. And then there was Irena.

No matter how determined to contain her instinctive reactions, Pamela could not rid herself of the dismay generated by picturing her sister-in-law in her kitchen.

Mihail looked faintly puzzled when he arrived to take over after she had summoned him by telephone. "You all right, Mum? You're not coming down with 'flu or anything?"

"Of course I'm all right. Upset about Mrs Singer, naturally. But – well, I thought I'd better see how you all were coping."

"Annabel has everything under control. She's really domesticated, you know. Far more so than us lot!"

His mother smiled as she threw on her coat. "I know,

207

love, I know. Just humour me, for once, eh?" She wished she could explain that it wasn't thoughts of Annabel which produced these misgivings. But she must never mention to anyone her true reaction.

Irena was in the sitting room, Andre beside her on the sofa and Nikolai in one of the armchairs. They were conversing in Russian but immediately on seeing her the young man sprang to his feet and Irena rose more slowly and walked towards her.

"We disrupt your work, I fear," she observed, and took Pamela's coat from her shoulders then carried it out to the hall.

Returning, she smiled towards her sister-in-law. "And now you should sit, here beside Andre. I suspect that you will have less time than I today for resting."

Nikolai inclined his head towards Pamela, waited until she was seated and Irena had found another chair.

"Your husband is telling to us how you were responsible for the beauty of these rooms. I think is very unusual that a lady should have this kind of work, no?"

"It certainly was when I began, just after the war. There weren't many women then did any decorating."

"And the work you accomplished here was so much more than a matter of applying paint and paper," added Andre and smiled as he turned to his sister. "You must notice the panelling in the hall out there. You would not believe how neglected it had become, yet my Pamela restored it to such a high quality."

Annabel interrupted, calling them through to the dining room where she had set out bowls of soup, together with some of Mrs Singer's final batch of bread.

"There is also a cold game pie which Mihail found in the fridge. And I made a salad of sorts. Just with the things that were there."

"You've done ever so well, love," said Pamela, and thanked her. "Talk about being thrown in at the deep end!"

"I'll do anything, anything at all."

It was Irena though who insisted that she would tackle the washing-up afterwards.

Pamela felt something inside her resisting, stiffening instinctively. She drew in a deep breath, made herself smile. "Thank you, Irena, how nice. But I'll go into the kitchen with you, show you where things are kept."

Her sister-in-law refused to don rubber gloves, and Pamela noticed evidence in the capable hands that some Russian women at least did not trouble with such protection. It occurred to her suddenly that Irena was accustomed to work, would most likely feel deprived if she were denied the opportunity to be useful.

Drying the dishes which her sister-in-law washed, Pamela began stacking them in her cupboards. As she put cups and plates and soup bowls away she told Irena where she was placing them.

"It won't matter terribly if you don't remember exactly where everything belongs," she assured her. "Neither Mrs Singer nor I ever managed to train the children to maintain any degree of order!"

Irena turned to her and smiled as she finished emptying away the dirty water. "And I feel certain that you would forgive them a great deal." She paused for a moment, thinking. "You are fortunate to have such a lovely son and daughter."

"A stepdaughter as well, we're both very proud of Tania. Which reminds me – have you seen Tania yet?"

Irena shook her head. "Andre telephoned to her house, but no one was there. He is promising that we shall visit her for tea."

"I must remind him that nobody's told Tania about Mrs Singer yet. She'll be upset, they'd known each other such a long time."

Leaving the kitchen with her sister-in-law beside her, Pamela experienced a curious sensation of déjà vu. Impossible though that could be, she might have carried out such domestic tasks with her before. It was as if completing those few minutes of humble routine while they talked re-enacted a previous encounter, one which had been important.

In the hall Irena paused to admire the panelled walls, ran her fingers over the wood. "That is good," she said, and nodded. "Very good."

Pamela smiled as she crossed to pick up her coat. "Afraid I've got to get back to the shop. You do understand?"

"But naturally. You have your own busy life. I hope that I do not disturb it too completely. And you will have your friends – you need not neglect them because I am here."

Walking down the drive Pamela thought What friends? and realised how rarely she saw Dorothy these days. They both had become immersed in family and work, to the degree that neither thought to arrange to meet and relax together.

Recalling the old days when she and Dorothy had shared so much, Pamela felt her scalp tingle. That sense of kinship which had existed with her friend was precisely the feeling engendered those few minutes ago with Irena.

Christmas with Mrs Singer's loss so recent would have been appalling had they not been obliged to make the effort to appear festive for the sake of their guests. The fact that Irena had emphasised that she understood their natural grief, must not encourage them to become miserable. And besides, Mihail and Annabel were spending their first Christmas together at Stonemoor.

Throughout the preceding days both young people had helped tremendously with the preparations. Several times Tania had joined them, eager to spend a few hours at the house becoming reacquainted with the aunt she had left behind in Russia all those years ago.

From that first afternoon when they had rushed to hug each other in the doorway of the cottage, the pair seemed thrilled to be reunited.

Tania swore that Irena had scarcely altered at all, while

her aunt asserted that her beloved niece had changed completely.

"She was such a difficult child," she later confided to Pamela. "Having her mature into an elegant and talented young woman is a wonderful surprise."

"Tania's not had an easy life, but she seems no worse for that. And now that she's looking forward to another child she will have an even stronger marriage."

"With your brother, yes? I have always learned from Andre all that was happening here."

"Aye. Our Ian married her while Pamela Anichka was quite small. Pity they didn't get together in the first place, but we all thought they were much too young."

"And Pamela Anichka is in London now, yes? Shall she be coming here during the holiday?"

"I'm afraid I don't know. You'll have to ask Tania."

Pamela Anichka did not arrive, but both Stonemoor House and the cottage often seemed full nevertheless. With the rush of airport traffic over for a few days and most children discharged from hospital, Sonia was allowing herself more free time.

Nikolai *was* an attraction, she could not deny. No matter how distressed she had been by the shattering of her dreams about Rupert, she could not remain indifferent to this charismatic Russian. He was interested in her work – indeed, one day he'd accompanied her to the airport where he'd been fascinated by being shown around. Learning of her desire to travel, he began to quiz her about the countries she longed to visit. They sat together for hours while he explained the vastness and the variety of his homeland. And then Sonia began telling him of the places he should visit during his stay in Britain.

"You could take me there perhaps?" he suggested one evening while Sonia was describing the scenery of the Lake District.

"I should love that," she replied, and was surprised to discover that might become true. "Although we'd better wait a while; it's likely to be too cold for comfort up there in winter."

Nikolai laughed. "You forget perhaps that I am accustomed to weather far more severe than any we may encounter in your country."

Despite his remarks, they were reminded by Andre that it would not be sensible to begin touring the northern counties of England amid threats of the snow which would inevitably fall during the next few weeks.

"And, Sonia," he added seriously. "You must not overlook the fact that Nikolai is over here to work, just as you have a job demanding commitment."

But before work recommenced for Nikolai he became even more interesting to Sonia. Among the many things which her Aunt Irena was unpacking gradually were old photographs of Russian cities, among them many of Moscow which Irena herself had never visited.

"My mother sang there, I know," she told them. "Did you ever visit there with her, Andre?"

Although her brother shook his head, Nikolai was able to tell them about Moscow which he knew well. Describing the old buildings and some of the art and artefacts he had seen, he awakened in Sonia a longing to learn more about the culture that was a part of her inheritance.

"One day I want to see all that," she exclaimed. "We could go, couldn't we, Dad?"

Andre was frowning. Had this child of his no sense whatsoever? Did the time which had elapsed before he was able to get Irena away from the USSR tell her nothing?

Nikolai could not bear to see that attractive young girl so crestfallen. "Travel is much less difficult now," he reminded them. "Before very long I feel sure it will be more easy still."

There, thought Sonia, and gave her father another look. Andre appeared no happier about the prospect. But it is one half of me, she reflected; without learning what Russia

212

is about a part of me will remain incomplete. Refusing to be deterred by her father's attitude she encouraged Nikolai all the more while he examined Irena's pictures and described ways in which some of the major cities over there had altered.

By the time that Nikolai was obliged to take up his appointment at the embassy in London, the plans which he and Sonia had made were sufficient to sustain her. As soon as he was able to take time off for a holiday she would arrange to have all the leave owing to her. The sense of anticlimax normally descending after Christmas did not affect her. Even when the day of Mrs Singer's delayed funeral came, Sonia could feel anticipation of that holiday upholding her.

They were a pathetically small group in the church and afterwards at the crematorium. Andre and his son had located only four, quite distant, relatives of the old housekeeper. With the entire Malinowski family along- side them, they still appeared an inadequate gathering.

The church in Cragg Vale had a new vicar, one who evidently was causing quite a stir. Although none of them were regular members of the congregation, the family had heard about the Revd Robert Haverford's innovative services soon after his arrival.

Drawn by the feeling that his fresh approach might haul them out of the neglect of attending church, which was causing them regret, Pamela and Andre had joined the service one Sunday morning.

The first thing they noticed was the incense hanging in the cold air. Smiling to herself, Pamela was pleased to recognise an element familiar from her days of worship- ping in Halifax. When the service began with all the music and vestments of the Sung Eucharist she settled down to relish the experience. Beside her Andre seemed equally content. She tried to remember how long it was since formal religion had first been frowned upon in Russia, and whether he had spoken of ever being a practising Christian.

213

Despite the small size of the choir and the congregation, that day's service remained quite impressive. When the time came for Mrs Singer's funeral Pamela was feeling thankful that it would be conducted by this newcomer to their parish.

Even Robert Haverford could do little to overcome the sadness which was exacerbated by having so few mourners present. He had, though, persuaded six senior choristers to attend, and everyone there appreciated their lead during the hymns chosen by Mrs Singer's family.

The address was short, a carefully selected amalgam of the information Andre and his son had provided.

"We come here today to mark the life of Edith Singer, a woman who from birth was locked within her world of personal silence. An example to us all, she not only created a happy marriage with the man she cherished until his death – she also created her own, very special place within the family at Stonemoor House.

"When Andre Malinowski arrived in England alone and began making a home of that house, Mrs Singer soon became one of the keystones contributing to its happiness.

"With his second marriage and the growth of his family she more than fulfilled her role as housekeeper; she served them unstintingly and with – I'm told – affection.

"Their affection, in turn, is witnessed today, and will be in the future as, I am assured, she will live on in their memories."

"It could have been nearly as bad as when old Mrs Fawcett died," said Pamela to Andre, recalling the widow whose shop she had bought.

"But Mrs Singer was loved," Andre asserted gently. "By all of us, for a long number of years. Every word that priest said was true."

Pamela agreed, feeling thankful that after Mrs Singer's husband had died they had been able to provide all the home life she needed. Shivering, she had another thought, one which made her ashamed. How readily she might have condemned her own unmarried sister-in-law to loneliness, by denying her a place at Stonemoor.

Having Irena there could be made to work. In some ways, had begun to feel better during Christmas. The only real trouble was, Pamela acknowledged silently, that she herself felt far more insecure than she'd ever believed possible.

It was the silliest things that seemed to cause her the most distress. Like going to the shops and coming home to find Irena setting the table for a meal. *That's my job*, something inside her would scream. *If you continue like this I shan't have a place here.*

She hoped to God she'd never be overcome by the impulse to express such unforgivable emotions.

In many ways, and quite frequently, she was discovering she needed the company of this woman who had come from such a different background. Adjusting to these early days without their housekeeper seemed so difficult. Mrs Singer's enforced silence had always rendered her unobtrusive. Never having heard her voice made it all the harder now to realise that she was no longer there going about her normal duties. Pamela missed all those written conversations, however brief and halting. But she was compensated by chatting with Irena.

And talk they certainly did; her sister-in-law often surprised Pamela with some comparison between her old life and this new existence in Yorkshire. Like Tania, she had memories of farming folk in her background, but Irena also recounted her own mother's life as a professional singer. Then there were stories of Andre's early prowess with the violin, incidents and situations which his reticence had withheld even from his wife. Gradually, she was learning to know him more thoroughly through his sister's words, and subsequently to like her increasingly.

The day that Irena asked to be shown around the antiques shop generated a more complete understanding between them. The suggestion had been made over

215

breakfast while Pamela was feeling rather less than happy.

Andre had departed the previous evening for London where he was booked to play with the London Symphony Orchestra at the Festival Hall. This was the first occasion that he'd been away since all the changes immediately before Christmas; Pamela was afraid that she might begin counting the hours to his return.

The shop felt to be less hers than her son's now that Mihail had taken up so readily her suggestion that he should spend more time running the business. Without really thinking of the effect it might have upon him, she volunteered that morning to take over.

"And what would I do, Mum?" Mihail protested. "You know I'm up to date with any clocks and watches needing attention." He had repaired some of those at home during the Christmas holiday.

Annabel was going out almost every day now, driving over the hills to sketch various parts of West Yorkshire which were providing landscapes very different from her familiar Cotswolds. When the long dark evenings forced her to turn her little car towards Stonemoor, it often was in order to spend a few hours at her easel before their evening meal.

Mihail could be pleased that she was so contented there without denying his own disappointment that they spent so little time together.

Conscious now of his need to save for a home as well as to have an occupation, Pamela apologised. "Sorry, sorry – just wasn't thinking. Suppose I'm not adapting awfully well to having less to do."

"And what it is about your antiques that interests you so?" Irena enquired. "Their beauty perhaps?"

"Some of the time, yes. But some things are rather ugly. It's their history most of all. And the way you can see how various items have developed."

"That's especially true of clocks, and of watches," Mihail put in. "I suppose that's one reason I love them."

216

"I also am interested in history," Irena told them. "Since I was a girl and our grandmother told to me how it was in the old days, before the Revolution. There were many fine buildings in Russia, you understand, and great craftsmen. I must show to you pictures that I have of items created by Fabergé."

Inviting her to the shop was the best idea Pamela could have had. After Mihail had shown his aunt some of his favourite clocks, and turned away to attend to customers, Pamela took over and brought out silverware and paper-weights, cut crystal scent bottles. From her mahogany framed showcases she took jewellery, châtelaines, and thimbles.

But Irena was standing before a display of glassware.

"*Bakhmeteff!*" she exclaimed. "I am certain – or almost certain that this piece is from their glass house in Moscow."

Pamela had been unable to identify that particular item, and was delighted now not only to have its likely source, but to have discovered a common interest to be shared with Irena.

"You must come here again, whenever you wish; we will show you everything you'd like to see."

Irena beamed, her grey eyes alight. She was beginning to believe that Andre's wife was opening her heart to her.

Fifteen

Tania could not believe how swiftly the time had passed. It seemed only so recently that she had delighted Ian with the news that she was pregnant. And now her labour pains were starting.

She had suspected earlier that day, long before he went off to work, but she had let him go. Everyone these days seemed to believe that their husband must be present at the birth. Tania herself was less than happy with that particular prospect.

It might be twenty years since Pamela Anichka came into this world, but the time which had elapsed had failed to eradicate her own recollections of the event. She had looked a fright, and fright had been her predominating emotion! She was certain she had screamed out – if she screamed today, she would not have her beloved Ian witness such total cowardice.

Pamela would be with her. This stepmother of hers had been there for her that first time, and Tania had discovered she could have wanted no one better. Together, they had endured those hours, and had arranged already that for this baby they would endure again.

The biggest difference was that the infant must be born in hospital. These days, forty wasn't considered all that old for becoming a mother, but it still meant that extra care should be taken. Although she didn't mind too much about going into hospital, Tania was worrying about Ian.

"You will keep an eye on him, promise me?" she insisted between contractions in the car.

Pamela smiled. "I will, of course. But you shouldn't be

fussing about that brother of mine. Ian's coped on his own before, hasn't he?"

"Not like this, though, when he will be in a state about the baby. And when it is here he will be dashing back and forth to visit us. I am sure he will forget to eat anything."

Her stepmother laughed. "Nay, love – our Ian's not daft, he'll get something when he's hungry. But I promise I'll ask him to come to Stonemoor for a meal every night while you're not at home."

The pains were more frequent by the time they reached the ward, and growing quite intense. Pamela hoped that Tania wouldn't have a long labour. The poor lass looked so fragile despite that lump. And she knew how exhausting giving birth became. The easy time she'd had with Mihail had in no way prepared her for the struggle before their Sonia had appeared.

They had brought books and magazines with them today, but exchanged rueful smiles when they both recognised that neither of them could concentrate.

"As if we could think about anything else!" Tania exclaimed. "Even though they have told me that nothing will happen for some while yet."

"Are you going to work next season?" Pamela asked, and hoped suddenly that Tania might wish her to look after the baby, if only for a few hours while she performed on platforms close to home.

Tania shrugged. "I do not know. It seems sometimes that I have been singing for too many years already. Even when there are new pieces to learn, the routine of rehearsals and performances does grow a little wearisome."

"Really?" her stepmother was astonished. To her, the careers which both Andre and Tania pursued always seemed so glamorous, and rewarding.

Tania waited while a fresh onslaught of pain subsided then nodded. "If perhaps there was opportunity to sing as I used to with a contemporary band, I might enjoy doing lighter songs. But then there is the quality of my voice – that is not so good as it used to be."

"Nay, I'll not have that! The last time I went to hear you, you were just as brilliant as ever."

Another pain gripped Tania, but seemed somehow less racking. The warmth generated by Pamela's remark felt to be easing her through it.

"God, but you are a wonderful mother!" she exclaimed. "I can hardly remember a time when you were not around for me. Had my own mother lived, she could not have been more reassuring." And if Pamela's words regarding her voice were generous rather than accurate, they were exactly what she needed. Even before becoming pregnant, Tania had grown concerned about her future career. Her range was diminishing, she felt sure, and there were occasions when the original clarity no longer existed.

"Do not tell my father of my feelings about my career, please. Not any of it – he would hate me for liking my singing less, and would be anxious if he learned how my skills are reducing."

"And what does Ian say?"

"Ian?" Tania shook her head. "I have told none of this to him. Only to you have I been completely honest."

"Thank you," Pamela murmured, her eyes filling with emotion.

Her stepdaughter chuckled ruefully. "I am glad that you view it as a compliment. Certainly, confidences do witness to a person being very good at listening."

As a further surge of pain seized her, Tania wanted to laugh, even though she could not. Life really was so strange – contriving so completely to turn on their head all those evil thoughts she once had entertained towards this woman now beside her. She could have hated no one more, yet now Pamela was the one person with whom she never dissembled.

Her father cared too much ever to be entrusted with her innermost doubts and fears. And Ian she loved too well for disturbing him with her misgivings.

"Perhaps I am a sham," she murmured aloud. "Since I was a girl I have hidden behind my singing. I wonder now if I should recognise myself without that ability."

Pamela grinned, reached out and stroked the dampened hair away from Tania's forehead.

"Happen you might find that doesn't matter too much, so long as we all recognise you. And I'm looking forward to seeing the capable little mother you were before, especially now this baby'll be our Ian's as well!"

Tania could only nod. The pains were taking her breath, tearing at her insides, following so rapidly now that she no longer counted seconds. The midwife came while she was willing herself not to scream.

And then she could contain the yells no longer. "Help me, Mother!" she cried, and felt Pamela's fingers in hers.

Her stepmother wept, moved beyond speech by that final word, from a forty-year-old woman who originally had resisted acknowledging the nature of the relationship that bound them. I shall tell Andre, she thought. And hoped he would understand her feeling that she might have succeeded with Tania.

Guiltily, Pamela dismissed her own emotions and intentions, and wished there was more she could do while Tania battled through the final stages of labour. She wasn't here for her own good, was she, to have her own ego boosted! She was here for Tania, and for that child now forcing its way into the world.

"It's a lovely little lad!" the midwife exclaimed eventually, beaming around and holding the blood-spattered infant aloft for Tania to see. "We'll just wrap him up nice and warm then you can hold him."

"He looks a bit like Mihail," Pamela observed when Tania was holding the baby for a few moments before resting.

"And so he should. It was seeing Mihail that made me want babies all those years ago. Ian will be glad to have a son." And, Tania thought, a boy should cause us less anxiety than we have had over Pamela Anichka.

"Will you tell everyone?" she asked her stepmother. "And that I shall be all right. Dad has PA's number. I believe Ian will be too busy rushing here to think of ringing her."

Pamela Anichka's response was a surprise. Having been told her reaction to Tania's pregnancy, Pamela antici- pated indifference, even irritation. Instead of that, PA began crying.

"I'm very pleased for them, I am truly. And I am so thankful that Mum is okay. I've been so afraid . . ."

"Eh, love – you ought to have said. One of us could have reassured you that the doctors were happy about her. Forty isn't old nowadays for having a youngster."

"I know, I do know. I was just that scared I might lose her. Not living at home doesn't mean I've stopped caring."

Pamela told Ian that night, although she was unsure how much he was taking in of anyone's conversation. He had spent most of the day at his wife's bedside, and was enraptured with their infant.

"We're going to call him after our Tom and Andre," he said. "Thomas Andre Baker. Tom's already said he wants to be a godparent."

"And who else will you have?"

"Do you think Mihail would like to be? And Sonia?"

"If she's at home when the time comes. She's set her heart on showing Nikolai around the whole country by the sound of it. I'm sure Mihail would be pleased though."

Pamela wished that Sonia might be so happy to become a godmother that she would reorganise her plans if necess- ary, but it was a vain hope. Both she and Andre had been surprised by the change in their daughter when Nikolai rang to say that he was visiting Yorkshire and wished to call on them.

From spending hours in that children's ward at the hospital, Sonia became obsessed by arranging all the free time she could to be with Nikolai. Working shifts at Manchester airport meant that she quite often had mornings or afternoons off, and they used them to the full, travelling all over Yorkshire.

The proposed trip to the Lake District was another thing to make Andre deeply anxious.

"I do not like this at all," he told Pamela one night in bed. "Who can say what their arrangements for sleeping will be? She is an attractive young woman . . ."

"And he's a gorgeous-looking chap, but not the first she's ever seen," Pamela went on. "We can only trust them, Andre. We brought her up properly, and will just have to hope that she will be sensible."

"Sensible? I fear that good sense will not be among the senses which will dominate their time together. We know what these times are like, do we not – have seen it all throughout the past decade."

Andre might have been reassured had he known that Sonia had insisted to Nikolai that they should book separate rooms. But even that fact would not have alleviated a prospect fast developing into Andre's greatest dread.

He knew his younger daughter. He had seen how she had so readily become friendly with Rupert Atherton-Ward, and guessed the cause of her distress following their last meeting at Mihail's wedding. Had Nikolai been an Englishman, Andre might have been thankful that his sudden arrival had cheered Sonia so completely. But Nikolai was not English, nor was he a permanent resident here. However firmly established his position within the Russian embassy might seem, the situation there could alter in a moment. Nikolai might be on his way back to Moscow at any time, and Andre needed no imagination to supply the notion of what Sonia's reaction would be. She would not let Nikolai just go off there, or not without a fight. Conversations with the pair of them simply confirmed that they were growing devoted to each other. And so Andre had tackled his daughter alone, sounded her out.

"I have nothing against Nikolai, you understand," he had begun.

Naturally, Sonia had groaned. "But?"

"I wonder if you have contemplated what the future may hold for him, my dear? These embassy situations are notoriously unstable – even where the Iron Curtain does not create additional difficulties. I do not want for you to become too attached to someone who might before all that long be obliged to leave this country."

Sonia had said nothing, but she had smiled. And in her steady gaze Andre had read that his daughter had already faced this possibility, and had reached a conclusion which did not dismay her.

She would go, he knew that now. If for some reason that young man should return to Russia, Sonia had no intention of having him go out of her life completely.

It would break his heart. He was no longer young – at sixty-two he was beginning to feel tired by concert rehearsals; most of all by the travelling so often obligatory. He felt stung by the irony of having this new anxiety occur as a result of his determination to have Irena live safely with them in England. And yet he could never wish that anyone might have chosen differently concerning his sister.

Sonia would never comprehend the dangers and the insecurities he had endured before leaving his homeland; he could not make her understand the reasons behind his alarm. Unable to express these deep-seated fears for her, he must lock them within his soul and allow her to enjoy her journeys around Britain with Nikolai. And hope that nothing occasioned their journeying any further. He could only pray that Sonia would somehow change her opinion of that young man.

And pray Andre did. He and Pamela were attending the local church regularly since meeting the new vicar there. Becoming a part of the congregation had brought them several acquaintances, and best of all a young woman who was happy to come in daily and help with household chores.

For Pamela's sake, Andre was glad, and not only to have her relieved of additional work.

"You seem very happy now, my darling."

Andre was smiling that particular evening, delighted that Pamela was spending more time at home. Most of all, he was pleased that she was more content to be there. He had had a reasonably good concert season, but now they were into the summer of 1970 and he was glad to relax.

She grinned back at him. "All right, say it – you could have told me that I'd be thankful for Irena's company!"

He shook his head. "Indeed not – I admit quite freely that I was concerned that you and she might not get along. Concerned also that you would not readily hand over so much responsibility for the antiques business to Mihail."

Pamela laughed. "Always poor at delegating, is that what you think I am?" When her husband thought better of replying, she continued. "Mihail has proved himself, that's all that matters now. He couldn't be more keen, and it's good for him. Sitting over timepieces he was repairing didn't provide much company."

"Whereas he now manages to do both."

"The interesting restorations, yes. And he enjoys teaching that young apprentice."

Andre nodded. Accepting that his only son should choose such an undistinguished career had taken years. Only Mihail's satisfaction had convinced him they had been right to go along with his ambitions. These days, Andre's private longing on Mihail's behalf went no further than yearning to have his skills find greater recognition.

Regarding this son of his, Andre had a great deal to make him deeply thankful. Within days of Mrs Singer's funeral service, the family had again become disturbed when Mihail was called to be a witness against Ivor Smith and his former tutor Jack Denham.

Determined to do everything possible to support his son, Andre had insisted that he would accompany him to court. Initially, Mihail had protested that it was quite

225

unnecessary – Lance Atherton-Ward had provided ample professional advice when the trouble first emerged; he would be there for him again.

"I don't want any fuss, Dad. Shall feel embarrassed enough being called to give evidence, as it is."

Andre had refused to listen. Mihail was *his* son, was he not? It would be a poor father who neglected to stand by him. And as for Atherton-Ward, he could like the man and respect his professional ability without wishing to surrender Mihail to him!

Mihail surprised his father in court. Although speaking quietly as was his custom, his voice was steady as well as clear; his entire demeanour revealed a maturity which jolted Andre into sudden recognition of fresh qualities.

He really does not need me, he was right, he thought, and was torn by conflicting emotions. Pride, yes – of this young man standing so calmly to give evidence as eloquent as it was concise, he was proud. But somewhere along the way he had lost that boy – the golden-haired youngster who more than either of his two daughters seemed always to have shown Andre Malinowski what he himself was about.

They talked on the last evening when the case was over, sitting over their wine in a hotel. Relieved yet still perturbed on behalf of his former friends, Mihail tried to express the division of loyalties which seemed to exist deep within him.

"Is it because of who we are?" he asked his father. "Is that why I feel unable entirely to condemn what they were doing? Is a part of me somehow hankering to experience the quality of allegiance which makes men behave with such disregard for their potential safety?"

Andre shook his head. "It is nothing to do with us, no part of who we are, my son," he stated fervently. "White Russians are not the ones who fight . . ."

"But I thought they did," Mihail interrupted. "You told me – your own father joined that volunteer army."

"A long time ago," snapped Andre. "Nothing to do with our attitude now, with who we are."

Mihail let that go. While wishing to spare his father attendance at that trial, he had been touched by his insistence on being present. He owed him now the peace in which to accommodate the effects of the whole experience. It had been easy for no one, and Mihail could only guess at the emotions it might have aroused in someone plagued for so many years by the need to avoid all possible links with Communism.

They talked instead of Lance Atherton-Ward and of his family, into which Mihail had always been welcomed so unstintingly. Glad though he was to learn more about them all, Andre found his concentration wandering.

Perhaps Mihail was not so dreadfully wrong, after all – it could be that their Russian ancestry created within them today a conflict far greater than any among English people. Someone who had suffered less than he had might feel a certain sympathy for men who chose either side. The Revolution had been provoked when people felt oppressed, when they sought a more just future.

Suddenly Andre smiled, raised his glass. "To you, Mihail, you have a fine head. Perhaps you are not altogether wrong. It may well be that inherent in us we find the very conflict which permits men to see the other side of the argument."

Andre was thinking back to that conversation when Irena came in from the garden to join them for supper, and they switched on the radio as usual to catch up with the news. Pamela would have preferred to turn on the television, but Andre had never been happy about viewing during mealtimes.

They were sitting over coffee when the telephone rang. "Could be Sonia," said Andre and rushed to answer it.

"He is anxious once more, I think," Irena said, her smile understanding.

"It is over a week since we heard," Pamela remarked.

227

"And even if they're no further away than the Lake District we'll never stop him being a worried father."

"No doubt you also worry about Sonia."

"Not quite so diligently! She's a sensible girl, and Nikolai takes good care of her."

But the caller was Ian, wishing to speak to his sister.

"What is it, love?" Pamela asked, taking the receiver. "Tania's all right, isn't she? And the baby?"

"Both fine. It's nothing like that. Just thought you'd be interested in seeing this house that Canning's is to renovate. Same period as Stonemoor; could be a candidate for similar decor. And it has a quantity of original oak panelling."

"Don't say you're asking me to advise!" his sister exclaimed. It was ages now since she'd done more than sit on the board of her old firm. She knew how much her brother relished the fact that he was in charge, while the other directors were little more than sleeping partners.

Ian laughed. "No, I wouldn't say that! You know as well as I do how long it took for me to gain a bit of responsibility. Joking apart, though – thought you'd enjoy taking a look. And you might prove more persuasive if they need convincing about style . . ."

Outwardly, the house was beautiful. Constructed in sandstone which, if it were cleaned, would gleam in the sunlight as pleasingly as Stonemoor House. Built as it was on a hill, where it had received decades of soot from the mills of Huddersfield, its exterior did witness to the distinction between country air like their own and a town's.

Internally, the hall instantly reminded Pamela of home, making her smile widen while Ian introduced her to the owner. Felicia Raven started to explain her ideas on restoration.

"Did Mr Baker, here, tell you antiques are my line of business? Used to work in one of the major auction houses. These days, I'm developing a programme in

228

conjunction with a television company." Beginning to show them around, Felicia continued that she could not consider anything less than an authentic appearance for her home. "I understand you did something very like that with your own place?"

Pamela smiled. "Years ago, and before it was mine, yes. Actually, I then married the owner."

"Good way of getting precisely what you want! But I gather you're no longer actively engaged in restoration?"

"No, I leave that to Ian and his team. But I could, of course, advise on methods, especially for this lovely panelling. Just so long as no one wants me to tackle it myself," she added ruefully. "Renovating ours really was a job and a half."

Felicia swiftly agreed to having the oak panelling restored. In each of the rooms she invited them to indicate what they believed would be the most appropriate decoration.

"What do you think, Pamela?" Ian prompted. He was used to having his head now, so could be generous about other people possessing ideas.

She considered for a minute or two. Internally, this house was different from Stonemoor; no trace of any original wall coverings had survived which meant there was no opportunity purely to renovate their condition. That fact, though, need not prevent them from adopting the period style.

"When I began on Stonemoor, I had the advantage that several walls retained designs incorporating lots of symbols from the Egyptian campaign," said Pamela.

"Scarabs, you mean, and sphinx heads?" Felicia suggested.

"That's right. I managed to clean and touch them up, and replaced only the decor surrounding the panels. Here – well, we might consider panels again and outlined with such devices. If none of our employees could reproduce them, we'd employ somebody freelance."

"Sounds good."

"I also used a lot of striped wallpaper – that was popular in Regency times. Glad to see you've still got the windows with those narrow glazing bars," she added. "They do enhance the period feel."

When every room had been discussed, Felicia Raven proved a ready listener, and soon was agreeing to be guided by their suggestions. Leading them back to a ground floor reception room, she offered coffee.

Pamela was standing in front of an elaborate clock when their hostess returned with a tray. "Forgive me, but I couldn't help noticing this. I specialise in clocks, you know, in my shop. This is one of those mystery clocks, isn't it?"

Felicia nodded. "And the biggest mystery is why it refuses to work! I've had it taken to a very good man who normally solves every problem with timepieces, but unfortunately, this baffled him completely."

"They can be tricky. My son could have had quite a time with the one he tackled not long since, but he managed it in the end."

"Did he indeed? Sounds as though he's a person one should cultivate."

"He's certainly worked wonders with just about everything I've put his way. But then, Mihail's very keen – has been since he was just a bit of a lad."

"Do I take it that he only does work for your own business?"

Pamela grinned. "Think he's got more sense than that! Though I must admit since he came down from Oxford, he's not had much opportunity for repairing things for other folk."

"But he would do – for me? I would pay above the going rate, of course."

As soon as Mihail saw the clock his blue eyes lit up. "Gosh, that is superb! I thought that other one I did was a lovely piece, but this is even better quality. I shall enjoy getting to work on that."

With a characteristic grin, he tried to reassure his

mother: "I shan't neglect the shop, mind. Nor any clocks you need restoring."

From that day, however, Felicia Raven's timepiece took precedence over any other work. Annabel teased him when he came home late of an evening, but the attention she devoted to her painting helped her understand his sense of priorities.

When the clock was working again and the figure suspending its pendulum cleaned, Mihail was delighted. He also rather wished that he might have it for his own. One day, he promised himself; one day when we've completed furnishing the house and may purchase luxuries. He and Annabel were to buy the cottage that Ian and Tania were now vacating for a larger detached home near Mytholmroyd.

Felicia Raven was thrilled to have the clock working again, and visited the shop to thank Mihail personally.

"When your uncle brought it home to us I was ecstatic. And I also became determined to see what you have on offer here. I gather your mother's the one who opened up this business."

Mihail nodded. "When I was a baby. She used to bring me here; I had a playpen in the back of the shop there. I always believe that's how I became so interested in things like this, sort of grew up with them."

"And you're self-taught?"

"Mainly, yes. I read a lot of books about old timepieces, of course. And I got a wider experience of mending them while I was at Oxford." Mihail stifled a sigh. He rarely let himself think about that tiny shop there, much less speak of it. He'd never really accept being responsible for the sentences Jack Denham and Ivor Smith had received.

"And when you're not in the shop, do you have an assistant who comes in?"

Puzzled by her question, he shook his head. "No, I've an apprentice, though, learning the repair work. He's on holiday this week."

"And if you take holidays yourself – does the shop have to close?"

"Oh, no, no. Mum comes in then, it's still her business really; I just run it for her."

"There is a reason for asking," Felicia continued. "Your mother or uncle may have told you – I'm working on a project for television, a programme scheduled for next year. About all manner of antiques. Wondered if you'd be willing to appear – with some of the watches and clocks you've restored; tell viewers about them."

"Well, I – well, this is a surprise! I suppose I might. Thank you for suggesting me, but I don't quite know if I'd be any good. I mean – all I do is—"

"Give new life to beautiful objects like these which otherwise would remain inert, dead. I'm sure you feel as I do that clocks are living things. You might also think about discussing items which are brought onto the programme. The idea is that people will come along with treasured possessions, learn their history and so on, share with the viewer their excitement when they're told of their value."

Excitement was the emotion inflaming Mihail now – contrary to his usually reserved nature, and to a degree which astonished him.

"I'd love to do it, yes. Thank you, thank you so much. I still don't know what I'll be like, but I do want to have a go."

Sixteen

A pilot for the television series was to be shown in the early summer of 1971. The entire family was delighted that Mihail had been asked to appear in that very first one, but he was less wholehearted about the occasion. Given time to dwell on appearing before the cameras, he had concluded that he had been insane to agree. The worst part of the whole business was the fact that most of it would be unscripted. Felicia and he, along with all the other experts, would rehearse any introductory passages, as for instance when the presenter questioned him about restoring clocks. When the general public brought items forward for information, however, they would be speaking off the cuff.

Sensing how afraid his son was that he would stammer or dry up altogether, Andre took him aside one Sunday morning.

"You have got away lightly, you know," he told Mihail. "Never until now have you been expected to perform in public. But there must be something of me in you somewhere. Just as there is in Tania – we learned to present ourselves tolerably well in front of an audience; you will do so also, in time."

"But television, Dad, think of all those millions of people . . ."

Andre grinned. "Ah, but in their own homes, do not forget. You, Mihail, will not be able to see them!"

Still not really reassured, his son gave him a rueful look. Andre considered for a moment, smiled his

233

understanding. "I know, Mihail, I do know really. You are an unassuming young man who has never sought publicity. But maybe the time is here for you to make people more aware of your skills. Your skills and your tenacity. Too many young people today are only eager to pursue glamour, or easy money. You are not like that, and I thank God for that."

It was a long speech for Andre, one which indicated more faith in his son's qualities than Mihail expected. And it changed his attitude. He knew that he hadn't altered basically; appearing in that show would be difficult, an ordeal, but he would do it. He had to, if only to prove his father's words could be justified.

Sonia was watching in Pamela Anichka's London flat. She had been told the date and time of transmission, naturally, and reminded of it on each occasion that she had telephoned home. Nikolai wasn't with them. He was busy at the embassy. Increasingly now, meetings there were arranged suddenly, with scarcely any warning.

Sonia was disappointed that he would miss the programme. She needed him to see what her family could achieve. All along she'd been acutely aware of how little she'd done with her own life. Whereas Nikolai had this important position, so important that he'd been brought over to England from Russia.

She had never met anyone like him, and still felt surprised that he seemed so interested in her. They'd had a fabulous time together, right from that first day when they set out for the Lake District.

On that spring morning over a year ago now, they had chatted throughout the drive over country roads that meandered up into and beyond the Yorkshire Dales. Stopping for a meal when Borrowdale was in sight, they'd continued talking until it was time to head towards their hotel beside Windermere lake.

Just on the fringe of Ambleside, the grey stone house stood near the water's edge, the view from its windows magnificent as a faint mist hung over the distant mountains.

Nikolai, who'd considered the scenery around Stonemoor beautiful, had stood immobile, barely able to speak.

"I shall never forget this place," he had said eventually. "And never forget you for showing it to me."

Their relationship reached a different plane. They spoke rather less during dinner, yet somehow communicated more because of sharing such an exquisite spot with each other.

Nikolai had kissed her that night, a real kiss, quite unlike the fun kisses exchanged beneath mistletoe during that first Christmas at Stonemoor. Parting to go to their rooms, Sonia had recognised how mature he was, and silently thanked the circumstances that had brought her this young man, who awakened attraction while leaving her unafraid.

Their tour of the Lake District had progressed with fun and laughter, and many moments revealing deep affection. They had walked the fells, strolled through villages and beside the many lakes, at one with the tranquillity and with each other.

As that holiday was ending Sonia's only consolation had been the plans they were making to visit Stratford-upon-Avon in the autumn. There again, they each had relished the other's company while exploring the glorious countryside. And Nikolai had insisted they must see every possible production at the theatre.

His love of Shakespeare became so strong that while visiting Stonemoor House for a second Christmas he suggested they should return to Stratford as soon as the 1971 season started.

They celebrated the anniversary of their trip to the Lakes there, and talked as they never had in the past – of the future which they might spend together.

Nikolai never revealed much detail of his homelife back in Moscow; Sonia knew only that he had neither brothers nor sisters. He mentioned no word of what his father did, but the occasional hint had suggested to her that he might be attached to some aspect of the diplomatic service.

Nikolai's background had seemed to matter less to her as weeks again went by and she recognised how fond she had grown of him. When he rang her late one night, she could only agree to what he was suggesting.

"I am missing you quite terribly, my sweet, and I cannot get away to come to Yorkshire. Can you think of any means of spending some time in London?"

Sonia was elated to learn how much Nikolai needed to have her with him. She reached the decision after only a couple of hours' deliberation. This year she would be twenty-one. For so long she had planned to leave her position on the ground staff at the airport in order to begin training as an air hostess.

She would quit her present job just as soon as they would release her, and then spend time with Nikolai before commencing her training. Explaining to her parents wasn't easy, but she chose the simplest route through her mother. And she tried not to listen while they argued over the wisdom of her decision.

Nikolai's delight when she rang him with the news reassured her completely. "We shall have the happiest of times together in London. And although I will be obliged to go into the office, that need not be every day. During the rest of your visit I shall concentrate on assuring you that we should be equally happy anywhere in the world."

It was further reference to their joint future, almost a proposal of marriage, Sonia thought, a glow of utter contentment warming her. This seemed to be the culmination of all her dreams – dreams which had begun such an age ago when she was longing for some person who would be special only to her.

Here in London they visited theatres too, and the occasional concert. They saw a play by Anton Chekov which encouraged Nikolai to tell her more about Russia.

This led to a more serious discussion about their future, and how and where it might be shared, and if she would be prepared, when the time came, to go with him to the land of her ancestors.

"You cannot ignore that part of you forever, Sonia. I wish only to make you feel complete – and I belicve that will come about when you experience the country which is your inheritance."

More almost than his declaration of needing her with him, these words made Sonia long to agree. She'd always wanted to see Russia. Nikolai was fun and he was kind. He was so attractive that she already spent hours imagining how it would be to love him. Her parents might not be too happy about such an arrangement, but they should not be surprised. All along she had felt this urge to see more of the world; and these days travelling between East and West really was growing easier.

She would soon come of age; they should be reassured that she was old enough to cope. Even if Nikolai did not feel ready to marry immediately.

"Would we stay with your parents perhaps, is that what you intend?" she asked. That way, her own people would realise the situation was no different from the occasions when they had welcomed Nikolai at Stonemoor.

"We shall decide such details when the time comes, my love," he responded with a smile. "But you may be assured I shall take good care of you wherever we are."

It was almost time for the programme in which her brother would appear.

"I wonder what Mihail will be like, PA? Can't imagine him coming across as any different than my rather quiet brother."

Pamela Anichka gave her look. Was Sonia testing her? Was she desperate to learn how she still felt about Mihail, after all this time? PA shrugged, sank onto the sofa, lit a cigarette, stared at its flare of fire.

237

Was that tiny red glow the cause of this wateriness in her eyes?

She blinked. "He'll – be all right. Yes, definitely all right. Don't forget he went to Oxford. That gives you a certain poise." So they say, PA thought, and reflected that she might have benefited from university. She often wondered recently if she hadn't been an almighty fool. She wasn't thick – she could have got to Oxford if she'd tried, couldn't she? A year later than him perhaps, but she'd have been there. He'd have shown her the ropes. That way, he'd not have got tied up with that Annabel . . .

Oh, her job in Carnaby Street was exciting; she never tired of selling fashionable clothes to such colourful people, and even if it wasn't *hers* – the boutique she'd once dreamed of owning – she'd made herself indispensable to her boss.

The thing that had upset Pamela Anichka, arousing this discontent, was the news Sonia had brought. Learning that Mihail and that woman were now living in her old home perturbed her. The cottage would always remain too familiar, presenting too many remembered scenes of evenings spent with Mihail. And fresh scenes too – of Annabel with him.

They'll be watching at Stonemoor, thought Sonia, picturing them all seated around the set. Grandma might be there, unless that husband she'd acquired had bought them a television. She missed Grandma Baker, or Vickers as she'd become. They rarely saw her since she'd been taken to live in that unfamiliar house those few miles away from the cosy terraced one.

Annabel would be at Stonemoor tonight. Neither Mum nor Dad would let her watch the broadcast alone. Although the programme had been recorded, Mihail had been invited to view their efforts along with the other experts who'd participated.

More strongly than ever during any absence from Cragg Vale, Sonia could see her home, the large sitting room refurbished so beautifully by her mother, the longcase clock which had inspired Mihail's career. She could smell logs blazing in the Regency fireplace, hear the breeze rustling that nearby tree, its branches tapping on their windows.

"It's starting at last."

PA's words brought her back to the London flat, and Sonia grew aware of the other girl's tension. She does still love him, she thought, and caught herself wondering if she felt as much for Nikolai. Would she still care if their love were forbidden, if he married someone else?

Pamela Anichka watched Sonia, envying her the freedom to go after some chap who offered her such a fresh beginning abroad. She herself had made too many mistakes, without willing them to happen. Too young to begin to understand, she had so easily become enraptured. And here he was now – within that tiny screen. In *her home*, as he never would be in reality.

Standing, in profile, Mihail appeared fatter, yet rather shorter than she recalled, but was that by comparison with the longcase clock he was describing? No one but she would notice that the smile he gave its owner was nervous. His voice was achingly familiar.

"Yes, indeed, a splendid example – by Jeremiah Standing of Bolton, circa 1780. Someone has cherished this clock for centuries, just see the exquisite condition of its carved mahogany case."

"Isn't he clever!" Sonia exclaimed when Mihail paused to take in the owner's comment.

Oh, yes, PA thought. Clever enough to get himself noticed now, to acquire a bit of polish too, doubtless to impress his wealthy in-laws. But then, he always had one advantage, being the favoured son.

"I'd miss my brother, you know, if I didn't see him pretty often." Sonia exclaimed when the camera focused on another expert.

Pamela Anichka gave her a look. "He used to think you were terribly soft when you were little."

The other girl laughed. "That's what brothers do – got to, haven't they? And we've got on well ever since. Never scrapped like lots of siblings."

Maybe not, thought PA, but he and I were sharing so much that he didn't give you much attention.

A while later Mihail reappeared on the screen. A collection of pocket watches received his attention now; he was inspecting each in turn, his commentary even and composed. The information meant little to the girls, or only as confirmation that he had done his homework.

As though for the first time ever, it occurred to PA that Mihail had passed beyond her reach. Not because of any dubious elevation engendered through appearing on TV, but by choosing a life where she featured no more strongly than as a part of his history – of his growing-up.

"He looks fatter, don't you think?" she remarked quite sharply. She did not suppose that woman of his knew a thing about sensible eating.

Sonia grinned. "Actually, I thought he seemed older somehow, rather distinguished. Very like Dad – as he always used to be."

Tears sprang to eyes which moments ago had been laughing. She hoped Dad would be thinking of her, missing her, wondering if she was watching Mihail. And Mum – she would be so proud, so thankful that for this moment her son was showing the world the knowledge he'd acquired. Was showing them that he hadn't been misguided in insisting on a job where he felt fulfilled.

I wish I was there, Sonia thought. London is Pamela Anichka's world, it isn't mine. Stonemoor is where I belong.

Mihail appeared one more time, with some complex marine chronometer which sounded so intricate that Sonia could not follow his description. That did not matter. He was her brother, and she was full of emotion because of seeing him in this other world of his, and knowing that he, as much as she, belonged in their Yorkshire valley. She would see him there soon, needed to tell him – tell them all – as much as she could of what she was feeling.

Never once while she was with Nikolai had she felt homesick, but homesick she was now, and to a degree that even the prospect of seeing him the next day was making precious little difference.

Coming to London had been a mistake. Oh, she could enjoy the lively ambience, love visiting theatres and restaurants; but she wasn't entirely comfortable in a huge city.

The thought of being near to Nikolai had ceased to sustain her. Moscow could be far worse, with no prospect then of dashing home for a break . . .

Andre could not sleep. For once in his life, he was too full of sheer joy to be able to rest. Since the day earlier that year when he'd opened the door to find Sonia on the step his relief had increased and developed into this immense elation.

"I'm home, Dad," she had said. No other words mattered.

Beside him in the bed Pamela stirred, sighed, and glanced towards him. "Still not sleeping properly, are you, love? What's wrong?"

His chuckle was quiet. "You will not believe it – I am too happy, I think. Too full of emotion. It is not good perhaps to be granted so much of what one wishes."

"What a funny thing to say, just when everything's come right. Getting Irena over here, having our Sonia arrive home."

"I knew you would think me mad, or a little deranged. I do not understand myself."

"I'll make us a nice cup of tea," Pamela suggested, reaching for her housecoat. She would enjoy a private few minutes with Andre before everyone else was about. Fond though she had grown of her sister-in-law and

241

greatly as she would love hearing about Sonia's training course, she needed this time with her husband.

"I would prefer that we walked; would you mind terribly, my darling?"

She gave Andre a grin and began looking out yesterday's clothes. They were fortunate this was Sunday; she could take a bath whenever she wished with no prospect of rushing to open the shop.

The morning was cool even for September and they walked briskly uphill towards the moors. Andre reached for his wife's hand, squeezed her fingers. Remembering was so good, and they had so much to remember. So many years had rolled on since they first walked these paths together. Years bearing as many ups and downs as those contoured within the valleys and slopes surrounding Stonemoor.

He gazed now over to the right, looking back towards that obelisk which directed their eyes towards the heavens. And then ahead lay the craggy summit near which he had poured out his heart, *his love* to this dear woman. From all these familiar hills, as he well knew, the view spread wide into a distance so great that he imagined one might almost reach towards infinity.

"You are not hungry, I hope?" Andre enquired, yearning to continue upwards until they gained the moors where one major route into Lancashire converged with their own road. It was at that point where he always felt he stood at the top of the world; where he experienced such a massive awareness of freedom.

"Actually, love, I do feel ready for breakfast," said Pamela. "And we don't want everyone wondering where we've got to."

Andre smiled, however ruefully. "Then just up through the fields here to our left, instead. That will take only a few minutes."

Her hand still in his, Pamela felt the energy driving Andre as he set a good pace, striding up the grassy incline. Secretly, she smiled. He called this a field, but

242

it was closer in texture to the moors themselves, had witnessed, she suspected, no cultivation in centuries. The scrubby turf sprang from uneven ground, a mass of humps and hollows. Low growing plants formed clumps which in season would produce bilberries.

They reached the hill's crest and, satisfied, Andre gazed all around them. If not quite so dramatic here, the view conveyed an equal symbol of space, of liberation.

"This is all I need," he murmured, drew their clasped hands to his chest. Standing there, a breeze stirring their hair while it cleared sleep from their eyes, the realisation came to him; dispersed the final strands of his unease. "I have been a fool," he confessed, startling Pamela into staring in surprise.

"Not you, Andre, you're too cautious for that."

He laughed, the glint in his grey eyes wry. "But that is exactly it – I have been too cautious always. For Tania, since I extricated her from Russia, and for Mihail – you will never know how torn apart I felt over him. How deeply I cared that he must go to Oxford, yet all along yearned to keep him safely with us at Stonemoor. And Sonia as well – poor girl, how I struggled to prevent her from travelling!"

"Only because you were worried for their safety. You're too hard on yourself, my love."

Andre shook his head. He knew, saw more sharply today than ever in the past. This place, this whole expanse of Yorkshire had made him free, free to be himself. Why had it taken him so long to permit his family that same liberty?

Unperturbed, Pamela smiled, teased him into running downhill with her towards Stonemoor.

She did not understand, Andre knew, could not comprehend how selfishly he had attempted to hold his children to him. He would not try again to explain; he preferred that she should not realise how misguided had been his reasoning.

Irena was eating bacon and eggs, sipping from her glass of Russian tea, and smiled as they hastened in through the kitchen door.

"Good morning," she greeted them warmly. "I have cooked some food for you also. You will forgive that I could not wait."

"Of course." Pamela hurried across to kiss her. "Andre wanted a walk. I hope you weren't worried?"

"I heard you go out through the door. I was sure it must be you – I did not really expect that young Sonia would be dressed so early."

"Especially during her hard work training to be an air stewardess!" Pamela exclaimed. "She looked tired out. We're hardly dressed, anyway, we just flung on whatever was close to hand. I haven't had a bath yet."

Irena's smile was wide. "That is good – it shows that you no longer consider me a visitor, no? You feel comfortable enough now to behave as though I was not here."

Andre looked rather uncertain whether that might or might not be good, but Pamela was sure.

"Aye, love – that's just it. You fit in that well here, that I don't have to bother."

"Aunt Irena's a dear," Sonia agreed from the doorway to the hall. "She'd make herself useful anywhere, and just sort of – blend in."

"What is this 'blend'?" Irena teased. "Are you saying I should be making your fruit juice?"

"Thanks for offering! But you *know* what I mean," Sonia protested. "We haven't yet caught you out failing to understand."

Looking towards her brother, Irena winked. "But of course I must understand everything that you say – all of you – you always tell me such nice compliments!"

Pamela went to have a hasty wash, her heart all but erupting with pleasure. This sister of Andre's truly was so special, had endeared herself to them all. Despite every one of her own early misgivings.

They were lazing with the Sunday papers before lunch – a meal cooking itself now after Pamela's preparation, aided by both Sonia and Irena. Sonia had talked, cutting up vegetables, and earlier during breakfast, telling them incidents from that intensive course. Pamela suspected that their daughter was throwing herself so readily into it in order to obliterate all thoughts of misgivings. She had known how entranced by that young Russian Sonia had become, could understand that the decision to come home must have hurt her.

Andre was the first to read the news. He was the one always to study the serious pages of any newspaper. Two days ago, on 24 September, ninety Russian diplomats and officials had been expelled from England for spying.

Perhaps he had not been too dreadfully wrong, after all, to be concerned for Sonia's involvement with Nikolai Trepliov. If she had not of her own will returned home, she might have been caught up in that mass expulsion.

And now, he wondered, how do I protect her from this news?

"What is it, Dad?"

He remembered then. Only that morning he had been so sure – sure that he would free his family to live their own lives.

"You'd better read this." Andre handed across the paper.

Sonia read the article, nodded. Outwardly composed, she faced him. "I knew this was on the cards. Nikolai rang me last Thursday."

He hadn't known that they were keeping in touch. For one appalling moment Andre wondered if there still existed a possibility that Sonia would wish to go to Moscow.

Her eyes had a gloss of tears, but she smiled nevertheless. "It's better than their being arrested. He'll be home now."

And my home is here at Stonemoor, Sonia thought, thousands of miles away, but home.